Torn by the Code

Torn by the Code

Eureka

URBAN BOOKS

www.urbanbooks.net

Urban Books, LLC
300 Farmingdale Road, NY-Route 109
Farmingdale, NY 11735

Torn by the Code

ISBN 13: 978-1-64556-078-4
ISBN 10: 1-64556-078-3

First Mass Market Printing September 2020
First Trade Paperback Printing December 2018
Printed in the United States of America

10 9 8 7 6 5 4 3 2 1

Distributed by Kensington Publishing Corp.
Submit Orders to:
Customer Service
400 Hahn Road
Westminster, MD 21157-4627
Phone: 1-800-733-3000
Fax: 1-800-659-2436

Torn by the Code

by

Eureka

Chapter 1

My Son Is Missing

Sitting at the long table adorned with marble and smoke-colored granite, I had a million and one thoughts going through my mind. Thinking about my son being missing, then thinking about the ones who were claiming responsibility for it made me even more furious. I tapped my fresh and very expensive manicured nails against the table, trying to come up with my next move. Someone was going to pay—and pay dearly.

"Lady Dutchtress, where do you want the package?" one of my highly trained murder-team members nervously said as he walked into the room.

The one thing my team knew was that when I was furious, no one was safe. I would sacrifice the first person I saw if I wanted to, so they all knew to walk on eggshells. I looked up at him and leaned back in the chair I had positioned right at the head of the table. With an inquisitive expression on my face, I said, "Is this the evidence of the snitch?"

"Yeah. I mean, yes, it is. He is the very one who told them where they could find you and your family."

"Good. Bring him to me, but before you do, assemble the cleanup crew. I want to prepare this place first. *No one* will cross me and live to tell about it! As a matter of fact, go and round up his entire family. I want *everyone* from his momma, daddy, and grandma down to his seeds. Leave no family member untouched. I want them all!" I said with venom dripping from every word.

He politely nodded his head and rushed back out the door.

I slowly stood up and walked over to the large bay window to take in the view. "Aaah! It's days like this I wish for the simple things in life," I said aloud as I took in a deep breath. I looked at the downtown area of Chicago from my office suite located on top of the Deloitte Towers on Wacker Drive near the lake. The view was simplistic yet breathtaking . . . high above the clouds where nothing mattered. During the days, I watched the hustle and bustle of the crowd below and the glimmering lights throughout the skyline. It was just as incredible to watch as it was to be there. The feeling of everyone moving around while they did not know who was watching . . . I watched as the busy crowd below went about their daily routine, unaware of the empire that was built right in their grand city.

Chapter 2

The Queen Is in the Building

I drove to the warehouse where all the suspects would be lined up. I have mixed feelings about this. First, my heart was overjoyed with the answers I would finally have to get my son back. Then my heart would sink because this may be a dead end like every other avenue I tried. But I knew my presence was needed, so I had to bury my feelings and boss up.

The warehouse served many purposes. The front of it looked like any other mechanic shop. Cars parked outside lined up for sale. Wrecked cars waiting to be fixed. The building had five floors. The lower two floors were strictly dedicated to the mechanic shop. The upper floors were only entered by members of my crew and me. The top floor was my destination. The top floor was set up with one large room in the middle of the floor, then other rooms surrounding it. The only way to enter those rooms was through the large room. At the back of the warehouse were two entrances. One entrance led to the mechanic shop which had a key lock. The entrance to the upper floors had keyless entry, and the pass code was changed daily.

I walked toward the back and punched in the code. The door popped open, and I walked toward what looked like a metal door, but it was actually the door of an elevator. I pressed the small panel on the side of the door, and the elevator opened. As I entered the elevator, my emotions were on overdrive as I pushed the button for the top floor. I closed my eyes as the chimes went off. When the final chime sounded, the doors opened. I took a few steps and rested my hand on the doorknob of the metal door. I took one final deep breath and put on my ice-cold face. I was taking no survivors. I turned the knob and saw my soldiers standing around.

The room was lit well and was set up like a conference room. There was a large table dead center in the room with filled seats all around it. There were different colored doors around the room and a few windows which were lined with mirror privacy film. Plastic lining covered the floor at the front of the table. I was ready to get answers . . . and *nobody* was gonna stop me.

"I see everyone is in attendance. Let's start the show then," I said as I walked into the room. I took long strides with confidence, letting everyone know who the boss was as I reached the long table. I took my place at the head and looked every bit of the Queen Bee that I was. After folding my hands in front of me, I threw a menacing glare over toward the snitch, Polu. "So, what do you have to say for yourself?" I asked him, still studying his face for a reaction.

"I-I-I swear, Dutch, ma, it wasn't me! I would never go against family, man. You fed me. Why would I. . . ." He trailed off nervously.

I smiled and didn't say a word. I looked over at Flex, who was sitting on the other end of the long, regal-looking table.

"So what you sayin' is that all the intel we have on you is lying? You didn't tell the Nu-money organization the pickup time? And where li'l man would be? Nigga, who the hell you think you fuckin' with?" Flex said as he stood up, getting ready to walk over and deliver a blow to his head.

I held my hand out to stop him in midstride. "No, Flex, this is my show. Let me run it," I said sternly. I stood up and slowly walked over toward the weapons I had neatly laid out on a table to the side. "How long you been rocking with us? About a few years now, right?" I asked as I lifted the machete. I looked over and motioned for one of my team members to drag the chair where Polu was sitting to the middle of the floor. Then I slowly started circling his chair.

"Anthony—I mean, Polu," I said with a sly smirk on my face, "I have a very reliable source that screamed your name. Look, if you tell me where they are holding my li'l man, I will spare your life and your family's lives as well."

I turned my glare over toward Polu's mother, who was sitting and shaking in fear. His father and two sisters sat beside her, also trembling. I gave Flex a knowing nod. Two of the team members, Snook and Terrance, stood by one of the mirrored windows. I had Polu in the middle of the floor where the plastic lining was. His entire family sat around the long table. Their hands were tied to the chair, tears streaming their faces, but I didn't care. My heart was cold and wasn't gonna stop until I got the answers I came for. Even his grandmother was there. I didn't want to leave any of his bloodlines. *Everyone* must pay.

I stopped in front of Polu and leaned closer to his face, staring deeply into his eyes as I spoke. "You have one of two choices: talk or I'ma cut this ear right here . . . off." I lifted the machete toward his right ear, never taking my eyes off of him.

"Dutchtress, I swear to God, I haven't betrayed you like this. All this so-called evidence you claim to have on me is all a setup," Polu said, pleading.

"You right. It was." I lifted my body upward and looked over at Flex again and gave him a nod.

Flex turned and walked over to a metal red door and opened it to walk into another room. He came back into the room with three blindfolded females, one of whom held a newborn in her arms.

I looked over toward Terrance and Snook. "Do these people look familiar? Hmm? Let's see . . . Terrance Carter . . . T-baby is what you like to be called. Tell me this: Did you *really* think I wouldn't find out? Muthafucka, you turned on the family! *You* are responsible for my son being taken!"

I had found out that Terrance—not Polu—was behind the setup. I pulled a remote control up and pressed it. Immediately, a large screen appeared from behind a wall panel behind the head of the table. It was a feature I specifically requested when building this warehouse. It was to include numerous rooms and one very large room where I could deal with perpetrators in the open. Terrance looked on in fear as Snook slowly moved away in the opposite direction from him. All eyes were on the screen. It was blank at first; then a picture, followed by some audio, came on the screen.

"Yeah, I got the little muthafucka. You got my money?" Terrance asked a man dressed in all-black. He roughly shoved my crying son on the ground. We all watched as Terrance punched the child in the face.

I flinched, then pressed the pause button. Seeing my son suffer was pushing my feelings to the surface again. I took a deep breath and looked up, secretly praying that my heart would not be broken for much longer. I shifted toward Polu's family. "Untie them and take them to the other spot. I'll call you with further instructions," I said to Snook.

I didn't even think when I had cameras installed that it would prove to be vital. It never crossed my mind that one of my soldiers was involved. Money clearly trumped loyalty. If Flex didn't remind me of those cameras, I would have never looked at the footage since I'm the only one with the pass code.

After I made sure they were out of the room, I walked over to Polu and cut his ropes with the machete. "See, there is something that people underestimate me about. I leave no stone unturned and cross every T. The fact that this muthafucka was too eager to hang you out to dry drew my attention. He was more than ready to kill you and your entire family, and that started me thinking. Why would he be so eager to sell his boy out? I mean, you two were thick as thieves. So that had me wondering."

When my son was taken, I was a mess. I couldn't even think straight. I had everyone on my payroll turning over every stone, not caring who was killed, hurt, or came hunting for my crew or me. After a week, Terrance came to me and told me his suspicions, but my headspace was clouded and couldn't see that it was just bullshit.

I inched my way over to a now-terrified Terrance. "Money talks, homie. I paid your own blood to tell me the low. That's a shame when money will make a nigga kill they own mother. Oh, what's the matter now? You not so big, are you? Hitting a defenseless child . . . You bitch-made-ass nigga! Uh-uh. I wouldn't do that if I were you," I warned him as he tried to reach for his gun. My soldier knocked his hand with a bat and took the gun away with an extra wooden slap to the face. "Bring his bitch and that little bastard of his over here to me!" I spat through gritted teeth. I stood directly in front of him. I couldn't get the image out of my head of him punching my son in the face. It was fucking with me, and my heart was turning cold and hard.

Flex roughly shoved the girl and baby over to me. Polu stood off to the side and watched with a mean scowl on his face. I'm sure he would have killed Terrance with his bare hands if they were left alone.

The girl stood there crying and pleading. "Please, don't; please, don't kill my baby and me! I will do anything, please!" she pleaded.

"All right, bitch, what's your name?" I asked with one eyebrow raised.

"My-my name is Nahena. Please, I will do anything. Don't kill us," she said as tears flowed down her face.

"Okay, I tell you what. During this weak-ass nigga's pillow talk, did he ever mention anything about this to you?"

"No, I can't remember offhand," Nahena said hysterically.

I smiled at her and turned to look at him, then back at her. "I suggest you get to thinking because when I count to five, you better have something or I will be carving your little shorty up into pieces. One, two—"

In one quick motion, I swung the machete and sliced Terrance's arm right off at the shoulder. Blood was spurting everywhere. I jumped back to avoid some the spraying blood. He screamed out in agony. Nahena looked on in fear, screaming.

"Shut up, bitch!" I spat. "Now, I ask you—and this will be the *last* time—did he tell you where my son is?" I said as I slapped her across the face.

Nahena looked over at Terrance with pleading eyes. He returned her stare. He mouthed to her, "Please don't say a word." He held his shoulder with his left hand, trying to stop the bleeding.

"I told you everything I know," Nahena said in a pleading tone.

I quickly walked over to the table and picked up the same remote and pressed play once more. I watched Terrance stomp on my son as he lay crying on the ground. A female silhouette emerged from the side of them. I zoomed in closer. The female standing there motionless looking on as Terrance stomped my son unconscious was Nahena.

"So tell me again how you don't know shit, bitch!" I spat.

"I'm g-g-g-" Nahena tried to say.

But she was unable to get a word out because, in one swift motion, I waved the machete and sliced her across the throat. Nahena fell to the floor, gasping for air. Blood spewed everywhere. It covered my shoes and my clothes. Thank goodness the floor was lined with plastic because this was a bloodbath.

I looked at Terrance. "Now, muthafucka, tell me where my son is, or I will slice this little muthafucka up!" I snatched the baby from Flex and held the newborn upside down by his legs. Immediately, the baby started to cry and struggle. I ignored those sounds and movements as if I were holding a doll baby.

Terrance watched in agony as his newborn son dangled in front of him with a machete pressed against his tiny abdomen. He was holding what was left of his shoulder trying his hardest to apply whatever pressure he could to slow the bleeding down. Tears were spilling from his eyes as he watched the bloody blade pressed against his seed. Fear and anger didn't fit well on his face. He sure as hell knew I would do anything to get my son back and didn't give two shits about his.

I felt nothing. My heart was dead. This motherfucker had answers, and I was going to get them no matter what. If it took me slicing his child bit by bit and spilling his blood to get my son back, so be it.

I took a moment to count in my mind in case he didn't answer fast enough.

"Okay, okay, I'll tell you!" he said, full of fear.

"I'm listening." I pressed the machete deeper into the baby's little stomach. "Okay, you got two seconds or this fucka is dead." Small trickles of blood came flowing down the baby's stomach as the baby's screams became louder. I didn't care about his seed. The only thing that mattered is my blood out there alone without me protecting him.

Terrance's eyes widened in fear. "Please, don't kill my shorty, man. They are holding your son on the East Side, in the stockyard right off Cottage Grove. I'm sorry! I needed the money," he said, crying and pleading.

Flex walked over toward me. "Let me handle him."

I stood with an emotionless expression, then flinched as I heard the baby's screams. I coldly looked at Terrance. "So, did you feel like a big man stomping my son? Did you love the feeling? Oh, wasn't it grand when he cried for his mommy?" I asked, walking closer toward him with his son held close to my chest and rocking him. "That shit was priceless, huh? Did you like it when my defenseless baby cried for me?"

I turned and walked over to Flex, speaking to him as if we were having a casual conversation. "You know when you love your children, you will do anything to protect them, even sell out the ones who gave you everything you have." I nodded at Flex.

"No! No! Please, Dutch, I will do anything, please!" he pleaded.

I just ignored him. He knew it was over. I rocked the baby in my arms trying to calm him down. Having him in my arms reminded me of my son when he was born and how I used to tickle his little stomach with my nose.

"You don't get to call me Dutch. That's only for family. You have proven your loyalty lies with my enemy," I said through gritted teeth. The baby laughed and giggled as I tickled his little chin with my nose while I raised the machete.

Terrance lunged, trying to rush over to his son, but Flex caught him with a nasty right hook, punching him in the throat. Terrance fell disabled to the floor. In his mind, he knew his actions were the reason his family met their demise. He tried a last desperate attempt to get his son from me. He lay down on the floor, trying not to watch the sight before him until Polu came over and roughly lifted his head up and held it.

"Oh, bitch-ass nigga, you not gonna miss this show! You tried to set me up and get me and my family killed for your dirty ass? You gon' watch this!"

The blood from chopping Terrance's arm off and slitting Nahena's throat covered my white wife beater. "Hmm, the smack you gave my 7-year-old son was epic. 'Shut up, little bitch-ass nigga. Yo' momma ain't here to save your spoiled little ass.' Isn't that what I heard you say to my son?" I said, mocking him. "The way his little voice cried out for me must have made you feel like a *big* man," I smirked, standing at the balcony door. I stepped over the threshold, still cooing and cuddling the baby. "Bring him over here," I ordered with a mean scowl on my face.

Flex dragged Terrance over to me. "You want to hold your son for the last time?"

"Please . . . don't . . . please . . . I'm begging you!" Terrance screamed out.

"There is no difference when it comes to that between you and me. See, you beat my son and watched him cry. *My son!* Now, your son, on the other hand . . . I will be nice. I'm making him laugh and smile before I—" In one quick motion I twisted the newborn's neck without hesitation and dropped him in front of Terrance like a piece of garbage.

"No! No! You bitch, no!" Terrance screamed as he watched his 12-week-old son lying lifeless at his feet. His one hand stroked his son's body as he screamed.

I placed my hands together as if dusting them off. *Now he knows how it feels.*

Terrance's mother and sister stood trembling, still blindfolded and gagged. They were unaware of the gruesome sight in front of them. Nahena's dead body lay on the floor. Terrance had one less arm with blood spilling everywhere, trying to crawl away. It was clear he was losing a lot of blood and was probably weak at this point, but he kept trying to crawl away anyway.

Terrance yelled, "Momma, run!"

She couldn't get one foot in front of the other before I rushed toward her, wielding the machete. I sliced his mother's head clean off her body. Then I turned the machete on his sister. I swung the machete as if I were conducting a symphony orchestra. I didn't stop until nothing was left of the young girl but bone and gristle submerged in a pool of blood. When it was all said and done, blood covered the room.

I looked first at Flex, then back at Polu and gave them the nod of approval. They went straight to work, wasting no time putting Terrance out of his misery. As Flex reached for his gun, Polu pushed him aside and wrapped his hands around Terrance's throat, watching and feeling the life leave his body.

Chapter 3

House Built of Straw

"Hey, love, I see you've been hard at work again," my husband said as I entered our plush three-story home located in the Beverly area of Chicago.

This area was home to some of the most upscale people who were deemed prominent by society: doctors, lawyers, congressmen, and more. Anyone who was anyone owned a mansion in that area. Naheri was one of the most respected private practice doctors in Chicago. He was also very handsome. He stood at six feet even and had a nicely toned body with chocolate mocha skin. It made him real easy on the eyes, and he was every woman's dream catch: a hardworking family man. He hit the gym almost daily, which made his body well-defined. He wore his hair in long locs that stopped right in the middle of his back. He said it was his African heritage.

"How's Junior? I want to know what he wants for Christmas. I swear that little boy gets way more than the average 7-year-old. By the way, he is coming home for the holiday break, right?" Naheri said when he came into the room, unaware of the situation that his son was experiencing.

I took a deep breath and continued to take off my shoes. My thoughts were all over the place. I had to get to my son and fast. My husband was unaware that he had been kidnapped and could be dead. I couldn't find the words even to tell him such a thing. To him, his wife was a hardworking corporate attorney, and their son was away at a very expensive boarding school. At first, he was dead set against sending him because he felt he was too young to be away from his parents, but I convinced him that it would be good for his education.

"I spoke with him today, and he said he wanted that Xbox and a new Kindle Fire HD; he said the one with the front camera on it. It will be good for him to talk to us on Skype," I lied, managing to hold back tears. Not knowing exactly where my son was made it feel as if a million knives were being pushed deep into my heart. I slumped down in my chair.

"Elana, are you okay, love? Is everything okay? You look a little stressed," my husband said with a questioning look on his face.

"I'm okay, Naheri, I just had a long day is all." I gathered myself together to keep up the facade.

My cell phone vibrated in my purse. It was a notification letting me know I had a text message. I grabbed it out of my purse and read the message from Flex.

Everything is clean. Don't worry; we will get li'l man back safe; I put that on my life.

~ Death before Dishonor ~

I read the message, and my heart melted with joy and pain at the same time. He seemed always to know when I needed him the most. On the inside, I screamed for him to comfort me and let me know he had my back and that my son—our son—was going to be okay. I sent a text message back to him.

Thank you. As always, you are my right arm, and, yes, we will get li'l man back. Even if it takes me my last breath, I will get him back safe.

~ Death before Dishonor ~

I hit send and sat back in the chair. Sensing something much deeper was bothering me, Naheri walked over and began rubbing my feet.

"Whatever it is, Elana, it will be okay. Let me take care of you for a change," he said as he rubbed his hands slowly up my thighs.

I wanted to stop him. Sex was the furthest thing on my mind. But I knew if I didn't allow his sexual advances to play out, that would cause suspicion. I allowed his soft hands to roam up my thighs, then back down to my feet. He rubbed me gently, caressing my thighs and the small of my back. Kneeling in front of me, he planted soft kisses on my feet, making a trail with his tongue up my legs. I felt my tense body start to slip into sensual feelings.

The more he touched, the more my body relaxed. He stood straight up and reached out his hand to help me stand. When I stood up, his six-foot frame towered over me. He slowly unbuttoned my shirt, exposing my huge breasts. I didn't have the perfect body—I had a few curves here and there—but he paid special attention to each crease and curve. Then he slid my skirt down to the floor. I stood there with my dark skin in all my glory, displaying my size 14 waist and the hips of a goddess. Naheri took in the sight of my Victoria's Secret lace bra and panty set.

Biting down on his bottom lip, he leaned down to whisper in my ear, "You are so beautiful! I love you, my queen. Whatever you need me to do, just say the word. You are breathtaking, Got damn it! I love it." He looked me deeply in the eyes.

The lust he had in his eyes filled me with a passion I didn't intend to touch on that night. He kissed me deeply on the lips and gently laid me back on the chair. He took one of his fingers to slide my panties to the side. His eyes rested on my neatly trimmed pussy. Then he licked his lips and began kissing my inner thighs once more.

"Girl, I'm about to dive in," he said, trying to sing a verse from the Trey Songz hit song. I was so caught up in the moment. All of the problems that weighed heavily on my shoulders just ten minutes ago seemed not to exist right now. I placed each one of my legs on an arm of the chair until I was spread-eagle. "Come get your dinner, baby. The buffet is open only for you," I said as I seductively beckoned for him to come closer.

He looked me in the eyes. "You can have whatever you like," he said as he knelt down in front of me as if I were a queen on her throne.

Naheri lifted one of my legs over his shoulder as he lowered himself in front of me. He kissed my inner thighs, teasing me with his tongue through my lace panties. He slowly lifted my bottom from the chair to remove my panties with his teeth. He kissed the creases of my juicy, wet lips, teasing me with the tip of his tongue.

He kissed and sucked on my thighs until he allowed his tongue to rest on my swollen clit. He gave me pleasure and relaxation in slow, steady motions with his lovely assault on my clit.

"Shit, this feels so . . ." I trailed off, throwing my head back in ecstasy.

Naheri licked and slurped all of my sweet nectar as it came flowing down from my sweet spot. The sounds of him sucking and licking until I had no more to give echoed throughout the room. Once he gave me a moment, and only one moment, to gather myself together, he picked me up and carried me to the bedroom.

"I need you," he said as he laid me softly on the bed, panting and breathing hard.

"Anyway you want me," I said, filled with pure passion.

"Aw, no! No! Give him to me!" I screamed out.

"Elana, wake up!" Naheri said.

I screamed and kicked, punched into the air, narrowly missing his face. He grabbed me forcefully by the wrist.

"Elana, wake up; it's me. Damn! Here you go again with another nightmare. What the hell is going on with you? This is the third one this week," he said while holding the right side of his face. When he took his hand down to get a better look in the mirror there was a small scratch with blood.

"My fault. I don't know what's going on with me," I said as I composed my breathing. I gathered the sheets from the bed and wrapped them around my naked body; then I got up and walked down the stairs.

Slowly sitting down in a chair in the den and pouring myself a stiff drink, thoughts of my son once again entered my mind. I began to cry silently, almost uncontrollably. I got up and turned the radio down to the lowest volume possible. *Maybe some music will calm me,* I thought.

"*You are everything; I would give you anything. You are everything . . .*" Dru Hill's lyrics played softly from the speakers. My tears began to cascade down my face like a rainfall. I wouldn't have wished this feeling on my worst enemy. The more my tears fell for my son, the angrier I became. "I'ma carve every son of a bitch up that had anything to do with this," I said through gritted teeth as the tears continued down my face.

I got up and went to my purse, grabbed my cell phone, and powered it on. I noticed I had several missed calls and texts from Flex. My heart felt as if it had sunk to the bottom of my stomach. I loved my husband and felt that he was a good man, but a part of me felt as if I had just cheated on him. The feelings of guilt had plagued me for years when it came to Flex and Naheri. I felt in my heart that I was one's wife and the other one's woman. My heart had been torn between the two of them for years. I took a huge gulp of my drink as I read the last text from Flex.

He's not here, Dutch, but don't worry; I'm on it.

Out of frustration and oncoming drunkenness, I threw my phone on the floor, almost shattering the face of it. Then I slammed my fist down on the table. I wasn't much of a drinker, but at times like this, I felt it was necessary.

Chapter 4

Here What Lies in the Heart of Man?

I stood in the shadows watching every agonizing move Dutchtress made. My plan was on full throttle, and before long, I would have her and Flex right where I wanted them. I had had them both secretly followed for a while now. It was all too painfully obvious of their closeness and their extramarital affair.

For years, Elana kept me in the dark about their past. When I first met Elana, she introduced Flex as her cousin, but as the years went on, they seemed a little too close to be cousins. So I decided to get to the bottom of their so-called family relationship. I hired a private investigator. It didn't take long for him to come to me with video footage of Flex and my wife. That day, my life and marriage changed forever. I saw them with my own eyes together, and it wasn't no family embrace either. The shit fucking hurt, but I can't say I didn't have any suspicions. It just confirmed my worst nightmare. Then when she became pregnant, my doubt that I was the father was, unfortunately, plaguing my mind as her belly grew. There were nights where I paced the floor of our kitchen wanting to confront her. Show her the video and hear what she had to say. Would she deny it? When the baby was born, I had to get him tested just so that it would stop fucking with my mind.

While Elana was at work, I took him to my office and took the DNA test. It was a perfect time. No one was there, and I would be the only one who knew the test results. I knew the answer, but I needed the science to confirm it. My office had the equipment to do the test and get the results. It was an expensive piece of equipment, but when some of my patients had dilemmas of their own, it was a smart, profitable purchase decision. Elana didn't even know about it, or the ends I made from it. It took maybe about an hour before the results confirmed my suspicions. It was clear. I was 99.99 percent *not* the father. My heart was crushed. My trust betrayed. I looked at that baby, then thought about the rap sheet his biological father had. I decided to keep it a secret. I thought what better way to stick it to

... my wife ... watched for years ... the issue when someone ... why our son resembled her more than ... To add a nail in the coffin, she gave him my name: Naheri Hakeem Dolvan Jr.

I sat at my desk thinking back to the day where my whole life changed, which made me think about why I didn't just take him and leave. What hurts the most is that she has upheld this lie for years. What kind of person does that to the man they supposedly love? My only guess is my love was the only genuine one.

"All right, Bridgette, you can leave for the night!" Naheri yelled out to his receptionist as she cleaned up the waiting area in the office.

"Sure thing, Dr. Dolvan, but are you sure? I could stay and help you," she said seductively while remaining professional as she stood in the doorway to his office.

I smiled. Her flirting was flattering, but I would not cross that line, especially not in the

… in
and t… …ave a
seat, Doc, …

I stood and w… …imself in the seat in front of th… …don't know who you are and what yo… …ut this is not where you need to be. So I sugg… you walk back out of here the same way you came in here," I said, still standing by my desk. Although I'm a doctor and civilized, my days of growing up in the harsh streets of Jamaica never left so if this turned sour, I was ready.

The man had a smirk on his lips. "So, you don't remember me? Dem memory be bad for you, boi. Take ya seat and look at this envelope before you get into sum fyia," the man said, lightly chuckling.

Just when I started to make my move for my hidden piece stored in my desk, he moved quickly, and in a blink, I faced the barrel of his gun. I learned at an early age to always keep your piece next to you like a second skin. But there I stood . . . open for a bullet.

The stranger found it amusing for a second. "Go ahead, reach for ya piece. I promise ya won't be breathing in 2.5 seconds, rude boi. Dem family will get their Sunday clothes together, and you become a loving memory." Then he sat with a 9 mm Glock aimed right at my chest.

It took me a minute, but I slowly sat down at my desk and reached for the envelope. I opened it and pulled out the contents. My eyes widened. I looked at the man still pointing his gun at me; then I looked back to what I pulled out of the envelope. I saw my wife and her right-hand man, Flex. Then I picked out another photo, and it was another one of my wife. This time, it was a shot of her and Flex with some unknown men who looked as if they were of Jamaican descent. All of them had long locs on their heads. I stared at the photo for a minute or two. Then it hit me. It was the resort where we honeymooned. There were more pictures and a DVD. Immediately, I opened the DVD case and put the disc into the slot of my desktop. I waited for it to prompt me to run the disc.

I wanted to ask a question. Well, many questions, but I thought it might be wiser to keep my mouth shut and let him tell me what he wants. What the hell did Elana get herself into now? Why does this man feel the need to come to me?

I pressed the enter button on my keyboard and pictures began to appear. The first image came up. Elana holding a machete in her hand, covered in blood. She held the head of a corpse, adorned with the long locs, and the expression on his face would be forever etched in my mind. It was gruesome. Blood was everywhere. The headless body lay on the ground with blood oozing from where his head used to be. My stomach began to convulse. I had to look away before I threw up on my desk. The next screen was a video. It was my wife shooting a gun, hitting a man directly in the head, and his head exploded like a melon. I reared back in the chair with a shocked expression on my face. *What the hell?*

"What the fuck! Where did you get this?"

"Never mind all that. All dem need to worry ya self with is that this lickel beotch is gonna die by the next sunup, and ya help us kill her," he stated in a matter-of-fact tone with a heavy Jamaican accent.

"Man, listen, I don't know who you are and who you think I am, but who is this woman in the photos, and why would I help you kill her?" I asked, lying, trying to throw him off track.

"Look, Doc, ya really might wan retink some shit. Mi know this bitch in the picture is your wife, and the bumbaclot in the photo is her right hand—or shall I say, she's his woman?" He started laughing hysterically, then suddenly stopped. "Look 'ere, dis how dis shit gon' work. You gon' set dis bitch up. I-I mean, we-wah know exactly where this bitch gonna be at this time on this date." He slid a piece of paper across the desk toward me. "Leave the rest to we, Doc—or shall I say Dr. Naheri Hakeem Dolvan, son of Akbar and Nafesa Dolvan? Ya gran mudda is healthy, yes? In Ochie? I would hate to have to change that." He let me know he had done his background check. "See, mi did mi homework on you, and ya know she ain't been all the way one hundred, as you Americans say, with ya. So, let's kill two birds with one stone. Wha ya say?"

I thought about all the lies Elana had told me, and even the ones I told her. There was no way I was going to let this common thug ruin my plans. I looked down at the photos on my desk. The video stopped on my computer screen; then I looked back at the stranger. “Can you assure me no one else will be hurt?” I said with defeat, giving my best performance. “How will I know you won’t kill my parents and my son?”

“You don’t, but I can say this: if you don’t help, then dem will die for sure,” he said through clenched teeth. “This bitch has got to go! She murda mi brudah.” His heavy Jamaican dialect came through his raspy voice.

The man confirmed what I had already suspected. He was Jamaican and even looked familiar. I definitely could not let him know that. This stranger put the offer on the table. There would be no blowback on me, but as much as Elana had deceived me, I couldn’t bring myself to agree. “I ca—”

“To make sure you don’t have any second thoughts, look at this,” he said, holding up a cell phone to my face.

My face turned white as a ghost. It was clear. I could not talk or walk away from this one.

I lowered my head. *Damn, I didn't need for her to be caught up in the middle of this. Damn!* "Okay . . . Okay, I'll do it," I said in a low whisper.

On the screen of his phone was Bridgette, my secretary, being abducted in an unmarked van as she left the building. The kidnapper held up a sign that read, "COOPERATE, OR YA FIND SHE HEAD AT YA STEP." There was nothing left to do but to agree. If I refused, Bridgette, who was innocent, would pay the price for my wife's dirty dealings.

Chapter 5

The Real Her

I stood off at the side and watched my wife go through the pain of her son being kidnapped. One part of me wanted to come clean and let her know I would help look for their son. Yeah, I figured it out. She couldn't hide it from me too long with the way she was acting. It was obvious something was wrong every time I wanted to talk to him or go see him. She would have an excuse why we couldn't go or why I couldn't call him by phone. After all, he had a cell phone. I continued to watch her drown in her misery.

Then thoughts of all the pain she had caused me with all of her lies, and now, someone who had nothing to do with any of it could die. She swallowed drink after drink until she was in a drunken stupor. I made up my mind. I would go over to her and tell her everything so we can get our son back. I walked over to her and placed my hand on her shoulder.

Her reflexes caused her to flip me to the floor. "I'm sorry, babe. Don't sneak up on me like that," she said as she reached down to help me up from the floor, barely keeping her balance. She tried to pull me up and ended up falling on top of me on the floor.

I laughed at first because it was nice to see that smile. . . . The very smile I had fallen in love with. She still possessed that sex appeal, even in her drunken state.

I remembered the first time we met and how gorgeous she was to me. There was something more than her looks that drew me in. Her determination and drive captivated me on our first date. She wasn't like any of the other women I had dated. There was something about her which screamed *wifey*. No matter how I tried, I couldn't get her out of my mind or heart. I found myself an out-of-the-ordinary love for sure. I eased myself up, then reached down to help her up this time.

"Ba . . . baaabe, you love me? Would you still love me if you knew . . . shh . . . shh . . . I hear something. Hahaha, my bad," she said, stammering and laughing. "Baby, I'm so sorry. Do you love me, Flex?" she said.

Flex? My heart sank to the pit of my stomach. Here it is! I was about to save her ass, and all she wants is this common-ass nigga. I know the fuck she didn't just call me this muthafucka's name. In fact, she had done just that. I pushed her ass back to the floor. I was about to slap her across the face but held back. Since this bitch loves this nigga so much, she can die with his ass.

I think she realized what she said. "Baby . . . I'm sorry . . . I got so much going on, and I'm drunk."

"I don't give a shit!" She reached for me, but I just backed away.

I never thought my wife, the love of my life, would treat me, of all people, this way. With all the lies and murders she had done, it was only fair that Karma paid her a nasty visit. Fuck it!

I moved back to the entrance of the den, looking at her in her pathetic drunken state with disgust on my face. She was crying and slurred her words. I had no idea what she was saying, and I didn't give a shit. I had made up my mind. Whatever was going to happen to her—she deserved it. I looked down and spotted her phone on the chair. It was lit and vibrating. I picked it up and immediately, anger and hatred exploded when I saw the text flash across the screen. These two dumb muthafuckas deserve what they have coming to them! I threw the phone at Elana and stormed out of the room, leaving her on the floor crying. I was more than upset when I read the text from Flex.

Dutch, I got you, and I will never leave you. I know not knowing where your son is at is killing you, but believe me, ma, I got you. I'm moving heaven and earth to find him.

We are Bonnie and Clyde. You my ride, and I'm your die.

I love you, my queen

~ Death before Dishonor ~

Chapter 6

Nothing Comes before We ~Death before Dishonor~

"You mean to tell me my son is *nowhere* in this city? You have *got* to be kidding me! Or do you think I'm a fuckin' fool?"

"Aw, Dutchtress, no, I don't know. . . . They told me to bring the kid here; then I was paid to . . . Aww, shit!" the man screamed in pain as I took my slow, sweet time peeling the skin from his body.

I looked over at Flex. "He thinks I'm stupid." I started laughing hysterically. In one swipe of my machete, I took the man's head off, then walked over to the remaining man. "I will let you live. I'ma let you deliver your boss a message from me."

"I-I-I don't—" he nervously stammered.

"Shh, shh . . . Don't talk. You will tell him . . . I will say it plainly. If my son is not back to me by sunup, I will make sure he wishes he was never born. This city will have blood on the streets, and it damn sure won't be mine. He's got till 5:00 p.m.—not 5:01—not a minute later—to give me my son."

I leaned down to the man and whispered in his ear, and the look on his face was as if the devil himself or—in this case, herself—had just spoken to him. He nodded his head vigorously in agreement with what I had just said.

"You can let him go," I said, looking over at Flex with a smirk on my face. We had previously discussed that someone would follow his ass, and that would lead me closer to my son.

Flex smiled and moved aside. He let him run up out of the warehouse we had tracked them to. I had gotten a hold of every location the ones who were claiming to have my son were supposed to be. Flex did not rest until he found out something he could give to me to ease my pain. Every address he'd gotten would get us one step closer to getting my son back.

I looked at the rest of my crew. They were standing around the warehouse, ready to do what they did best.

"You all can go now!" I spat aloud, angry. They could see the frustration on my face. They probably thought I was becoming unhinged as the days went by after the kidnapping of my son. But they didn't know I was setting a plan in motion so that the other true snake would tip his hand.

Flex looked on, but never changed his facial expression. He nodded at the soldiers and silently dismissed them. "Come on, Dutch, let's go."

"No, you can go. I'll be okay," I said in a defeated tone.

"What you mean I can go? Dutch, you sound crazy as fuck right now! I'm not leaving you—not like this. I know shit seems like we not winning, but we will," Flex said as he placed his hand gently on my shoulder.

I jerked my shoulder away from his touch. "That's my son—*my* son! And these muthafuckas came in *my* space and took him. Every night since then, I've been wondering how and where he is. Flex, my son needs me. When I gave birth to him, he changed me. Money used to motivate me, Flex, you know that; but now, he is the reason I breathe. And . . . you know I can't . . ." I spoke until my voice started cracking. Every word dripped with pain.

Flex grabbed me up in his arms. "Dutch . . . Elana . . . Don't tell me. I can't feel your pain, ma. It's been you and me since day one. I feel you, and you can feel me. Listen, ma, I know Junior is okay. He's a survivor, just like his momma. I know he is made of some tough stuff. I also know he is still alive. They want to use him as a bargaining chip to get you and me. But we'll get him back safe; then they'll pay. Every fucking last one of them is gonna pay," Flex said as he held me closer to his chest.

I looked up into his eyes as tears began to form. "Kajaun, promise me I will get my son back safe. He's my world."

Flex was the only one to see me in my most vulnerable state. He looked me square in the eyes, filled with love and strength. He wrapped his strong arms around me a little tighter and said, "As sure as my name is Kajaun Michael Stanton, he will be back home with us safe and sound. Dutch. I put that on my life."

We stood in an embrace in the middle of this abandoned warehouse as if no one and nothing in the world existed. The love I felt in his arms was way deeper than what I shared with Naheri. Flex always made me feel safe, like a woman's equal. There wasn't a time in my life since I'd met him that I didn't love him except when we were around 16, but even then, it was an unspoken love.

Because of the paths we each chose for our lives, we couldn't have that fairy-tale life. I went off to college, then graduated law school. Flex stayed behind in the city and rose his way up in the ranks to become one of the most-feared enforcers in Chicago. When we lost touch with each other, it devastated us, but we knew fate would bring us right back together.

And it did. When I first started practicing law, I worked for the public defender's office. When I saw Flex's name come across my caseload, I knew in my heart it was him, and sure enough, when I entered the courtroom, I saw that it was. Kajaun Stanton—Flex—stood at my table on some petty charges I knew I could get dismissed, and that I did. All charges were dismissed for lack of evidence. When Flex noticed it was me, he moved heaven and some of the earth to find me and keep in touch, even though I was newly married to Naheri. His love for me and my love for him was a magnetic pull which brought us back to each other, even though I had a husband. I guess it was meant to be, and I couldn't stay away.

When I was working at the defender's office, there were a lot of drug-related cases that came across my desk. As soon as Flex was released, his relentless presence of making sure he would never lose me again was apparent. One night, I was working late on a major drug cartel case, and when I was leaving, someone was watching me. It turned out that it was, in fact, the cartel. As the man approached, Flex came out of nowhere and gun butted the dude to the ground. That's when I knew for sure he still loved me, and no matter what, he was willing to kill for me.

Flex wiped a lone tear from my eyes. "Let's go, Dutch. The cleanup crew needs to do what they do." He led me to the back door, where a black, unmarked car was waiting with the engine running. He helped me in the backseat of the car, and the driver began to drive off.

"Where to, Boss?" the driver asked.

I managed to compose myself. "Go by the hillside house. I need to freshen up."

We both sat back and rode in silence. We didn't need words to express the hurt and worry we felt. The pained expressions on our faces said enough. When we pulled up in front of a plush but modest-looking townhome, Flex opened the door for me. "Come on, let me run you a hot bath," he said as I walked up to the front door.

I opened the door, walked into the den, and plopped down on the small couch. My mind was in a million places. *How am I going to get my son? How much does Naheri know? What is he up to? When is this nightmare going to be over? Who else is involved?* Flex went into the bathroom and started the Jacuzzi for me. He knew this would help me . . . for a brief moment, at least.

"Dutch, baby, come on, let me clean you up." He lifted me from the couch.

I nestled into his arms as if I were a newborn and released all the pent-up tears I had been holding back. My mind and emotions were everywhere. My clothes were still soaked with blood, and I didn't even care. No matter what, I could always let my guard down around Flex. I wished I had that type of bond with my husband, but I didn't. Flex was like my oxygen to breathe, and I was the air he breathed. We had been through too much not to have a love like this, even if it had to be kept a secret.

"Dutch, babe, listen, this is hard as fuck! I feel your pain. Believe me, li'l mama, I got you." Flex planted soft kisses on my forehead. He carried me to the tub and lowered me down on the side of it. I couldn't move. It was as if I were stuck.

I allowed him to do everything, even undress me. I felt so helpless. Once I was naked, he lowered me into the tub; then he stood up to leave and give me privacy.

"No, Flex, please don't leave. I need you," I managed to utter, barely audible, reaching for his hand.

He stopped and looked at me with compassion and love. He didn't say a word. He just lowered himself into the tub behind me, fully clothed, and wrapped me up in his arms. "We gonna find him," Flex said, folding me up in a loving embrace.

Flex took his hand and gently poured water on top of my hair, followed with gentle strokes. He clearly felt my pain. He turned me to face him. I looked at him in his wet clothes and realized what he was willing to do for me. He had just sat down in a tub full of water in his True Religion jeans and matching shirt. He even had his shoes on.

"I trust you, Flex. You the only one I can ever trust. I remember when we were younger, and I didn't have anybody, and you stepped in. Have I ever thanked you for that?"

"Naw, you haven't," he playfully laughed. "But you have given me something that I have never thought I could have. I mean, from day one, I knew there was something between us, but I was too up in the streets to be caught up in domestic life. Then yo' ass came and knocked a nigga straight off his script. Before that nosy bitch on the third floor tricked off about your living situation, I was ready to give it all up and settle down, make some real shit happen with my life.

...had other ideas. If we'd stayed in that building, you wouldn't have graduated top of your class and become this big-shot-ass lawyer. This time around, you saved me, shorty. Man, life can be a trip sometimes. But on some real shit, Dutch, I love you, and I know li'l man is my son," he said.

"But I nev—" I tried to say.

"I knew from the moment you announced you were pregnant he was mine. He rockin' my genes hard. His eyes are my grandfather's mark. Every last one of us carries that, and the ones who don't, their kids do. What I'm saying is, I don't need any DNA test to tell me that is my son. I didn't put up a fight because I didn't want to bring him into our world. Both of his parents living this life was too much. I wanted to tell everyone and claim my family, you and my son, but I knew it would hurt him in the long run. I love you to death, and there is nothing I won't do for you. I'ma promise you this: I will find our son, and we can start a new life somewhere. If I can't spare him the world's hurt, at least I can protect him and let him know I'm his father."

I lay my head back against his chest and wrapped his arms tighter around me. I never said a word to deny or admit to what he said; no words were needed. I knew every word he said was true. I had a love for my husband, but my heart would always belong to Flex.

I slowly stood up in front of him. The soap and water from the Jacuzzi bubbles dripped down my body. I looked at Flex and reached my hand out to him. "Come lie down with me, please. I haven't had any good sleep since they took him. I want to rest my eyes some before we go to the next address. Will you come lie with me?"

Flex placed his hand in mine and stood up to face me. Water and soap dripped from his clothes. He slipped off his shoes and slowly removed his shirt, exposing his well-proportioned chest. The soap on his chest area had his mocha complexion with a hint of vanilla glistening. He had a scar on the right side of his chest. He gazed at me with those eyes, the same eyes his son had: brown with a hint of gray. My hand roamed over his chest. I said aloud every word of his tattoo as I traced the letters with my fingertips: "*Forever is we, Death before Dishonor*." I touched each letter slowly as if I was reminiscing about the moment we got them. He caressed my shoulder and allowed his hand to rub across the matching tattoo I had that rested just above my right breast. I remembered we got matching tattoos when we were just seventeen: *Forever is we, Death before Dishonor*. It was the symbol of

our bond which not even distance or death could come between.

I unbuttoned his pants. Flex finished unzipping them for me, lowering them to his ankles. Once they were all the way off, he threw them to the floor, soaking wet. The water dripped from our bodies as the cool air stiffened my nipples.

"I love you, Elana," Flex said as he softly kissed my neck.

"And I love you, Kajaun," I replied, lifting up on my tiptoes to plant a soft kiss on his awaiting lips.

We kissed each other as if it were our last breath, the forbidden meal for the two of us. In a matter of seconds, we were wrapped in each other's arms. I wanted and needed the pain to go away as if my very life depended on it, and being with Flex was my escape from harsh reality.

We stepped out of the tub and walked to one of the bedrooms in this small on the outside but spacious on the inside, hideaway. He laid me gently on the bed, where we cuddled. He took his time and made sure I could be myself with him. We lay in the spooning position for a moment, and he twirled my hair in his fingers and kissed my neck. We lay there naked under the covers, just wrapped up in each other.

I looked over my shoulder. "Please make love to me. I need you, Flex. I want you."

He lowered his soft, thick lips to the nape of my neck and gently kissed all over the back of my neck and shoulders. He took his time with me and finally turned me over to face him. He positioned his six-foot-one frame on top of me and seductively invaded my lips with his tongue. He gently stroked my hardened nipples. Every stroke from his hot, wet tongue sent a welcoming sensation throughout my body. The nectar from my sweet, tight snatch started flowing down the creases of my inner lips. I moved my hips, thrusting to meet his massive nine-inch member.

"Not yet. I wanna taste you," he said as he placed my hands together over my head.

I loved when he would pin me down and make thug love to me. I released light moans of passion into the air.

"Open your legs wider," he said in a stern tone.

"Anything you say, ba—"

"Shh! I didn't tell you to speak," he said as he lowered his face down to lick and suck on my erect nipples.

I kissed his chest, making trails with my tongue to his neck. He gently began feasting on my nipples. I lowered my hands to rub his back, but he quickly put them back above my head.

"I didn't say move!" he said sternly.

It was the way he would take control, and it excited me more. He kissed my neck, and with his tongue, he made a long, sloppy trail down to my wet pussy. His mouth watered with anticipation at the lovely sight before him. My clit was exposed and hard as if it were about to jump right into his welcoming mouth. He took the tip of his tongue and tickled it, around and around in circular motions, making light strokes, then deeper ones. The sounds of him slurping and sucking me into bliss were like no other.

Before I could release my sweet juices all over his tongue, I pushed his head forcefully from between my thighs. I flipped him over on his back, and before he could protest, I took all his dick in my mouth. I relaxed my throat muscles and deep-throated his massive member with ease. I bobbed my head up and down and then side to side, stiffening my jaw muscles. I knew the spot to make his toes curl and his back arch. I gave him the hula hoop. I tightened my jaw muscles and suctioned his member like a glove, leaving no room for air. All he could feel was my warm saliva running down the side of his member. I sucked and blew on the tip of his dick until his back arched, letting me know he was about to release his load. Before he could release himself into my mouth, I slowly climbed on top of him.

"Damn! Shorty, your head game is the truth," Flex said as he wrapped his arms around my size fourteen waist in a bear-hug type of hold and began grinding his member deep inside of me.

"Mmm, yes, Kajaun, I love you! Go deeper; touch all of this pussy." I met him thrust for thrust, stroke for stroke. My hands rested around his neck, and he fucked me into a state of sexual bliss. He pounded soft, then slow. Each stroke was different; no two were the same. He rotated his hips in a twirling motion, thrusting deeper inside of me. I released soft moans into the air as he touched my sweet G-spot. The way he touched me and the long, deep thrust he delivered caused a tear to fall down my cheeks.

"Mmm, I . . . love . . . you," I moaned.

He tightened his grip a little more, grabbing a handful of each of my ass cheeks. He moved his hips again, this time thrusting deeper and deeper inside of me. My hot wetness oozed down his dick like smooth, melted butter. He couldn't hold it any more.

"Aaah, aaah, grr!" he released into the air.

It was as if we were singing in the same choir. Not even two seconds later, I joined him, almost in unison. "Oh shit, yes! Yes, mmm, yes, yes!"

We released the sounds of our passion as our sweet nectar mixed. He filled my walls with his thick nectar, and I painted his member with my glistening wetness.

After the last long thrust, breathing hard and panting, I rolled over from on top of him. "Oh . . . my . . . God, that was good! I *needed* that." I cuddled in his arms.

Flex released a long breath into the air as he tried to regain his composure. "Dutch, baby, I love you. You know that, right? This ain't just words a nigga say to anyone and don't mean it." Silence filled the air for a brief second. "Shorty, why didn't you tell me Junior is my son? I know you did what you thought was right for him, but I wanna hear you say the words."

I lay there wrapped in his arms. . . . The arms I always wanted to be in. There had never been a man able to touch me down to my very core besides Flex. It was as if he touched my soul. Our sex session just made it even better. But I couldn't seem to bring myself to say the words, "He's your son, Kajaun." I couldn't allow that phrase to cross my lips.

"Flex, please, can we lie here for a minute? I need to rest my eyes so we can find our son." Before I could take my last words back, just like that, I had admitted that Flex was indeed the father of my son. I couldn't say the exact words he wanted, but I made it clear in my own way. The way he would understand. It felt like a weight was lifted, but telling Naheri weighed heavier than ever now.

"Okay, Elana, I will let this go for now, but as soon as we find our son, we will leave this life and be the family we were meant to be. Can you at least *think* about that?" he said sternly as he hugged me tighter.

I couldn't answer. I couldn't even think about the future for us as a real family. What would happen to Naheri? He was the only father my son knew. How would I look in my son's eyes? I knew that I couldn't hide it any longer, and the longer I waited, the more devastating it would be for little man. I had to do it the right way.

We lay spent in each other's arms and drifted off to sleep.

Chapter 7

Reality over Fiction

"Help! Help me! Flex, please, they said if I didn't call you, they would—" Bridgette yelled in the phone as Rasta punched her right in the nose, sending the phone flying across the room.

"You tell dem what mi say or your head off!" he said angrily with a strong Jamaican accent as he walked over to pick the phone up.

Bridgette sat crying hysterically in fear of what would happen next.

Rasta picked up the phone and coldly spoke into it. "Aw, dis dem bad boi? Mi been searching 'round for ya. Now mi got ya and dat fuckin' witch, Dutchtress. She kills mi brudah and feel she gwan roam free! Nah," he said sinisterly into the phone.

I jumped up, still dazed and a little confused. "Who the fuck is this!"

"Aw, so ya don't know mi now, is that right?" Rasta spoke into the phone as he twirled Bridgette's hair with his finger. "Just know de bastard boi of she will die. She will feel pain like mi when she cut mi bruda's head clean off. De bloodclot. Tell me sumpting, where de fuckin' bitch?" he asked, referring to Dutchtress.

I sat straight up in the bed. "Listen, you Rasta muthafucka, when I get my hands on you, I will squeeze the life right outta yo' ass with my bare hands!"

"Ya bad, now, huh? And when she find de likle boi head pon she office door, ya still bad?" He started laughing, then hung up.

Dutch was now at full attention. She didn't say a word. She got up as if in a trance. She moved swiftly, rushing to the bathroom and taking a quick wash. I had already anticipated the move, so as she left one room, I went in just as quickly. After a brief couple of seconds, we were both dressed and ready.

"Call Jorge. We need his assistance," she said as she remembered their close ally. "Maybe he can help." It was a long shot, but they needed all the help they could get. Dutch strapped on her Glock 9 mm with nothing but murder on her mind.

After I got on the phone, going into specific details with Jorge about the whole situation, he told me he would get back to me in a few with some information on the whereabouts of Junior.

Dutch looked over at me, immediately wanting the scoop. "So, what did he say?"

"He said he'd get at me in a few with some intel."

"Well, I hope so! I need my baby. I know he's scared. I should have chopped that nigga's balls off when I had the chance," she said through gritted teeth as she remembered her last encounter with Rasta and his brother. She had wanted to kill him too, but time was not on her side, and he got away.

When Flex's phone first rang, that woke me up; then hearing a female's voice screaming through the phone, I became wide awake. I lay there motionless, listening to the entire phone conversation. When I heard the man's voice on the other end, I knew it was Rasta. At that moment, I cursed the day I had let that pussy get away. I broke one of my rules: Leave no witness. Now it had come back to bite me in the worst way. My baby, my son, the very reason I breathed every day, might pay for my mistake with his little life.

I looked over at Flex with a mean scowl on my face. "Tell me, where does that white chick on the other end of that phone call fit into our nice and neat little future?"

Flex lowered his head. At that moment, he thought about how he and Bridgette had been hooking up for a good while—a little over a year, to be exact. He had never mentioned it to Dutch because when he was with her, no other woman mattered.

I had met her one night at Naheri's office after a Christmas party he gave. I only came because Dutch begged me. She thought a change of scenery would be good for me, so reluctantly, I gave in. After about an hour, I was ready to leave. I got tired of standing around and acting phony, kicking it with some of the most bougie black people I'd ever seen or been around.

I couldn't take being in there, and it was becoming stuffy. I watched all the so-called elite, phony muthafuckas act as if they ruled the world. I walked over and tapped Dutch on her shoulder. "I'm stepping outside for a smoke." She nodded her head, and I stepped out a side door.

"Hey, you gon' share that shit?" a soft voice came from behind me as I lit the front of my Kush-filled blunt.

I needed to get a hit if I was going to continue to stand in that room keeping an eye out for Dutch and anyone who might think it was sweet to come at her during the party. I was there as her bodyguard regardless of whether she wanted it. "Yeah," I said turning around to face a honey-blond, thicker-than-a-Snicker, nice-shaped white female standing behind me. I took a moment to take in her semi-sexiness.

"Hey, my name is Bridgette. I work for Dr. Dolvan."

"Oh, okay. What you know 'bout this good shit right here?" I inhaled a long puff of the blunt and watched her as the smoke from the blunt drifted in the air.

The smell was so euphoric that it only made Bridgette want it more. Often, she hit a blunt or two, but sometimes she would lace it with some cocaine to get a deeper feeling from the weed. "Look, give it to me and I'll show you what I can do with this so-called good shit. Hell, I probably have had better."

I lightly chuckled. "Is that right? You make it a habit of stepping up to strangers and asking them for they weed?" I waited for her response.

She laughed. "No, I don't, and you are hardly a stranger. I've seen you before with Mrs. Dolvan. Is she your sister or somethin'?" she asked with a knowing look on her face.

I smiled, showing her some of the brightest teeth she had ever seen. She inhaled the blunt and released it into the air. Then she seductively smiled at me. I knew what that look meant.

"Hey, I'm a straight-up kind of girl, and right now, I want to be honest with you. I wanna fuck you, point-blank. I see no need to bullshit around. I find you sexy as hell, and I would love to blow the top off that dick."

I was taken aback a little by her straightforwardness. "Damn, shorty, you really that chick, huh? I find you attractive and all, but I don't think right now is the ti—" I looked inside the office through the window and saw Naheri plant a passionate kiss on Dutch. Although she was married to him, I never liked to see her in a passionate embrace with him.

I looked on with a mean scowl, then quickly turned back toward Bridgette, who was standing with a smile on her face like a cat that swallowed the canary. "You know what?" I said in a stern tone. "I changed my mind. Let's do this. I would love to see those juicy pink lips wrapped around my dick."

Bridgette bit down on her bottom lip. "I can't wait to suck that big black dick! You got some more of that Kush? That shit was fire."

"Yeah, I got some more in my car. Follow me over to the parking lot."

We walked over to my 2011 custom-made black-on-black Chevy Suburban. I hit the alarm and opened the door for her to climb in. Then I pulled out the second blunt and lit it up.

My thoughts were not on the sexy white beauty sitting in the front passenger seat but on the sight of my one and only love kissing her husband and looking as if she enjoyed it. My heart was heavy. Dutch held a piece of me that no matter how hard I tried, I couldn't shake it.

Bridgette broke my deep thoughts as I inhaled the blunt. She rubbed her hands up my thigh until she reached my manhood. "I see you play with big toys." She smiled seductively.

I smiled, "Yeah, big toys for big boys." I took another pull from the blunt and flicked the ashes in the ashtray.

In one quick motion, Bridgette went to unzip my pants. The nice linen suit I wore that night made for easy access. She wasted no time exposing my massive nine-inch python. Her eyes widened, and her mouth spread even wider as she lowered her head, placed my manhood in her mouth, and went to work. She bobbed her head up and down and side to side as she deep-throated my entire penis in her mouth. She massaged the sides with her hands as she worked me into an orgasmic rhythm. When she felt her gag reflexes, she slowed her pace and slowly made love to my manhood with her mouth.

I threw my head back on the seat in bliss as she worked my manhood into a sexual explosion. All of my sweet, thick load released into her mouth. She didn't slow her pace. She slurped and swallowed every drop.

"Aww, shit!" I said, making a slithering sound.

Bridgette sucked and sucked until I became hard again. She lifted her leg to climb on top of me.

"Wait, let me grab this condom." I lifted the console and placed the condom on my rock-hard manhood; then she climbed on top of me and rode me as if she were on a mustang. She shifted and grinded her hips deeper on my dick.

"Aw, aw, shit, this feels so fuckin' good! Oh, fuck me, fuck me, fuck my cunt!" she screamed in ecstasy.

I was thrown off a little by her sex talk, but I kept a steady rhythm, diving in and out of her wet, tight, juicy box.

"Aaah, shit, aaah, shit!" I released another relaxing load inside of the condom.

We sexed in the truck for a while, smoking most of the night.

I hadn't noticed that Dutch had come outside to look for me.

Where the fuck did he go? I looked at the parking lot to see if his truck was still here. When I saw his truck rocking wildly, I thought for sure something was wrong. I rushed over with a small revolver in my hand. It was my little backup in case something popped off. I lived by the code "never get caught slipping." I had the gun cocked and ready to murder anyone who was in the truck. When I eased up to the truck, I heard the sexual moans of a female, and when I listened closer, I heard a familiar moan. Motherfucker!

I couldn't see shit, so I lowered my gun and stared for a brief moment. My first thought was to go off and shoot him and whoever the bitch was in the truck. But I ultimately decided it would not be a good move.

I was ready to tell Naheri it was over and my son was not his. I knew for certain the baby was Flex's. We'd been together almost every day that month, like two wild animals. I made up my mind that Flex, our son, and I were going to be a family, and we were going to leave this dangerous part of our lives for good. At least, that was the plan . . . until I saw his truck rockin' and heard sounds only he could make deep in some pussy. I turned and quickly stormed off back to the party. I walked over to the area where they'd set aside for drinks and grabbed a nice tall glass of champagne and downed it like it was water. I drank glass after glass until the euphoric feeling took over, and I couldn't feel my face anymore. I got so drunk that I thought the baby would die or be born with a birth defect.

Flex came back into the party a few minutes later with the blond female right behind him. Both of them tried to play it off as if they weren't just in his truck busting nuts all up in there. I watched as Flex adjusted his clothing discreetly as he made his way to the restroom. When he made eye contact with me, I cut my eyes and looked away. He continued to the bathroom, and I continued to play the good wife in front of Naheri and his colleagues.

Inside, I was seething with anger. I wanted to confront Flex. I was about to make strides toward the bathroom but decided against it.

Thoughts flashed to the child we already had. I thought we would never be able to have a happy life. Living a lie was getting to me. There were so many days I planned to come clean because the guilt was eating me alive, but I got too deep into the game, and there was never a right time.

Chapter 8

Light It Up

"Dutch, I'm a man, and I had needs. Li'l buddy was something to do. I never loved her. She was good for me to fill those days and nights when you were with your husband and our son playing family and shit. What else was I supposed to do? Baby, I couldn't have you, so what was I supposed to do?"

"You know what? Fuck it! Fuck it, fuck it! I don't have time to think about this shit right now. I need my son back in my arms. Nothing and no one else matters," I said as I walked out of the room.

Flex almost lost his footing as he rushed behind me and swung me around to look him straight in the eyes. "You serious right now? Really? How the fuck could you say that, Dutch? All this time you have been married, and I had no one because I could never get past the love

I have for you. How could you just say fuck it—fuck us? I didn't have you, and I especially didn't have *our* son," he said, emphasizing the word "our." I have sat back and watched how the choice we both made and the lifestyle we chose to live caused us to be lonely. "Yeah, I banged the broad. But she meant nothing to me. All I wanted was you. All I have ever wanted was you. How the hell did you think I felt when you gave birth to my firstborn, *my* seed, and I couldn't even be in the room? That shit damn near killed me! When I first laid eyes on him, I *knew* he was mine."

He looked into my eyes as my tears began to fall down my cheeks. I had to think about every word he spoke, and my heart went out to him because he was right. How could I be mad at him for trying to find a piece of happiness while I stayed in a marriage of convenience?

"You're right, Flex. But you didn't find that odd that Bridgette would call you? I mean, if you weren't official, why she would call you? And for that matter, how did Rasta even know y'all were messing around? Some shit not sitting right with me about this at all." I always thought out every detail. That was how I had been able to escape and live another day and not get locked up . . . by staying one step in front of the rest.

"You're right; we were not exclusive, and out of the whole time we saw each other, I never took her out too much in public. If we did go out, I would always get a quick drive-through meal, and every car I had always had a dark tint with bulletproof glass. The more I think about it, the more things really don't add up." Flex paused a moment. "Hey, Dutch, how long ago did that shit happen with Rasta's brother?"

"Man, that shit was over two years ago. I knew I should have hunted him down and killed his ass. Why you ask that?"

"I think this sh—" He stopped midsentence as he answered his vibrating cell phone. "Yo, what's the word?"

Chapter 9

My Screw Face

"Ow, why the hell you hit me like that? That shit hurt!" I yelped and rubbed my face.

"Mi sorry, Bridggy. Mi had to make it sound good. Besides, that fool boi not gonna come just for ya ass alone. Mi had to make it real fo dem," he said as he leaned over and kissed me on my face. "Pretty soon dis be ova. You did good, me vanilla bean. Mi would never have known anyting about the son if you hadn't told me. So the bitch is more dutty than mi thought. How she lying to this doctor husband, and he be lying to her? These Yankees are so treacherous. Mi no trust none of dem."

Rasta sat there with a smirk on his face. His plan was coming together. He had set Naheri up right where he wanted him. He played on the weakness of any man in love: a woman. "Seems to mi de bad boi has a hidden motive," Rasta said as he shrugged his shoulder, smiling widely as he looked over at me. At that time, I was partaking in the drug of my choice. He watched me as I reared my head backward and pushed a white substance up my nose. The night I was "abducted," we staged everything. Rasta needed me to make his plan work in exchange for some of the purest cocaine Jamaica had to offer. It was a win in my book. I didn't have to do much to keep my expensive habit afloat.

Rasta told me after Dutch or Elana killed his brother, it put him in a position where he was reduced to poverty. He was back down to scraps and pennies, which made his thirst to kill her even greater. No one would deal with him. Word was out that he was a snitch, and he was the one who set his own brother up to be robbed and killed. When he did find one of his brother's old connects that was willing to deal with him, he ran off with over ten kilos with a net worth of $250,000. When his spot got robbed, he was stuck. They wanted their dope or the money. The only way around it was to pay up . . . or die.

The only other thing they wanted more than the money or dope was the Great Dutchtress. He promised to deliver her head to them in a gym bag, and that would wipe his debt away. I wanted to ask him who "they" were, but I thought I was already in it to the point of where if I knew any more, my life would be in jeopardy. It made me shiver when he said he wanted her son to be there when her head rolled across the floor.

"Make de boi some food and bring it to him. He need to eat someting before he see his moma dead," he sternly said to me. Then he sat back in the chair and watched me move to obey his orders. I was half high and only semi-aware of what his orders were. Slowly, I got up, barely standing, sluggishly grabbed a sandwich from the counter, and carried it into a small, dimly lit room.

Little Naheri lay there in the same clothes he had on for a week already. His little face was swollen from the beatings he had been receiving when he would cry out for his mother. Rasta showed the small child no mercy. In Rasta's mind, the boy's mother was the reason for his downfall, and he would make her pay by any means necessary.

I threw the plate next to his head, barely missing him. Then I stumbled back out of the room. Rasta looked at me with a frown on his face as if he smelled something rotten.

"Fuck this! I ain't no fuckin' babysitter! Give me my shit so that I can go!" I said in protest.

"Shut up, stupid crackhead. Ya be who I say ya be. Now come 'ere and do the ting ya know well, bitch."

I walked over and dropped to my knees in front of him and placed his short, stubby manhood in my dry-ass mouth. I started bobbing my head up and down on his manhood like he told me. I couldn't stop until he came in my mouth. When he finished, he looked at me with a disgusted expression, laughed, then pushed me to the floor, zipped up his pants, stood up, and walked into the bathroom, making sure to slam the door.

I lay on the floor in an altered state of mind. The drugs had taken effect the way I wanted them to. I felt nothing: no guilt, no pain, no depression. I knew deep down that once his plan was over, he would have no use for me, and he would kill me just as quick as Elana's head rolled. I cursed my life and what I had become—a bottom-of-a-barrel bitch—and not in a good way.

My life was out of control and was unbearable. I had turned tricks for money and drugs before Naheri gave me the job as a receptionist in his office. I was grateful to him since all of my close friends and family turned against me. They could not take all the lying and stealing of their shit when they tried to help me. My family quickly put two and two together and figured out that I was on drugs and would do anything to get them, which included selling my ass on the street. Honestly, Naheri had a place in my heart. He was the only one who treated me with respect and gave me the tools to have some dignity about myself, and he didn't even realize it.

When Rasta first approached me with his plan, I didn't want to do it. But after a night of drugs and drinking, he gained some information from me about her family. Where they lived and where they worked. He was smart. Got me talking about my life and how much shit I went through with my family to have them believing that I was finally clean and living a good Christian life. He used that information to make me go along with the plan, and if I didn't, every one of them would die because of me. I couldn't have that on my head. I promised to do as he asked as long as my family was unharmed, and he kept my secret.

I lay on the floor with come still dripping from the sides of my mouth.

"Get up! And go wash ya ass! I swear you witch sure look ugly wen ya no dun up." Rasta shook his head in disbelief as he headed out the door.

Once I heard the door slam behind him, I slowly rose up and made my way to the bathroom. I caught a glimpse of myself in the mirror—and I immediately threw up. The sight of my worn and frail-looking image made me sick. *What have I done to me? Who am I?* I wiped the mirror thinking that it was my mind playing tricks on me again. Quickly, I splashed water on my face aggressively. Then I grabbed a washcloth hanging by the sink and dipped it under the hot, running water. I scrubbed my face, hoping it would rub this fucked-up look off it. After that, I stared at the reflection in the mirror . . . and started to rub my face again with the washcloth. I wanted to tear away my skin.

"This can't be life; this *won't* be my life." I continued to scrub my face as I yelled, "Oh hell, no, I'm out of here! Fuck this shit!"

I didn't know if it was the strength of the coke I was on or if I was really prepared to change. All I knew was at that very moment, I had had enough! No longer would I allow men and drugs to define me. I turned the water off, ran into the living room, and grabbed some clothes. That's when I heard him. The moaning and crying came from Junior in the other room.

"Mommy, Daddy!" his little voice cracked from dehydration.

I walked over to the room where the scared and battered child lay.

One part of me wanted to turn and walk the other way. I don't want no part of this crazy shit anymore! I'm not with hurting a child. Fuck this; I'm out!

I hurried to the door and slowly turned the knob, but it was as if something was holding me back. I looked over my shoulder, cursing myself for what I was about to do. I knew that either way, it meant certain death, whether it be by the hands of Rasta or Elana and Flex. Either way, I would pay.

But maybe, I figured Flex would show me some mercy and spare my sorry life. Then the thought popped into my head like a lightbulb. I'll call the one who has shown me nothing but respect. Naheri. I know he will be happy to see his son!

Quickly, I ran into the room and picked up the crying boy, then raced to the front door. I threw him over my shoulder like a fireman and cautiously opened the door. Two big men were standing in front of it with their backs toward the door.

Damn! I quietly closed the door so they wouldn't notice I had opened it.

I rushed back over to the room where Junior had been and closed the door. I laid little Naheri on the mattress on the floor and began searching the room for an exit. He started to moan and cry again. "Shh, shh, I'ma get us out of here!" I whispered to him to be as quiet as he could be.

I walked over to the boarded-up window in the room and tugged and pulled until I felt one of the boards loosen up. I was able to pry one of them off the window to create a space big enough for us to fit through.

"One more good pull. . . . Aaah!" Finally, I removed the board. I stood still for a moment to make sure we were the only ones in the house.

I stuck my head out of the space I created to make sure no one was watching the window from outside. Once I saw that we could get out, I grabbed Junior and climbed out of the window. As soon as my feet touched the ground, I took off running like a track and field star with Junior in my arms. I wasn't stopping until I got close to Naheri and got out of town before anyone could find me.

After running without stopping for at least five minutes, I looked up at the street sign to see where I was. I ran all the way from an abandoned-looking house on Sixty-third and Laflin Street on the Southside of Chicago to

Seventy-ninth Street and Ashland Boulevard. I ducked and dodged the main streets on my way to Naheri's office.

My heart almost skipped a beat when the office came into my sight. I stopped abruptly when I spotted Rasta's dark-colored wagon parked outside on the side entrance of the office.

Immediately, I ducked into an alleyway and hid behind a few garbage cans. Cautiously, I peeked above the cans to see if Rasta's wagon was still there. After a few hesitant peeks, I watched Rasta leave from the back of the office. Then I saw Naheri standing in the doorway with a strange look on his face. After I was certain Rasta left and was out of view of the office building, I headed that way, making sure to keep my eyes open for his wagon or any man with dreads in the area.

As I got closer, I remembered that it was Thursday, and there were usually no surgeries scheduled. It would be perfect to slip inside of the surgical suite and leave Little Naheri there. We were finally at the back entrance. I slowly crept over and opened the back door, which Naheri Sr. never locked. As soon as I walked in, I headed to one of the surgical rooms. I placed the little boy on the metal table and covered his body with one of the surgical gowns. The little boy was so tired and drained he just lay still, motionless, with his eyes barely open. Quietly, I closed the door.

I walked over to Naheri's office and stood in the doorway. I saw him in his chair, facing the window as if he was in deep thought.

"Dr. Dolvan, you got a minute?" I said in a voice just above a whisper. I wasn't sure how I was going to explain all of this to him, but I prayed he would understand.

Chapter 10

Care to Explain

"Hey, Jorge, did you get that?" I asked.

We had been out all day searching for Junior. We hit a few spots and even had one or two of them torched to keep sending the message. We found a couple who knew Rasta and really wanted to settle a few scores with him themselves.

"Yes, amigo, I found out where Rasta is laying his head while he has been here in our fair city. One of my *caliente reina negra* told me she saw him in the hood over on Laflin Street. You know, over there by our old spot? The one those punk police hombres had shut down?"

"Yeah, I know about that one. You mean to tell me that muthafucka been hangin' out in my city right under my nose with Junior?"

Jorge was silent for a moment. Then he took a deep breath. I could tell he had something bad to say, so I braced myself for what he was about to lay out. I took a deep breath. "Go ahead, amigo, spit that shit. It can't be no worse than what I suspect anyway."

"A'ight, homes. The *chica* told me they been doing the li'l boy bad, beating him and starving him and shit. I mean, some really fucked-up shit is what she said."

I looked over at Dutch, who was pacing the floor. I decided not to tell her this last piece, as it would surely send her over the edge. "A'ight, man, how this chick know about all this? Is she with them?"

"No, bro, she a party girl. She told me one night her and her friends were at the club up on Lawrence around Montrose in the Jamaican and Nigerian part of the city, partying and shit like they always do. She said she spotted these dudes with long locs and dark skin coming up in the club. She said her girl was on the dance floor when one of them approached her and asked if they wanted to party at the crib out south. Her girl, being one of them greedy-type hoes, agreed. Now I couldn't get mad. She not my wife, so, hey, she free to fuck who she chooses. She said all of them left and met up at this house on Sixty-third Street and Laflin. She said when they pulled up, at first the shit looked abandoned, but her girl talked her into going inside with her anyway. There she saw a nice setup, she said. So when she asked to use the bathroom, she accidently walked into the wrong room where she saw a little boy lying there like he was half dead. She said before she could get a good foot all the way in to help the boy, one of the men grabbed her by her arm and threatened her. She said he told her to forget anything she had just seen if she wanted to live. So when she heard me asking around, she put two and two together. These are some new dudes with Jamaican accents, and you know they asses stick out like a sore thumb in those parts."

I listened very closely to all that Jorge was saying. I had to get our son, and I will handle Rasta for good. It had only been a few days since Dutch told me about the scene she had with Naheri. She had been going back and forth to the hillside house, using it to shower, sleep, and eat. Her colleagues were handling her practice. There were no big cases, and her presence was not necessary. One thing I did notice was that she did not attempt nor made a move to see Naheri. I hoped that she was finally seeing the big picture of us and no one else.

"I'm going to shower," Dutch mouthed to me while I was still talking to Jorge.

"My man. I knew you would come through. You don't know how much this means to me. We'll meet up soon; and trust me, you know how thankful I am." I hung up the phone.

I smiled with the news I just heard. And I knew Dutch would be ready to go get this motherfucker. Then our life could start.

Staying at this hillside house with Dutch was great, but the circumstances weren't. The last few days we were together, hunting, killing, sleeping, fucking, eating . . . We never left each other's side for more than a few minutes. I thought of the day when we, she, our seed, and me, would be together and all this craziness would end. We would have to move to another country 'cause I know with the amount of destruction we have done, *everybody* would be looking for us.

Chapter 11

It Ain't No Fun When the Rabbit Got the Gun

"Hey, I'm not waiting anymore. I'm out," I said through gritted teeth. I didn't want to stand in that house one second longer. I was on my way out the door, with or without Flex. Then my phone rang. "Hello?" I answered, agitated.

"Yeah, I wanted to call and check on you. I haven't heard from you in days. Elana, what's going on? I know the last time we got into it, but we're going to have to talk about it like adults. We can't avoid our problems any longer," Naheri said with concern in his voice.

"I'm doing okay; I have just been . . ." I tried to say something but felt my emotions starting to overwhelm me. I released a sigh of frustration with a mixture of defeat.

"Listen, Elana, it's okay; whatever it is, it will work itself out. Your office called my office for you. They said they couldn't get a hold of you, and they haven't heard from you in days. Is everything okay, Elana? What's going on?"

"Yes, I'm fine. I'll give them a call soon. I've been working on a case that has me feeling somewhat like I'm in the mob. I mean, they have me so hush-hush. I'm sorry. . . . I'm sorry for the way I acted the last time. You're right. . . ." As the words left my mouth, the thought of lying yet again had my head spinning. This has got to stop.

"When do you think you'll be home? I need to talk to you," Naheri said.

"Ay, yo, Dutch, let's go!" Flex yelled, unaware that I was on the phone with Naheri.

"Is that Flex?" he angrily questioned.

"Yes. We were at a meeting with a few new clients," I said, trying to come up with a quick, believable lie.

"Why is he . . . You know what? Never mind; go ahead and handle whatever *business* you were up to!" Naheri said with a tone full of sarcasm; then he hung up.

My mouth gaped open wide in shock at the tone he had just used with me. In our entire marriage, he had never raised his voice like that to me. I probably would have sliced his head clean off his shoulders if he had. This was a first.

I didn't have the mind-set or the desire to deal with Naheri's attitude. But I dialed his number back anyway and reached the voicemail on the first ring.

Why do men always end up in their feelings? I threw my hands up in submission and shrugged my shoulders as I turned and walked out the door.

By the time I made it to the car, Flex had it running and almost in drive, ready to pull off. He didn't say a word to me. He just pulled off into traffic, heading toward I-290. He entered the ramp, headed east on his way to the South Side of town.

"Where we going? What did Jorge say?" I asked.

"This will be over very soon. It's time you start thinking about where we gonna live," he looked at me smiling.

I didn't know what to say. My emotions were on a high. Will this be the day my son is finally in my arms? Are we going to get him? I looked toward the backseat of the truck and saw my blade. At that moment, I knew it was finally going to be over.

Chapter 12

Back to the Beginning

We pulled up on the block—the block I used to call home. When I was younger, that was where I gained my street smarts and learned the survival of the fittest. I started looking around. The more I saw, the more things looked like they had not changed. I spotted the old swing in the park, the same park I spent so many days and nights in. I began to remember back to the times when my mother would leave to feed her nasty crack addiction, sometimes for days at a time. I was forced to take care of myself until the state came and took me away. It was either be a ward of the state, or else a ward of some family member.

I would have rather been in and out of foster homes than living with my horrible aunt Baelene. She was just as bad as my mother on drugs. She was what you would call a functioning crack-head. That's when someone appears to have it all together to the outside world, but to those of us who had to experience their horrible habit up close and personal, we knew the real deal. It seemed in those days that was all everyone did. If it wasn't marijuana, it was crack or that other nasty drug of choice: heroin.

I always had to survive on my own, trust no one, and let no one in—that was until I met Flex and Ms. Ruby. When I turned the tender age of 16, we met and instantly fell in hate. I was not the type to let anyone come around me and get up in my space. Flex was the neighborhood dope boy. At the age of 18, he had been in and out of jail so many times that everybody just knew when they saw him coming that trouble was close behind.

I looked around my old neighborhood and started reminiscing again on the moments and times that made me who I am today. The lawyer, the mother, the lover, the wife, and the killer that I am today . . . I owe it all to this small Englewood community right here in the heart of Chicago.

We drove down a little farther. We were about to pass right by 6125 South Morgan. That building held bittersweet memories for me.

"Pull over right here," I quickly said to Flex, causing him to come to an abrupt stop. He looked at me confused but did what I asked.

I slowly opened the car door and got out. I looked around the old, raggedy building that still had people living in it. Nothing looked like it had changed or even been fixed. In fact, it looked like it had the same paint on it from when I was a little girl living here. I held my head down as feelings of sadness rushed over me. This was the very thing I was trying to keep my son from, but here it was. He was right in the thick of it all because of my way of life.

I turned my head to the left where the corner store used to be and thought back to the time the neighborhood sex offender tried to get me and my friend Marla. We fought like hell and got away. I inwardly laughed because if I saw him today, I would cut his eyes from their sockets.

I stood a little bit longer, getting ready to end my trip down memory lane. I had to stop and get some perspective. For me to defeat my enemy, I had to think like them, and what better way to get in their mind-set than by getting in their element, back to the place where I started? No matter where my life had taken me, this was the place where I learned how to survive. By running off of my emotions, I had made some costly mistakes. I needed to go back to the beginning where my motivation was survival, back to the place I learned to do that. That was the only way

I would be able to get my son back and regain my life. To kill a rat, I had to think like an exterminator, and this was right where I learned to do that.

"Elana, is that you?" I heard a light voice call out my government name.

I turned in the direction of the voice to see who was behind it. My eyes fell on Ms. Ruby, looking not a day over 55. She still looked the same, for the most part. She had a few wrinkles here and there and gray hair, but it was her.

I was so excited to see her. Ms. Ruby was the one who took care of me when my aunt would leave me for days at a time and let her drug dealers have their way with my young body. "Yes, Ms. Ruby, it's me, Elana," I answered.

"Baby, I wasn't sure if that was you or not. You look good, chile. My old eyes ain't what they used to be. How you been, baby? I always wondered what happened to you."

"I'm okay, Ms. Ruby. I went on to college and got a degree in criminal justice, which later led me to become a lawyer."

"Aw, now, look at God! I always prayed you were doing all right, and from the looks of you, you're doing just fine. Baby, I searched for you, but them people would never tell me nothing about you. I called and called . . . and nothing. They said because we weren't no kin, I couldn't get you." She paused for a second. "You know they found your mother and aunt dead? Yeah, baby, they owed some money to some of those dope boys. Uh-huh, they found them with their throats slashed awhile back almost right after them folk took you. They had it on the news and everything. They ain't never found who did it. Some people 'round here said them gang-bangers over on Sixty-ninth Street did it 'cause they owed some money, but who knows. Yo' aunt and yo' momma was a mess. I remember the nights yo' grandmother cried and walked the streets looking for them girls," she said, shaking her head in sorrow. "Anyway, did they ever find your little brother and sister?"

I wasn't sure if it was old age or what, but I didn't know of a little brother or sister. "Ms. Ruby, I don't have a little brother or sister," I said, confused.

"Oh yes, you do, baby. Yo' momma gave birth to them when you were about 13 or so. I don't know what happen to them 'cause when I saw her that one time, she was pregnant and clean. She looked real nice like she been off drugs. Then the next time I saw her after that day, she looked like she was back on that mess and didn't have those babies with her. She told me she was having twins. Judging from the look on your face, I take it you didn't know this."

I didn't know whether I should show any remorse or emotion about the fate that my mother and aunt had met. I wasn't concerned about my so-called brother and sister. Hell, from where I sat, they were better off without her trifling ass. I hope they ended up in a good place. At least they didn't have to put up with the hell I did. Honestly, I didn't care, because I was the one who sent my mother and my aunt straight to hell.

One night after one of my aunt's suppliers and one of his friends raped me, I decided I'd had enough. I went in search of my aunt. My first stop was to her usual dope spot, and there she was, sitting at the table smoking her pipe and looking high as hell as if she didn't have a care in the world. She nodded and twirled in her chair, high as that thang. The one guest who joined in on her smoke session, to my surprise, was my mother. She sat right next to my aunt. I watched both of those sorry-ass excuses for caregivers nodding and laughing as if the pain they had caused me in my life was just a joke. I was furious! I watched as they smoked up all of the state money that was sent to me and left me to be fucked and sucked by anyone who would front my aunt some drugs. I watched until something snapped inside of me. I reached in my back pocket and pulled out a box cutter I kept on me for protection. I held a grip on it so hard it almost pierced my skin.

I waited until all of them inside the house were good and out of it. My aunt and my mother continued to sit at the table. By now, the drugs they'd just put in their bodies had them zoned out and not on point—as if they ever were. I slowly crept in the door. The first one I went to was my high-ass mother. I stood right over her. She looked up, then dropped her head back down to the table. She was so high she didn't even know who I was.

A part of me hoped she would say, "Baby, I'm sorry. I'll be a better mother." But that was all in my imagination because when she put her empty, unstable eyes on me, her reaction was as if I was a total stranger. I frowned at the fact that she didn't even know her own daughter. She didn't give a shit about me, and she chose drugs over her child. Before I knew it, I had grabbed her by the hair and lifted her face off the table. In one long, swift swoop, I sliced her throat open, then slammed her head back on the table. All I could hear was her making a gurgling sound as she took her last breath.

My aunt sat there dazed like she was a mummy or something. She didn't scream . . . She didn't flinch. Nothing. All she did was sit there with her eyes wide open. All I could see was her leaving earlier and telling me, "*Now, you let Mr. Jacks and his friend have some fun. I'll be back in a little while.*" She smiled and left me to the wolves. That man and his friend wasted no time having their way with me. I walked over to her and punched her in the face. Here I was, 14, and they had done stuff to me only seen in porn movies. Every image flashed in my mind. After I punched her in the face, I grabbed a fistful of her nasty, disheveled hair. She tried to fight me, but her swings were off.

I took my time dragging the box cutter across her throat. I even paused once so I could make sure her blood was spilling from the hole I put in her neck. I took great pleasure in watching these two miserable, low-grade bitches known to me as mother and aunt take their last pathetic breaths.

Once the last stroke was done, I made sure neither of them had a pulse. I wasted no time stuffing their bodies under a floorboard in the old trap house. All of the rest of the people in there were so high that they didn't even know what day it was. One of the men in there even offered to help me drag my aunt's body, he was so high. They wouldn't tell the police shit out of fear that it would bring heat to their beloved crack house. I lived on my own in that same apartment taking care of myself with the help of Ms. Ruby some days. After Flex and I got close, it was me, him, and Gelow. We were all like the three amigos until Gelow was murdered by his own brother over some drug debt. Sad to say, that was one of the worst days of my life. I cried more for his death than my own family.

I went to school by day and trapped by night. That was the only way I could take care of myself until Flex came to move in with me. After almost getting robbed by the stick-up boys, Flex was like a bodyguard to me. We weren't intimate with each other at first. Our love/hate relationship blossomed into a good business arrangement. But after a year or so, the more we hung out, the more our feelings grew. It became more than just him protecting me and the trap house we built. He was everything I needed. We had one of those unspoken attractions that developed as we spent more time together. He watched my back, and I watched his. I'd never experienced anything like it. Not even my mother showed me a love like that. If anyone would even touch a hair on my head, Flex did not hesitate to drop them like a bad habit.

After we both realized we had more than just a business arrangement going on, I decided I would give in to my desires, and I gave myself to him. He already owned my mind. I thought of him daily, and I could damn near finish his sentences. He made me feel complete, and he owned a part of my spirit. It seemed only right that he'd have my body too. He was my first true relationship.

When I spent the first time with him, all of that bad stuff that had happened to me didn't even enter my mind. We had it all set up, the operation, the relationship, and the love . . . until that nosy bitch on the third floor called the landlord, who then called the Department of Child Protective Services. They came and found out I was alone and that my mother and aunt were both missing.

"Ms. Ruby, you still live here?" I asked, bringing myself back to my reality. "After all these years? Wow!" I said in amazement.

"Chile, where am I gonna go? This neighborhood been here before me and gon' be here when I'm gone. I won't let nothing and nobody run me away from here."

I looked down at her and her clothing. It wasn't the most expensive, but she wore it like it was designer made, and I had to respect her for that. She even still had that bright smile she had when I was younger, that smile that would make me feel that all was right with the world, even when it wasn't. "Ms. Ruby, I'm so glad I saw you! Will you allow me to do something for you?"

"What's that, chile?" she asked with one eyebrow raised.

"Here, take this. I want to help you get out of this place. I own a couple of houses, and you can have one. Will you let me do that for you?"

"No, I will not! Listen, baby, nothing in this lifetime is by chance or just happens that the good Lawd ain't meant it to. All the money and nice thangs ain't gon' get me into heaven. Now this here is my community. I was born here and more than likely gon' die here. But I will take them couple'a dollars 'cause, yeah, see, times is hard," she said with a slight chuckle. "But for the most part, I love living here. I done watched all these kids and they kids' kids and even some of they kids' kids grow up. I done seen four generations in one family been raised here. So, no, I can't leave here. But what brings you 'round here, Elana? Not that I ain't happy to see you."

I smiled as I remembered how I could never get anything past Ms. Ruby. "Well, to be honest, I'm looking for some new guys that I heard live here in the neighborhood. They took something that means a lot to me, and I need to find them. Someone told they were over around this way. They have some strong Jamaican accents."

Ms. Ruby's eyes grew big, and she held her coat close to her chest in fear.

"Ms. Ruby, you okay? What's wrong?"

She looked at me in a hushed manner. "Elana, you don't want to mess with them, baby. Them men is dangerous! I saw them the other night terrorizing one of the girls around here. They beat her up pretty bad. I closed my curtains and called the police. I didn't want them to see me. I heard one of them say as he stomped her, 'Bitch, you told where I am,' but it didn't sound like the way we talked. He said it in that foreign voice, like 'you de tell' or something like that. I heard they were over at Mr. Johnson's old place, you know, the one down by Ogden Park. The place went down after he died. He left it to his daughter, and she let her kids sell drugs out of it. The city eventually took it."

I turned in that direction. I knew which house it was. Then I turned back to Ms. Ruby. "Okay, I'm not going by there," I lied. "Listen, for what it's worth, I never got the chance to thank you for everything you did for me when I was coming up. Do you remember that program you made me get in when I was in high school?"

"Yeah, the one that said they could help you get into college and will help pay for it?"

"Yeah, that's the one. Well, they gave me a full scholarship to Stanford. I graduated top of my class, and I owe that to you because you always told me I could be anything I wanted in this life. I used that advice to make something of myself and to get the finer things I wanted out of life. For that, I will be forever grateful to you." I reached out to hug Ms. Ruby. "I thank you, Ms. Ruby, for showing me love when my own family didn't. I sing that song you taught me when I was younger to my son, Naheri Jr. One day, I'ma bring him by to meet you if that's okay," I said as I thought about my son and how Ms. Ruby was the only one I could count on besides Flex. Because of her, I was able to show my son some motherly love.

After our hug, she leaned down and looked at Flex in the driver's seat. "Is that that hardheaded li'l Kajaun?" she called out with a smile on her face.

Flex got out of the car, walked up to her, and hugged her. "Ms. Ruby, you looking just as good as you did when I was younger," he said with flattery and a huge smile on his face.

"Look at you!" She looked him up and down. "Mr. Fl . . . Fo . . . Flex? Oh yeah, Flex is what they called you. But I'm calling you by the name your mother Fredericka gave you. Kajaun, you look just as cute as you were when she brought you home. How you been, boy? Stayin' free and out of trouble, I hope."

"Yeah, Ms. Ruby, I'm good."

She smiled, looking at me and then at him. "I see the good Lawd kept y'all two in touch," she said with a knowing smirk. "Well, let me get to this house. These old bones ain't like they used to be. Y'all come back and see me soon. Ya know I ain't gon' live forever, and I would love to sit down and talk with you."

I reached out and gave her one more hug and promised to be by soon.

Flex and I watched her walk down the street to the gate of her building. It was the push I needed to get my mind right. I had all the people in these streets I paid, and none of them could give me the information I needed. But here I was, and the very person who gave me love and asked for nothing in return could give me all the information I needed.

Just as Flex got into the driver's seat and I opened the car door, I noticed a young man walk up close to Ms. Ruby. Then she suddenly fell to the ground. The guy ran off as I rushed over to her. When I got closer, I saw blood covering the front of her coat, and she was holding her hands close to her chest, gasping for air.

Flex took off chasing the guy. I placed Ms. Ruby's head in my lap. I wanted to scream. All I could do was watch one of the few who helped me in this world take her last breath. I sat rocking and holding her and noticed a small knife wound in her chest, close to her heart. "Ms. Ruby, why? You didn't deserve this!" I yelled with tears rolling down my face.

"Come on, Dutch. There's nothing we can do for her. Come on before them boys in blue get here. Come on!"

I gently laid her head on the cold concrete. I knew this was a hit on her because they knew she saw them beating that girl the other night. In the street, rules don't apply. It was leave no witnesses. I said a silent prayer for her and got in the car.

"Ms. Ruby, I'ma get these muthafuckas if it's the last thing I do!"

I couldn't get the image of Ms. Ruby, then Junior's little innocent face, out of my head. I knew I was losing my grip on this whole situation. First, they caught me slipping and took my son. Now, the only person that had ever shown an ounce of motherly love was just taken from me. Suddenly, it hit me. I grabbed my phone and placed a call.

"Ah wa yuh a deal wid, ah lang time wi nuh link up, mi need a fayva. All of Rasta man's roots in my house there. Mi wah send clear message," I said as I spoke in a heavy Jamaican dialect. I called to have all of Rasta's family members, the ones that were left, assembled in my home in Kingston, Jamaica. I wanted his two kids, his father and his new wife, and his half brother. I would not make the same mistake I did before. This time, *no one* would be left to carry his bloodline. Then I hung up. "It's done!" I made a critical mistake with Rasta. His brother was my target at the time, and I thought he was alone, but when Rasta showed his face, I didn't have enough time to murk his ass too before the Babylon arrived. At that time, my ass couldn't get caught. Now, Rasta's entire bloodline will be taken out. Even the fucking dog is going to get it. I don't give a fuck!

Flex looked straight ahead as he drove with a sinister smirk across his lips.

"Dem dead soon," I said through clenched teeth.

Chapter 13

The Real You

"Dr. Dolvan, do you have a moment? I need your help." A low-toned, soft voice startled me from my thoughts.

I turned to see a disheveled Bridgette standing in the doorway. She was slightly trembling. I quickly rose and rushed over to help her into a chair in front of my desk. I peeked out into the hall to make sure no one was straggling in the hallway. It was the end of the day, and everyone was leaving.

"Bridgette, I have been worried sick about you! How did you get away? Did they hurt you? Did they rape you?" I fired question after question, not giving her a moment to breathe or answer them.

Bridgette looked over her shoulder, then all around the room. She wanted to make sure they were alone before she told him everything.

She took a deep breath. “Dr. Dolvan, what I am about to tell—” She stopped.

“Come on; it’s okay. You’re safe now. I’ll close the door. Have a seat. Nobody’s going to hurt you. He left and is long gone. You’re safe, I promise. Everyone has left for the day.” I spoke calmly to ease her and gently rubbed her arm to give her a sense of security; then I sat next to her.

“Dr. Dolvan—Naheri—what I’m about to tell you will change everything. I first want you to know how sorry I am for the part I played, but I didn’t have a choice.”

I looked at her, not knowing what she was about to tell me, but whatever it was, I knew it was big. Never before had she called me by my first name.

“I was part of this whole thing. I was the one who set up your wife and Flex. The man I’m working for is Rasta from Jamaica. When I met him, he held something over my head and forced me to help. I didn’t want to help him hurt you like this—not you, of all people. You are the only one who has ever treated me like I mattered.” She cried uncontrollably.

“Okay, Bridgette, it’ll be okay. Calm down and tell me all about what you have taken part in to destroy my family and me.”

"I had to—or else he was going to kill my family and tell them about my addiction." She dropped her head low, ashamed.

"What do you mean? Are you still on drugs? I thought—"

"I know . . . but after you helped me get off of the drugs, I reached out to my family to show them that I was not the same person I used to be. I was clean and living a good life. They finally allowed me to visit on the regular, interact with everybody, even invited me to family events. Naheri, you don't know how much this meant to me. I was finally good in their eyes."

"But, Bridgette, what made you start using again? Were you high at work?"

"No, I was never high at work. I met this guy, and at first, it was just a sprinkle in the blunts we was smoking, which I didn't think was a big deal because I wasn't smoking every day. But then the little sprinkle wasn't cutting it; then I took my first hit in a long time, and it felt really good." She started to cry again.

"What the hell, Bridgette . . . I'm sorry . . ." I grabbed her hand. "It'll be okay. Now tell me, what did you do?"

"I helped him."

"Helped who?"

"The man that just left your office."

My head dropped, and my anger started to show. “You *helped* that man? The *same* man trying to kill my wife?” I stood up and started to pace the floor from the door to the chair she was seated in. “What the fuck did you do?”

“I told him about you and your wife after he told me his story. I told him where you lived and that you had a son. That’s when he came up with a plan to get to your wife, and the only way to do that was to take your son.”

I stopped pacing and stood directly in front of her and lowered my face inches from hers. “Where the fuck is my son?”

“I promise I didn’t do anything to hurt him. I fed him.”

At this point, my anger overcame me. I yanked her right up out of the chair and tossed her ass against the door. “I’m *not* going to ask you again. Where the fuck is my son?”

Bridgette lowered her eyes and fell to the floor in tears. “I know he is not your biological son. I found out right before Rasta kidnapped him. I wanted to tell you, but I didn’t know how. I ran across the DNA test on the little boy.”

“Oh, did you? Well, you also know he is my junior. DNA or not, he is my son. I don’t care what his mother may or may not have done—he is *my* son.” I punched the door above her head with anger oozing from every word.

She eased up carefully and wiped her tears. "Come, follow me."

I started to cut off the lights and close the window blinds at a hurried pace, thinking we would be leaving the office to get my son.

"Lock the front door," Bridgette urged me.

She walked toward a room with me following close behind. Together, we walked to the surgery area. I had no surgeries scheduled for today, so the area was empty. I only hoped I wasn't walking into another trap. We entered an unoccupied surgical room. Then I stopped dead in my tracks when I spotted my son through the window of the door. He was lying on the metal table with a gown thrown over him.

I almost knocked Bridgette over to open the door. I rushed over to him. "What the fuck? What the hell did they do to my son?" I cried hard. At that moment, I wished I never met Elana, or Dutchtress, a ruthless murderer that fooled me for years. She led me to believe he was ours. The child who carried my name and knows only me as his father. It sank in. Elana was not the person I thought she was. Everything was a lie from the start.

I should have listened to my mother when she told me she didn't trust Elana. I tossed her doubtful comments out of the window. I could hear her voice loud and clear now. "*I don't like her. There is something about that girl I can't put my finger on it, but something is not right with her.*" It hit me like a ton of bricks. I made up my mind right at that moment that neither my son nor I would be subjected to Elana's lies and her deceit any longer. I was truly done. There was no talking through it. Sitting down like adults working out our problems was *not* going to happen.

"Bridgette, close the door. I need to examine him. I need to make sure he has no internal bleeding or anything. Help me quickly."

"Of course, Naheri," she said moving at lightning speed.

I wanted to wrap my hands around her throat and choke the life out of her. I have never been a violent man, but this right here could turn any man.

I removed the gown from him and started to examine his body, making sure he had no broken limbs.

"Daddy?" his little voice called out.

"Yeah, son, it's me. You're good now. Daddy's here."

"Daddy, my face hurts. . . ." His words groggily trailed off.

The bruises on his face, head, and chest almost made me break the stethoscope. I didn't want to scare little man, so I started to hum one of his favorite songs from *Lion King* to ease him. The wound on his head looked like someone hit him with something hard. My heart fell into the pit of my stomach. Seeing my son like that was too much for me.

It was a relief that the bruises were just on the surface and no limbs were broken. I know I would have to do some more tests and have his body x-rayed to make sure there were no minor fractures that a physical exam would not reveal. "I'm going get him something to help him with the pain. When was the last time he ate? Do you know, Bridgette? When did you feed him last?"

Her face turned white. It looked like she was about to throw up. The look on her face had me wondering. Did she partake in his torture, or did she stand by and watch someone treat him like an animal? I had so many questions, but time was of the essence. I walked over to the locked medicine cabinet. I remembered that I didn't have the room restocked after my last surgery, so I hoped some pain meds were still in here. I quickly searched through the medication and came across some Oxycodone. It was strong, so I had to be careful. If given enough, it could make a patient feel like they were on cloud nine, but too much could kill my son because of his weight and size.

I picked up the bottle with the seal still fresh on the top and grabbed a syringe. I held the bottle to the light. I wanted to make sure to give him the correct dosage. Every thought of anger, lies, and deception from everyone but my son flashed in my head. I pulled the plunger back farther to fill the syringe, growing angrier and angrier. I didn't plan for things to go like this. It was not supposed to be like this. I emptied the bottle that was full of medicine into the syringe.

"Bridgette, stick your head out of the door. I thought I heard something."

"Sure, Naheri . . . I mean, Dr. Dolvan," she whispered with a smile on her face. She walked back over to the door and reached for the knob.

As soon as she slightly cracked it, I quickly walked toward her and plunged the syringe deep into the side of her neck. I watched her body fall limp. I caught her before she fell to the floor. Her eyes rolled to the back of her head. I pulled her body into the room; then I walked over to the medicine cabinet and filled the syringe with Propofol. I didn't want any loose ends, and she was most definitely a loose one. Then, I walked back to her limp body.

"Die, you fucking bitch—die!" I emptied the syringe into her neck. I could see her body falling to the drug. She would die peacefully. "Sorry, Bridgette, you had to be a casualty in this, but you were a part of this mess."

Anger overwhelmed me. I didn't want to kill her, but there was no way I was going to let her live after she told me she helped that man. Did she *really* think she was going to come in here with my son, tell me some half tale and walk out with a smile on her face? I was no hardened criminal, but I sure as hell wasn't a fool and would allow this bullshit to happen.

I dropped the syringe into the red box by the door. Then I dragged her body closer to the washing station. There was a cabinet underneath big enough for her body to fit in. I stuffed her in there and walked back over to the medicine cabinet. There was some Ibuprofen in liquid form, so I grabbed a new syringe and filled it to give to my son. "Okay, buddy, this may pinch a little bit, but I have to give it to you so you can feel better." I gave him a small amount, but enough to ease his pain.

"Daddy, where's Mommy? I want Mommy."

"You'll see her soon, son. I promise, but now, we have to get out of here quickly. I don't want anything else to happen to you. So for now, you can't see Mommy." I dropped the syringe into the red box. Then I scooped my son into my arms and held him tightly. Tears fell from my eyes. There was no way I was going to let him out of my sight, and I definitely wasn't telling that bitch of a wife I got him either. She can slaughter and hunt down whoever with that motherfucker, Flex. Let *him* clean up her mess.

Cautiously, I left the office building. Since I parked my car in the back, it was easy to get my son to the car without being seen. I gently laid him down in the backseat. Once I got into the driver's seat, I pulled out my cell phone.

"Meet me at the airport, and have the jet gassed up and ready. My guest and I will be leaving for an extended stay in Kingston." I hung up the phone.

If she doesn't die on American soil, I will make sure the last breath she takes will be in my homeland.

Chapter 14

Hell Hath No Fury . . .

Flex and I drove at top speed over to the address on Laflin Street. We pulled around to the back of the address, and just as Ms. Ruby said, the place looked abandoned. We snapped the clips in our 9 mm Glocks. We had them cocked and ready to blow anyone's head off if they decided to make a run for it. My main concern was getting my son out safely. I slowly crept through the gangway on the side of the house. Flex circled on the other side. When I came up to a window, I heard shouting. I knew it was Rasta's men from their heavy accents.

I heard one say, "How dem get away? Boss gonna kill mi dead for dis fuckery!"

Slowly, I crept to the door, which was partially opened. I could see the two fuckers standing there with their backs turned to the door. I nodded to Flex and pointed to the door with my gun. Quickly, I kicked the door wider, and we shot at their heads. Both their bodies hit the floor immediately.

Flex rushed throughout the house, searching every room for our son. Suddenly, bullets were flying from the back of the house. He dove headfirst through an open door. "Muthafucka!" he yelled. I hid behind a wall and ducked low. I could hear Flex returning fire. The hail of bullets seemed endless until I heard someone screaming in agony. I listened carefully to make sure it wasn't Flex. When I was sure it was safe to come out from behind the wall, I rushed toward the screaming and saw Flex standing over a heavyset man with dreads crawling toward the back door. Flex kicked him in the head. "Where the fuck is the boy?"

"He not 'ere," the guy said as he moaned and groaned from the pain of a bullet lodged in his right side of his body and his left leg.

Flex stepped on his leg where he was shot. "Fuck you mean he not here! *Where* is my son?" he said through clenched teeth.

I went to every room in the house and looked in every closet. Junior wasn't there, but when I went into the last room, I saw a mattress in the middle of the floor, and the board was off one of the windows in the room. I looked at the floor and saw something shiny. He was here; we were just too late. I rushed to the back of the house where Flex was.

Just as he was about to pull the trigger and end this fucker's life, I shouted, "Flex, Flex, he's not here!" I had found the little bracelet I gave to him when he was 5. I had it engraved: "*None before we, death before dishonor.*" I held the bracelet up in the dread's face. "Where the fuck is my son?"

"Mi not know! Ow! Dem gon' wen mi got 'ere."

I cocked my Glock and pressed it close to his temple. My face contorted into a frown. "So you think this shit is a joke, huh? You think it's okay to fuck with what's mine? Hey, Flex, they think this shit all good, I see." I smiled from ear to ear with a chuckle. Then I leaned closer toward the man's face and lowered my lips to whisper in his ear. "I'll make sure to find your family and kill them just so you can see your family on the other side, motherfucker!"

I stood up and walked to the kitchen by the stove where I turned on all of the gas burners and blew the flames out. I turned on the oven and blew the pilot light out too. Then I walked around the kitchen and found anything that was flammable and set all the items in the middle of the floor.

When I walked back to Flex, I noticed the dude was still trying to crawl his way out the door. Flex had one of his hands under his chin as he stood watching the dude in his last-ditch effort to escape. With a sinister smirk, he aimed his gun at the dude's right ankle and fired.

"Shit, Flex, you could have blown us the fuck up!"

"My bad, Dutch, but he was getting on my damn nerve with all that moaning and crying and shit," he calmly said as if he hadn't just shot the dude when he was already down.

I finished throwing everything flammable on the floor. When I was set to walk out the back door and throw a match to this bitch, I could hear someone yelling in front of the house.

"Wha di rass!" I clearly heard the voice now. It was Rasta yelling. "Where dem? Bridggy, why ya nah call me yet?"

Flex and I hurried and hid on the side of the door, guns ready. When he came out of the front room, I came from around the wall. Our eyes locked in a deadly stare . . . mine full of rage and his full of fear.

I pointed my gun dead center at his head. "So, muthafucka, you behind all this? Did you *really* think I wasn't going to find your weak, whack ass? You're heartless, bitch boy. Where the fuck is my son?" I hit him over the head with the butt of my gun.

"Mi nah know. He was 'ere when mi left. Ask Bridggy. She gwan wit' 'im," he said, rubbing his head.

The fact that he stood in front of me with this foolish look on his face made me want to bust his face wide open 'til the white meat showed. But, first, I had to find out where my son was. I thought about it for a second. "Okay, since you wan' play, I'll play your game, you fuckin' bullah," I said, mocking him in my broken Jamaican dialect.

I shoved him toward the front door. I could hear Flex kicking the shit out of the dread still on the floor in the back. "You wan' fuckery? Well, ya go get fuckery." He attempted to swing his elbow back toward my face, but I ducked and popped him right on the head again with the butt of my gun.

"Ah wah di blood clot!" he spat in his heavy Jamaican dialect after feeling the butt of the gun connect with his head again.

I hit him hard enough to make it hurt, but not knock him out. He held the fresh gash on the back of his head and kept moving toward the front door.

Flex met us at the front. "You go out; I got this," I said. He headed toward the back of the house as he pulled out a lighter. All he had to do was ignite the lighter and run out the back door. I was already smelling the gas so I knew it wouldn't take long for the house to explode.

I rushed Rasta over to the other side of the street, pushing and shoving him all the way to where there was a huge black truck parked. I pushed him down to the ground and ducked for cover. I used the truck as a shield as I watched the flames start to come through the windows of the raggedy, old house. It didn't take long for the windows to explode. Then the house ignited into flames. I heard screeching tires. It was Flex racing around the corner from the back of the house, doing about fifty miles per hour in his car.

He stopped in front of me. When I rose to get Rasta and put him in the car, he kicked me in the leg, causing me to buckle to the ground while he took off running. I raised my gun to shoot him in the back, but Flex yelled out to me. "No!" I could see people were starting to come out to watch the house burn to the ground. I hopped up and jumped in the car before anyone noticed we were there. We rushed from the scene, but then circled back around to see if Rasta would show his face. For an hour we went up and down the surrounding blocks. We even parked the fucking truck and walked around going into restaurants, stores, even buildings that were open. But we came up empty.

Fuck! I was so fucking close! This added to my anger. Now, Rasta will not only die by my hands, but he will also feel what he put my son through. I didn't mention it to Flex, but the room where they kept him was awful. Boarded windows, filthy mattress on the floor, a smelly bucket in the corner of the room, and one plate covered with roaches. No water bottles on the floor, so I knew they wasn't doing him right. This motherfucker is gonna pay!

We finally gave up our search and headed back to the West Side. I wanted to see if my people over there had heard anything. I reached for my cell phone to contact them, but instead, my phone was vibrating. "Hello?"

"Hey, mi got someting for ya," the connect I had over in Kingston said as I answered the phone.

"Yeah, what you got for me?"

"Well, dem rude boi you be lookin' for, 'im roots right where ya wan' dem to be, but there is someting else, boss lady."

"Yeah, go ahead," I said as we drove onto the highway.

"Well, mi found out that Rasta not workin' alone. He got some Yankee blood helping 'im, and dey say he helped set up the kidnap for ya son and dem murder of you and Mr. Flex."

"Did you get a name?"

"Yeah, 'im name Fraught or someting like dat. Mi find out more from 'im roots we have on ice. We link when ya come, boss lady." He disconnected the call.

"I want to swing by my house. I haven't been there in days, and I know Naheri is going to start to worry about me."

Flex didn't respond. Instead, one side of his lip curled up from the mention of Naheri's name. I knew Naheri was a good man, and some part of me did love him, but I could not give up Flex. I struggled with the decision I had to make on a daily. At some point, I would have to make things right, but first. I had to find my son.

"Don't do that, Flex."

"Don't do what?" I could tell by his tone that he was not feeling me going to see my husband.

"Don't look like that and don't answer me like that. The first order of business is finding our son. After that, we will handle us . . . and Naheri."

"Yeah, okay. Whatever you say, but be sure my son, *our* son, will know who I am soon."

Chapter 15

I Can't Stop, We Won't Stop

After driving in silence for what seemed like hours, Flex pulled up to the front of my house. I turned to him and said, "Look, let me figure this all out. I know this is one big mess, but let's find Junior first, please. Then we can come to what will happen after that." I wanted to get an understanding from him about where we stood at this moment. We couldn't think about us when our seed was out there. Thinking about us would be selfish, and it sure as hell wouldn't help the situation. "Right now, you have to understand that I can't focus on us. I have to find my son. Our son."

I looked around as I opened the car door. I didn't see Naheri's car parked in the driveway, as usual. He should have been home by now. It was already six in the evening, and it was a regular workday. Something seemed off, but I couldn't put my finger on it. I didn't even get the car door closed before Flex was pulling off, screeching his tires. I knew he was upset. Every time I mentioned my husband, home, or anything to do with my husband, he would act like a 2-year-old who didn't get what he wanted. Over the years, I thought we had an understanding, but I guess when Junior got taken, and I confirmed that he was Flex's seed, it became different. I remember once, before Junior was born when Flex didn't talk to me about anything but business, and after I left his ass alone to calm down, he finally came to me to talk.

"What's going on with you? How come you only talk to me as if I'm just your boss? What the fuck is that about?"

"I don't know if I can do this. I can't sit here and hide my feelings for you. I love you, Dutch. I can't watch another man hold you, kiss you, show you off like you're his world."

"Flex, when we linked again, I thought you understood my situation. I can't just up and leave my life 'cause you came into town. Do you even think about how it would look? I could see the headlines now 'Up-and-Coming Lawyer Finds Herself in a Love Triangle with

the Town's Prominent Doctor.' Do you not see what I'm trying to build?"

"So it's about image now?"

"Yes and no. Yes, my image can't be tainted with all the side shit. I'm helping too. Remember when you stepped in and handled that cartel dude. Well, what happened? We had that shit all wrong, didn't we? The cartel wanted to retain my services, right? And when I sat down with them, who was by my side? Was it not you watching their every move and making sure I was not getting pushed around or forced into something? And because of your knowledge of who was who and how they moved throughout the city, didn't we lock down a huge ally which made your movements easier to run your guns and drugs through the city? I know, Flex. You are down for me and will do anything for me. But for us to continue getting this money and growing, you can't act like this when you see me with him.

"Flex, you have to look at the bigger picture. You can't become a hothead 'cause you see me with my husband or screw your face up at the mention of him. Besides, if you start acting up, this will only make him suspicious of us, and that would mean only one thing. He would want to see us apart. Now, I know you

wouldn't want that, and you have to know I wouldn't want that, either. So can you put all that shit to the side while we get this money? And one more thing . . . You can't keep my dick away for too long." I gave a nudge and a smirk while I reached for his manhood.

"Dutch, I have one question. Do you love him or me? Answer me truthfully."

"What kind of question is that? I love you with all my heart." I planted a long, wet kiss on his soft lips. After that day, he never showed his anger or dislike toward my husband or the situation.

I snapped out of my trip down memory lane. I needed to finally fill my husband in on what had been going on with Junior. I didn't see anything obviously out of place, but his car not being in the driveway was suspicious, so I proceeded to walk into the house cautiously.

I put my keys down on the table in a bowl near the door. The pressure of everything hurt my head, and my feet felt even worse. The more I searched for my son, the harder it was for me to keep a grip on my sanity. I felt that at any moment, I could snap. Every place we searched came up empty. To think I was so close; then—

boom!—my hope was snatched away in an instant. I thought back to when I had Rasta right in front of me. The only thing that kept me from pulling that trigger was that he had my son. I sure as hell didn't believe that he didn't know where he was. How could I be so stupid and give him the opportunity to get away from me? Now, he's in the fucking wind! I sighed loudly.

I walked over to my new best friend, my liquor cabinet. I drank now more than I ever used to. I always thought liquor and weed wouldn't solve anything, but with all of this, I found myself leaning more toward the alcohol.

"Ah, where do I start? How would he get the word that his family is seated at my table ready for the slaughter?" I asked aloud while I grabbed a short glass and headed to the fridge. I filled the glass with some ice and looked in the fridge to see if there was anything to munch on. There was nothing, and I mean *nothing*. I headed back to my liquor cabinet to pour my drink.

I took a big gulp from my glass of Henny VSOP. It always calmed my nerves. I twirled the ice around in the glass to get it nice and cold. I took another drink, then another. I found myself in what seemed like seconds calmer and ready to handle business around the house.

During all of it, I remembered that I'd neglected to pay a few utilities and finalize a few of my cases. I hadn't been in my office for days, but the fact that I was a senior partner in the firm worked in my favor. I walked into my home office next to the kitchen and called one of my junior associates I knew that I could trust with the caseload I had. I needed her to take on a few of them that didn't require me to be in the courtroom. I logged on to my computer and started to draft the email with the files she would need to handle the cases.

"Hey, Courtney, do you think you can handle the McCavour case for me? And give the Frasier caseload to Peter. I don't know how long I'll be out of the office. A family emergency has come up that needs my undivided attention. I wanted to make sure every case was being handled by someone who would work like I do. Can you guys handle that?" I talked into the phone as I walked toward my kitchen.

"Yes, Mrs. Dolvan. Is there anything else you need from us? We're here; take as much time as you need."

"That'll be all. Just make sure you do a good job on the Frasier case. The firm has a lot riding on this case. If there is something you can't hammer out, please contact Shena Danil. She's aware of each of those cases." We finalized everything and ended the call.

I walked back to the liquor cabinet and poured myself another drink, then headed upstairs to my bedroom. As I was walking up the staircase, it dawned on me . . . Why was the fridge empty? Usually, the maid would go shopping and have it filled to the max with all the shit we liked. It made me think, and I stood at the step for a moment. It was almost the weekend, and she's not around on the weekend, so the fridge should be fully stocked. What the fuck? I let it go and continued up the steps. I walked past Junior's bedroom, and something caught my eyes. I almost walked right by it, but I had spotted a pile of clothes on the floor of the room.

"That damn maid! First, the fridge ain't stocked, and now all these fucking clothes on the floor! What the fuck are we paying her for?" I placed my glass on top of the dresser close to the door and walked into the room to pick up the clothes. I was a little baffled because one of the shirts I picked up was the shirt Junior had on that night he was kidnapped. I knew it was the same shirt because I remember him begging me to let him wear it to the restaurant.

"Mommy, please, I always wear that uniform, and I'm home now!"

I reminisced about the sound of his little voice. I kept the image of his handsome little face smiling and those eyes—his eyes, looking just like his father's—in my head. I couldn't help but give in when he flashed those puffy little cheeks.

"Okay, li'l man, anything for you."

"I love you, Mommy."

That conversation stayed in my mind, especially those last words I heard my baby say. They rang in my head like a CD on repeat. It played over and over again.

How did this get here? I was confused. I held the shirt up to inspect it more. I knew I had had a few sips, but this shirt is real. I looked closer and spotted some bloodstains on the bottom of it.

I threw the shirt back on the floor, running down the hallway to search the house. "Naheri! Naheri, Junior!" I yelled from room to room. But there was no answer. There was no way this shirt just appeared out of nowhere. *He was here*. "Naheri!" I yelled out one more time in desperation. I ran back downstairs and grabbed my cell phone to call Flex.

"You know who this is . . ."

"Shit, his voicemail!" I cursed. I quickly hung up and called my husband, Naheri.

"Hello? Hello? I can't hear you, Elana, hello!" he yelled into the phone as if he couldn't hear me.

I heard him just fine. There was no choppiness on my end, and I could understand him perfectly. "Naheri! It's me, Elana!" I yelled back into the phone right before the call dropped . . . or at least I thought the call dropped. I immediately dialed his number again, only to reach his voicemail on the first ring. I frantically ran through the house once again, searching every room, even under the beds. I knew he was here. There was no way that shirt would appear out of nowhere without him being here. When he was taken, his room was kept nice and neat, so why would there be clothes all over the floor?

I rushed into my bedroom, taking rapid steps over toward our shared walk-in closet. When I stepped inside of it, there were hangers and clothes sprawled everywhere . . . and most of Naheri's things where gone. "What the fuck!" I said as I stood there in confusion. I picked up my cell phone and tried dialing Naheri's number again, only to be met with the voicemail once more. Then I tried to call Flex again, but his phone went right to voicemail as well.

"What the fuck! Both these muthafuckas have lost their minds!"

I grabbed my keys and ran out the door. I hopped in my BMW and sped off, on my way to Naheri's parents' house. "Call the hell-laws," I said aloud to my voice-activated dialing system.

"Calling hell-laws," the computerized voice chimed back as it dialed their house number.

It rang for a while. "Shit, no answer!" I banged my hand on the steering wheel. Now, something seemed *real* off to me. Naheri's clothes were missing. It was as if he left in a hurry. I knew he couldn't possibly know what was going on. Could he? And now his parents weren't answering.

"Something is not right. I'ma get to the bottom of it, even if I got to kill every bottom-feeding-ass fool to get to it."

Chapter 16

This Right Here Not What You Want

"Yeah, yeah! I got it! Well, keep fucking looking!" I was more than frustrated and far beyond mad. I banged my fist on the dashboard. I called around and hit every block I could think of trying to find the bitch-made-ass nigga. "I'm not answering shit right now!" I shouted as Dutch's number flashed on the screen of my cell phone. I was in no mood to even talk to her right now. The timing might be off, but hell, she had some decisions to make.

I pulled over to the shop on Madison and Pulaski in the strip mall. I knew that if anyone knew anything, I would find it up there. I pulled into the lot and parked. As soon as I stepped out of the car, several local hustlers came running up.

"CDs and movies!" they all yelled out in unison.

"Naw, I'm good," I said, shrugging them off. I was used to that back in the day. That was how they fed their families or their drug habit. Either way, they hustled for what they needed instead of stealing and robbing people . . . at least, most of them did. "Hey, Banks, is that you?" I called out to a scruffy-looking hustler. I could see some of his features underneath all the dirt and bags he had on him.

"Yeah, who wants to kn—Flex? My nigga, is that you?"

"Yeah, buddy, it's me. What it do, money?"

"Nothing, man, everything still everything 'round these parts. I see you living well. Nice ride."

"Yeah, I'ma maintain. My nigga, Banks! Man, I ain't seen you since the county, nigga! How did you end up out here? I mean, no disrespect to you, but damn! You was the man. How the hell you get here at this point?"

"Flex, man, life happened. This shit ain't like it used to be. I was all good until I got popped off by the Feds and went down for a seven year bid. Me and my boy Chilo—you remember him, don't you? From over on Lockwood?"

"Yeah, I remember that square-ass nigga. I always said there was something about him I didn't trust. Why, what up? What about him?"

"Well, you were right not to trust him. That nigga set me up to take the fall. Homie came to me with some new shit from these Jamaicans from up on the North Side. I told him I didn't really wanna fuck with buddy, because something about that nigga didn't sit right with me. But he convinced me all the shit was legit. I saw dollar signs instead of using my head. Yeah, but that's water under the bridge. Anyway, when I got to the meeting to cop that work, these muthafuckas got live on us. I did what I had to get out of there: I busted back at them."

I listened to his every word. Banks sounded as if he was filled with regret for making a foolish mistake.

"But in the process, I wasn't wearing any gloves, so my fingerprints and DNA was all over the place. So when these fools got away with all the money and drugs, this dude cut a deal with the prosecutor and named me. He got two years, and I got hit with seven. When I got out, I seen this muthafucka and he was living well. He was in on setting me up. He took that little time so that them Jamaican muthafuckas could rob me and take over my set, and they paid his snitch ass in work and part of my shit."

"Man, that shit is fucked up! I swear you can't trust a muthafucka for shit. So where dude at these days?"

"Man, them muthafuckas killed his ass about a year ago. He thought shit was sweet, and them same muthafuckas let him run shit for a little while; then they popped his ass. I guess Karma is a bitch." He laughed, then diverted his attention to some other hustlers across the street. He never took his eyes off of them. "Man, shit real out here! This shit reminds me of prison. You have to stay alert and never turn your back on these thirsty bitches. Hey, what you doing down here?"

I looked around, taking in the surroundings. The days I used to spend on the streets hustling were far behind me. "Yeah, man, I'm out here to find this nigga who done took something real important to me. Man, and it's ironic, this nigga Jamaican too. I wanted to put my ear to the ground and see if the streets was talking. I need to touch this fool in the worst way." I was seething with anger.

"Man, I swear, I just seen some new niggas up here the other day. They were over there shopping in Tops and Bottoms when I walked up to them to sell some of my movies and CDs. I remember them having that Jamaican accent. I could barely understand them. Hold on, let me ask this nigga right here something. Hey, Weasel! Slide on me right quick."

I stood to the side while Banks was conversing, and my cell phone rang again. I sent Dutch straight to voicemail. When I saw Banks dapping the dude up, I walked back to him.

"Hey, Flex, my dude just gave me some info on them Jamaican niggas you might be looking for. Look here, my guy just told me them niggas had a spot on the South Side, working for some nigga named Rasta, and this dude supposed to be big shit. But word is he crossed some bad people, and they gunning for his head. They done placed a reward on his head, and a lot of muthafuckas looking for him." Banks started coughing and spitting out thick, disgusting mucus.

"Man, you good?"

"Yeah, man, ain't nothing some good medicine won't cure. Anyway, they say dude holed up in this loft up on Clark Street. He got security and everything. They say this bitch almost took his ass out a little while ago, but he got away, though. I guess the nigga got nine lives." He started laughing and coughing again.

"Banks, you sure you a'ight? Man, you been coughing and shit like you about to lose a lung. Dude, you ain't looking too good."

"Aw, man, Joe, I'm straight. I got a checkup the other day, and they saying I got cancer, but I'ma be a'ight. I got this bad-ass cold with it right now, but I'ma be good."

I looked at his red, sunken eyes. I could see he was well beyond being okay, but I wasn't about to argue with him. "Okay, man, look here, thank you for the info. This might be the guy I'm looking for. Here, man, take this and my number. Hit me up if you need anything. Get you some place to lay your head, man. Fuck this street shit! It ain't where it's at no more."

I gave him some dap and slipped a wad of cash in his hand. Banks was the type of nigga that when he had it, he would give you the shirt off his back. To see him like this did something to me. I remembered when my mother put me out on the street. Banks let me come to his crib for a little while and lay my head there. He even put me up on the game. There was no way that I wasn't going to return the help.

"Aw, thanks, youngblood, you a'ight with me." Banks smiled, showing his rotting teeth. "Come back and holla at me, dude. I'm up here er'day. It was good seeing you. Thanks again." Banks rushed off, no doubt on his way to get some drugs.

I wasn't about to stop him. It was his life and his call.

I got back in my truck and drove off. When I hit the corner, I spotted a car that looked familiar. Thinking back, it looked like the same car I had seen around Naheri's office awhile back. I looked closely at the driver, but he didn't seem familiar, although I remembered that car.

I went with my gut and slowly followed the car, maintaining a two-car distance. I followed the car all the way to the expressway as it got off on the exit ramp toward the airport. Then I watched the car pull into the car lot. A few seconds later, the driver got out and opened the back door. I noticed two older-looking people, male and female. The female was holding something that looked like a small child or a baby tightly wrapped, rushing toward the gated area where the private planes were. The way they were moving, I assumed they were late for a flight.

I swear I have seen them before, but I can't put my finger on it. Then suddenly, it hit me. "Oh shit! What the hell is going on?" I said out loud as I looked on from across the parking lot.

I watched Naheri's mother and father moving onward in a hurry.

Chapter 17

Ya Really Don't Want to Test Me

I pulled up in front of Naheri's parents' house. Their cars were parked in the driveway. I got out and took a deep breath. His mother and I were not the best of friends, and we might never see eye to eye when it came to her son, but right now, I needed to talk to Naheri. I looked around, and again, something did not feel right. Usually, their big, old-ass dog would come barking on the porch. There was no sign of him, and that was odd. Sometimes, their nosy neighbor Mrs. Burton would be on the porch looking to see who was pulling up, and she wasn't out either. Ever since the night of Junior's kidnapping, I had been out of my element. My emotions had been all over the place. I was ready to murder any and everything that I could think of.

When I got closer to the front door, I stood there for a moment to listen. The neighborhood was a quiet one, so anything popping off could be heard. I looked out at the street. There were no cars parked on the street. There was, however, a huge truck parked in the driveway across the street which made me wonder who the hell owned that 'cause the people who lived there were an old couple. My gut was telling me shit ain't right. I knocked on the front door. No answer and I didn't hear anyone in the house. The dog didn't even start barking. No dog? Oh hell! I banged on the door even louder. Still, no movement inside, and no one answered. I stepped back and walked to the side of the house. I opened the gate and went around the back. I pulled my Glock out like I was on an episode of a detective show. They had sliding glass doors in the back. At first glance, you would think someone had robbed them. I got closer and saw that everything was all over the place. Furniture was flipped over, and papers were sprawled everywhere. I tried to open the glass door, but it was locked. I took the butt of my gun and hit the glass by the lock. I knocked the pointy glass out so that I could stick my hand in to unlock the door without getting cut in the process. Then slowly, I opened the door and entered the house.

"Naheri! Nafesa! Mr. Dolvan!" I cautiously walked through the house with my gun ready. I didn't see any of them. I continued to call out to them as I took two steps at a time up the stairs to the second level of the house. I was looking in every room and still received no answer.

Just as I made it back down to the bottom of the stairs, a loud crash came from the front of the house and bullets started flying everywhere. I managed to dive over the couch and get off a shot or two myself. Then I lifted my head to see Rasta standing there with a Desert Eagle, airing the house out.

I shot back, then heard sirens coming toward the house. In this quiet, middle-class neighborhood, gunfire and illegal activities don't go down. If you so much as walk on the side of the street the wrong way, the police are down your neck. It's called walking or living out here while being black. I thought to myself, *How in the hell did he know where Naheri's parents stayed, and why would he come out here for them when his beef is with me?*

"Muthafucka! I know you got the boi! I want 'im back!" I heard him yell out. "Everybody dead!" he yelled again, then continued firing into the house.

There was no way I was going out like a punk. I stood up and fired two shots toward him, hitting him in the leg. The sirens sounded as if they were getting closer.

"Babylon close! Let we go," I heard one of his guys yell as he dragged Rasta to their truck.

"Dis not ova till dem all dead! Dem blood clot dead!" I heard Rasta yelling through his agony.

I rushed outside behind them and busted off two more shots at their tires as they sped off in the same truck I saw parked in the driveway across the street. My bullets hit nothing. I ran straight to my car and exited the scene quickly. I didn't want any part of the police, although I could have easily fed them the bullshit to seem like an unlikely suspect. I didn't have the time for games. Why the fuck hadn't Flex answered his fucking phone? I decided to try him again, and for his sake, he better answer his phone!

"Meet me at Naheri's office now!" I said through gritted teeth into my phone as Flex finally picked up my call.

By the time I pulled up in front of Naheri's office, Flex was already there leaning against the grill of his truck with a look of pure evil on his face.

"Oh, so *now* you come when I call? Humph," I said as I walked up toward his car with a slight attitude.

"Whateva, Dutch! Listen, shit ain't looking right to me. I went up on Madison Street and ran into Banks, and he gave me some intel. It's a damn shame how people in the street can get shit solved faster than these so-called highly trained niggas with college degrees and shit. When I was leaving, I spotted this car that looked real familiar. I remember seeing it at this office when I was here once. I decided to follow the car, and it went to the airport. I watched his people get out of the car in a hurry, carrying something. I couldn't make out what it was, but it looked like a baby or a small bundle of something. They were hauling ass too."

"Interesting. I just came from their house out in the 'burbs, and Rasta showed up. This fool stood in the front of their house and dumped at the house. I've been calling Naheri's phone, and he's not answering. I went by his parents' house because when you dropped me off at my house, mostly all of his shit was gone and Junior's clothes was all over the floor like somebody was looking for something. I found the shirt he was wearing the night he got kidnapped."

"Are you sure? It could have been some clothes that the maid forgot to put away, no? I—"

"Trust me, it was his, and since he was kidnapped, no one's been in his room. The room was cleaned to the max," I said while cutting him off. "Look, let's go in his office and see if Naheri's there, or if there's anything that can tell me what the hell is going on with him."

Flex just looked at me with his lips curled up on one side. "His car ain't even here. So, he ain't here. You got keys? 'Cause, it looks like the building is locked up tight."

He gave me pure attitude, and I couldn't deal with that shit right now. "Come on, Flex, now is *not* the time to be in your feelings. Something is off about this whole thing, and I need to get to the bottom of this fast. My son's life depends on it."

"You can't even say the words, can you?"

"What? What words are you talking about? I don't have time for this," I said, agitated.

He walked up closer to me, his six-foot-one frame towering over me. The smell of Kenneth Cole Black invaded my nostrils. His caramel mixed with a hint of mocha skin tone with the angle of the sunlight made it kind of glisten. I knew at that moment that it was not the time or the place to be fantasying about him like that, but he had that effect on me. He was the only man who could take me from zero to sixty in one conversation, and the next minute, have me ready to let him bang my back out.

"Flex, I don't know what you're talking about," I nervously said, trying to take my mind off my buckling knees.

I moved to walk toward the door, but Flex placed his arms out so that he could pin me against the car. "Say it! I want to hear you say it just one time out loud. I already know the answer, but I want to hear the words come from your lips. I want to hear you tell me he is my son—*our* son. We created him out of love, Dutch. I know he is; I just want to hear you say it."

I looked him right in his eyes, those pleading eyes—the same eyes as my son bears. My son always had a way of making me give in with those bright, beautiful, light gray eyes and a contagious smile. I intently held my gaze to Flex's, never blinking or looking away.

I felt my tears start to well up in the corner of my eyes. The fact that I missed my son was getting to me more and more. On the outside, I was a fighting, hard-core, sexy-ass diva who looked like she had it all together, but inside, I was in a million broken pieces. I lowered my eyes toward the ground like a shy schoolgirl. "Okay, Flex—Kajaun—you are his father. There, I said it! Yes, you are his father," I said in a defeated tone.

A huge smile flashed across his lips, and suddenly his facial expression changed. Sadness and desperation were written all over. "Elana, all I wanted was to hear you say it. I love you, and I have always loved Junior because he was—I mean, is—a part of you. I knew in the back of my mind and heart he was mine. I just wanted to hear you say it. Come on, let's go find our son."

It was crazy, but I felt better. I guess I really had to hear those words just as much as he had to hear them. Tears fell from my eyes, and he embraced me tightly. I didn't care anymore who saw us or if Naheri would see. I kissed his lips, letting him know our secret was no longer hidden, and we would finally be a family.

Chapter 18

No Stone Unturned

I opened the front door and walked straight to Naheri's office. Everything looked like it was still in its rightful place. I went over to his desk while Flex looked around the rest of the office. I turned the computer on and typed in his password. The words "password incorrect" flashed across the screen.

"Damn, he changed the password?" I said aloud. I tried one more password I could think of, and it still denied me access. I reared back in the chair with my finger on my chin in deep thought. I had to think: If I were him, what would I use? I thought about our wedding day, time, date, and location. I found a small flash drive in the drawer as I searched for a password.

I wonder what this is. What could he have changed it to? He wasn't the type of man that liked to change passwords on the regular because he would forget them easily. His usual password was his birth date. My mind was at a loss, but then I tried my son's birth date. "Yes! Okay, now let's see what the hell is going on," I said aloud.

I put the flash drive in the computer. The only things I noticed were all the regular things, like appointments and schedules. Nothing looked out of the ordinary . . . until I saw a folder labeled "deceit." As soon as I opened it, I saw photos of me at different locations, doing different things. I spotted one with Flex and me in an embrace. Has this muthafucka had somebody following me this whole time? Searching through more photos, I came across one of me holding Rasta's brother's head in one hand and my bloody machete in the other. I knew then that he knew all about my secret life. But how much more has he been keeping from me? I wondered.

I opened up more photos. In the same file was a footnote, kind of like a journal. He kept dates and times of my meetings and even Junior's sonogram. That made me smile a little bit . . . until I looked right underneath that and saw a folder named Test Results. *Test results? What kind of test results?* I opened the file, and it showed DNA results. *This motherfucker tested my son, and I didn't know about it? When did he do this?* I searched for the date. I wiped my eyes as if I was clearing something out of them. No matter how I tried to change what I was looking at, I couldn't. There it was: Undeniable proof that he had a DNA test done for him and Junior. I had no idea he did that when he was a baby. *This muthafucka has known the whole time.*

I was shocked, and more than anything, confused. It was as if I were in a bad movie and the starring role had my name on it. I knew the secrets I had kept would one day catch up with me. To find out he was on the same page as I was more than I was prepared to handle.

I couldn't bring myself to be truthful with him, and he damn sure wasn't truthful with me. I guess the old saying is true: I wonder, can you swallow the same mix you done made for someone else? I sometimes cursed those old wives' tales. Ms. Ruby always had one or two to teach me as I was growing up. Right now, I was sitting at this desk with the same medication I had dished out, finding it hard to accept.

I scrolled down some more and saw a video of Bridgette bound and gagged as a dark-complexioned man held up a sign saying, "COOPERATE OR FIND SHE HEAD AT YA STEP." I obviously really didn't know my husband as well as I thought

I did. I scrolled a little more, almost unable to take all that I had found out already, but my curiosity got the better of me. I went down, and what I saw next almost caused my heart to leap out of my chest.

I jumped up from the chair. "Flex! Flex! Come here!"

I ran down the hall of the office calling out for him, but there was no answer. I walked toward the back where surgeries took place. I saw Flex through a window in the door standing in a surgical room. When I entered the room, he was looking at Bridgette's body half stuffed under the sink. He looked at me, and it seemed as if he had tears forming in his eyes. I was thrown off because why would he shed tears for this bitch if she meant nothing? Or was she more than what he was telling me? If Flex lied to me about this bitch, what else did he lie about? I already had one man in my life lying to me for years. Now, if Flex was in that same boat, there would be no future with him. Ever. I decided to get to the bottom of that situation at another time because right now, the man I married has completely flipped the fucking script.

"Flex, you need to see this. Follow me." I walked out of the room and headed back to Naheri's office and sat in front of his computer.

Quickly, I opened the DNA file again and looked at the names listed. Dameon James. The name looked real familiar. "There is no way he could be a blood relative to that muthafucka!" I said, clenching my fists tightly together as I reflected on his birth name. Could it be that one of my mistakes was coming back to me on every avenue to bite me in the ass? If my suspicions were correct, he shared the same last name as one of my once good friend-turned-enemy.

"Look at what I found on Naheri's computer! He's been lying the whole time," I said in a huff and turned to him with my face scrunched up into a frown and frustration written on my face.

"What? You got a problem with me? This motherfucker ain't even who he say he is." He moved to the chair in front of the desk. He looked defeated.

"Why you looking like that? Like you lost your best friend or some shit." As much as I didn't want to know what the real reason was that he was tearing up over that lame bitch, I threw a slight jab to see his reaction.

He gave me a look like I was overreacting and overthinking shit. "Dutch, I went to the back to search around. I got in the room and started to open whatever cabinet doors I could, hoping to find something indicating that Junior was here. I walked around the metal table there and noticed a cabinet under the sink. I opened it, and she was stuffed in there, dead. Before you came in, I noticed her pocket was bulgy, so I pulled her out enough to retrieve what was in it. It was a small recorder. I pressed play. I guess she was using it as a journal or some shit. She had details on how she and that Rasta mutha-fucka set this whole kidnapping shit up. Not only did the dumb bitch help them, but, Dutch . . ." Flex stopped to take a deep breath. "What you saw was not tears of sadness, but I'm so mad at this bitch. . . ." Anger was etched all over his face this time. He stopped, put the recorder on the desk, and pressed play on it.

"I don't know who the fuck he thinks I am! I'm not a babysitter."

I could hear a small voice whimpering in the background. I listened closely. It sounded just like Junior. Then I hear a loud smacking sound. "Shut the fuck up crying, you little bastard! Your momma not here! I should burn your ass with this cigarette."

Suddenly I heard a cry I will never forget, one no mother could forget: the sound of her child screaming out in pain. I pushed past Flex and raced back to where Bridgette's body lay. "You cheap, stupid bitch! Die, bitch, die!" I screamed as I released my full clip in her body. I shot her in the face, hands, neck, anywhere I could shoot. Then I grabbed a small scalpel and started carving her face. "This bitch! She burned my baby! Flex, revive this bitch so I can kill her again! Bring her back! She needs to feel this shit! Stupid bitch!" I pushed the scalpel in deeper into the side of her face. There was no blood leaking. Her body was cold as ice, and she was still in that crumpled position.

"Dutch, come on, baby, she's dead! Hell, she more than dead. She gone. Damn, ain't shit left of her tired-ass body." Flex grabbed me by the waist to pull me away from her. I was trying to get one more slice across her face. "Come on; there's more you need to hear on this recording."

"Dumb bitch!" I screamed and kicked as he pulled me out of the room. I lost it. After I heard my son's bloodcurdling scream, I wanted—no, I *needed*—to kill her myself. "After all the times I spared this bitch's life! I noticed her all up in Naheri's face a time or two. Even after I caught the bitch smoking on the premises, I didn't say a word. Then, I mean really, then to find out she was fucking you! I should have kicked her ass underneath the truck that night!" I said as my anger intensified once again.

"Dutch, you need to hear this," Flex said again as he dragged me back to Naheri's office. He turned the recorder back on.

"Die, you fucking bitch, die! Sorry, Bridgette, you had to be a casualty in this," I heard Naheri's voice say in what seemed to be the final moments of her life. I guess she left the recorder on after her last entry.

"Flex, that's Naheri's voice. He killed that girl. Oh my God! This is *not* the man I married. And look at what I found on this flash drive. It's just the tip of the iceberg as far as what he's capable of. Come over here and look at this." I pointed to the name on the DNA test results.

"Dameon James? Who the hell is that?" Flex asked.

"Apparently, this is his real name. I've been with this man for over seven years and not one time did I suspect him of being a part of them muthafuckas."

"Part of who? Dutch, who the fuck you talking about? Who is this Dameon dude?"

"Flex, Dameon is Naheri's real name. Does the name look familiar?"

"Hell no! I don't remember it offhand. Should I?"

"Hell yeah, you should! Remember when we had to make that hit in Jamaica about five years ago?"

"Yeah, when we had to take care of Garland James, yeah. But what does this have to do with him?"

"The dude that was in the shit with Rasta's brother Jahele . . . Well, I remember digging up dirt on him right before they tried to set us up. Remember, that's how we were able to beat them to the punch. The guy's last name was James, born in Ocho Rios, Jamaica. I was sure we got them all. Damn! I can't believe I fucked up like this again! Fucking loose ends!" I said through clenched teeth as I slammed my fist on the desk. "Do you see anything else?" I said, pointing at the screen. "The muthafucka knows about Junior not being his biological son. He has known since my baby was damn near born. Flex, how in the hell did I get caught slipping like this? I have worked too damn hard to get to where I am."

"So, what you think? You think he married you to get revenge for killing his people? I mean, that is a little too far even in the name of revenge. Come on, Dutch, there has to be more to this."

"You might be right. I got to find this nigga and get some answers. I have searched everywhere I think he would be, and nothing. Then to come here and find this dead bitch in his office . . . I know he killed her. I don't know who the fuck

I'm dealing with. This is the worst type of enemy: the one you never see coming."

Suddenly a huge brick came through the window, and screeching tires were heard on the pavement. Then a loud thud against the front door caused us to leap over the desk and head toward the front door with our 9 mm guns cocked and ready. When I snatched the door open, ready to bust at anyone on the other side, Rasta's bullet-riddled body was at our feet with a note attached to his chest that read:

Hope you and your lover enjoy your stay in jail.

Next, I heard sirens coming from the distance. I looked up at Flex as I knelt down to read the note. "Get the fuck outta here now!" I yelled. He looked at me, confused, I had a strong feeling this was a setup to frame us.

"Dutch, I'm not leaving you! You not going down for this!"

"Go, Flex."

He paused for a second. "Hell no. Ain't no way you can beat this shit. The body back there is cold as ice, and you lit her up with your gun. Let's go! Now!"

I hated to admit it, but he was right. There was no way I could explain the dead body in the back. I do have a license to conceal and carry, so those bullets would have my name written all over them. "Come on, let's go." I hurried to Naheri's office to pull the flash drive out and grab Bridgette's recorder.

We made a mad dash toward the back entrance. I could hear the sirens getting closer. We ran to Flex's truck and pulled off in time. Two minutes away from the scene and we were safe . . . until I saw lights and sirens behind the truck. We were headed in the opposite direction, so I thought this was it. I looked at Flex, hoping he would say something to ease me. He slowed the truck down and veered right, then put it in park. I reached for my gun and tucked it under my seat.

The police car sped past us.

My heart was relieved, and I started to breathe again. Flex grabbed my hand and squeezed it.

"Thought we done."

"For a second, but either way, we was shooting our way out of it." I grabbed the gun from under the seat and put it beside me.

"Let's get the fuck outta here."

I said a silent prayer for my son and for forgiveness about what I planned on doing. Now I have to go to see my so-called husband, and he better pray to God he kills me first.

Chapter 19

Next Stop, Destiny

"Mi dun know why, but we almost 'ere," I said as I spoke with my cousin in Jamaica.

I ended the call and looked out the window and over the clear blue waters. My mind drifted to happier days when I was younger. The time I spent on the island taught me a lot, and it had been a long time since I had been home. When we honeymooned on this island, I was a bit nervous, and I did my best not to be seen. As much as I wanted to bring Elana back with Junior to show her and tell her who I really was, it became apparent that I needed to keep my identity close to my chest. At first, it was all about payback for what she did to my family. I hunted her. I found out who she was, where she was, and how I could get at her. After getting her, however, something changed. I built a life with her. I saw the hard-core killer she really was. I knew who she was. How dreadful she was. How cold she was. But I blocked it out. Then when this shit happened with Junior, it all came back in a rush. The lies she told. The deceit. I shook my head and cursed myself for allowing love to control my decisions. *Humph, relative, my ass! I could see the way he looked at her and the way she looked at him. I should have nipped that shit in the bud back then!*

I sat daydreaming and wondering what might have been if I could have done things differently, if my son was mine, and if Elana could have loved me and only me. Ever since I found out that Junior wasn't mine, and I saw Flex and her together, I wanted to choke both of them. They played me like a fool. This would serve them the ultimate payback.

"What's wrong, Dameon?" my mother said, bringing me out of my thoughts. "You look like you have something on your mind, son."

"Mother, I'm fine, but please don't call me Dameon. I left that name behind when I left this country. Besides, my son doesn't know me by that name, nor will he ever."

"Okay, Naheri, have it your way. I told you to leave that she-witch a long time ago, but no, you wanted to love her. The devil himself wouldn't love her treacherous ass."

"Mother, what Elana did to our family was a long time ago. And at this moment, my only concern is him." I pointed to Junior fast asleep stretched out in the seat.

"What do you mean? She lied! He is not your so—"

"Do not say that again! He *is* my son, and if I hear it again, I swear to God . . ." I was so upset to hear my mother speak those words. "He *is* mine. No matter what a test says, I will raise him as mine!"

I sat back in the chair of the plane while my mother sulked in hers. "Humph! All I'm saying is that you should have left her a long time ago."

"Nafesa, leave him alone! We have enough to worry about without you rubbing it in his face," my father said to her as he sat back in his seat and sipped on his glass of liquor.

"Humph!" she scuffed at him. "I still say he should have left her a long time ago." My mother was determined to say her piece.

I couldn't keep sitting in my seat. A hundred and one thoughts occupied my mind, causing my emotions to be all over the place. I got up to check on Junior. Watching his little bruised face sleeping made me feel the decision to come back to Jamaica was the right one. I watched him a little while. He slept from the medication I had given him earlier. I knew he would be okay, but I needed to get him out of the country and away from his mother and her lying, cheating ways. He needed to be away from all that mess, but my only hope was that I wasn't bringing him into a bigger one.

I walked over to the little bar setup and poured myself a nice stiff drink. I wondered what the repercussions would be when Elana found out everything. If she got out of that trap I set for her and her lover, she should have found the DVD I left for her.

I stood there for a few moments and closed my eyes, silently saying two prayers: one for protection and the other for forgiveness. If it came down to it, I would kill again to keep my son. There was no way in hell Elana and Flex were going to have a happily ever after—not if I had the last word on it. And with everything I managed to set up before I left, they wouldn't be skipping off into the sunset. Instead, they would be getting a one-way ticket to hell and misery.

"That got damn Naheri! When I get my hands on him, I'ma choke his ass out!" Flex angrily said as he stormed inside the house I shared with Naheri.

"Calm down. I don't know for sure if he was behind this. Besides, we dodged that bullet for now." I walked into the den and started thinking back to all that had gone down within the last 24 hours.

After the police stormed Naheri's office, I received a phone call from them. They told me I needed to come down to the station for questioning. As a lawyer of criminals, I knew this was a ploy to get me in front of them without a lawyer. I wasn't playing that game. I marched down there with a lawyer at my side. She was someone I trusted not to divulge my business to anyone, including the firm we worked for.

When I got there, two detectives met me. They were the total opposites of each other. One short, white, and fat and the other tall, black, and lanky. Their eyes almost dropped from their sockets when they saw that I had someone else with me.

"Hello, Mrs. Dolvan."

"Hello."

"And who is this?" the short fatty pointed to my girl.

"She's a friend and is here to support me."

"Where have I seen your face before?" the tall detective asked.

"Ah . . . Yes, I am Jessica Gomes, a defense lawyer. You may have seen my face on television speaking at press conferences."

"Mrs. Dolvan, there was no need for a lawyer to be present unless—"

"No way. I been in this business a long time now, and I have seen the headlines. You will not make me a stepping stool in your career."

"All right, Elana. I am not here as her lawyer. I am here as a supportive friend."

The detectives looked at each other.

"Now, are we talking out here or in a room? What happened? And why isn't my husband here?"

"Okay, Mrs. Dolvan, please follow me."

Jessica and I followed them toward a room. They ushered us both in. The room was cold and lit up like the North Star. We took our seats, and the tall detective closed the door behind us.

After everyone was seated, they told me that there was an "incident" at my husband's office.

"What? An incident? What kind of incident? What happened to my husband?" I grabbed Jessica's hand to show my surprise and concern.

"Umm . . . First, your husband was not on the premises. That's why you are here."

"Okay, what happened? Where is he?"

"That's what we don't know and were hoping you can help us locate him."

"Wait . . . What happened at the office?"

"Well, this is unofficial, and we are still in the process of investigating. We found two dead bodies. One at the front door and the other in one of the rooms in the back."

When the detective said that, I immediately started to cry. My acting skills were on point, and my girl Jess knew exactly what to say.

"Detectives, obviously, this is a shock, and she will need some time before answering any more questions, but I think her concern right now is her husband. She needs to make some calls and find out what exactly is going on with him. This is a little complicated because she and her husband have been separated lately due to his infidelity."

The detectives looked at each other.

Jessica looked at me and said, "Come on, Elana. I'll get their cards, and you can call them when you get a hold of Naheri."

"Ms. Gomes, is it? Here you go and please, as soon as Mrs. Dolvan can get in touch with Mr. Dolvan, have him call us."

I wiped my eyes as I got up and walked out of the room. Jess and I walked straight out of the building. I saw Flex's truck in the parking lot.

"That was interesting . . ." Jess said.

"Yes, thanks for showing up on such short notice. Again, I will keep you in the loop just in case I do need a lawyer." I gave her a quick hug and walked toward Flex's truck.

"Not a problem. Anytime."

When I reach Flex's truck, I opened the passenger door in the back and climbed in.

"What! I'm your driver now?" Flex said, laughing.

I said nothing. I just sat there.

"Dutch, you good?"

"Yeah, I'm good for now. Let's go to my house. I need to search that house better."

I stood in the doorway of my den and stared out the window looking at nothing when I jumped out of my trance at the sound of Flex's voice.

"Damn, I can't believe this man I married was nothing but a stranger!"

"Man, Dutch, I don't mean to sound insensitive and shit, but fuck that fool! Real talk, this shit seemed like he on some setup shit from day one. Now that we know his ass knew for the longest he ain't my son's father ain't no telling how much this fool has done."

I couldn't argue with Flex at the moment. I got up and walked downstairs into Naheri's home office. He called it his man cave. I rarely went inside there, but right then, I was about to see if he had left anything to lead me to where he was.

I had called his phone several times on the way over here, but I only got his voicemail. I even called the company to activate the tracking on it, and they told me it was not in range. I walked over to his desk. There was one of those sticky notes on the desk attached to a DVD case that read, "*Elana, watch me.*" What the fuck is this?

I picked it up, confused about what it could contain. "Flex, come here!" I yelled at him from the lower level of my house.

He came rushing inside the room, gun drawn and murder all over his face, "What the fuck? What happened?"

"Boy, put your gun down! I found something. Look at this." I passed him the sticky note. "Put it in the player. Let's see what this nigga has to say."

I placed the DVD in the drive and waited for the prompt. I clicked play once it came on screen and watched on the video as Naheri took a seat in his chair with tequila in his hand. He began gulping down a full glass. "*Elana, if you are watching this, then that means one of two things: I am either dead or have left the country. I wanted you to hear in my own words how much you and that no-good-ass so-called cousin-slash-lover of yours hurt my family and me. When I first came in contact with you, it was not a mistake or a chance meeting. I was sent to you. Do you remember the name, James? I'll give you a second. The good Lord knows you have come across so many people in this lifetime. I'm quite sure your enemies' list is as long as my dick, and we both know how long that is."* He busted out in laughter.

"Anyway, Lefette James is—or shall I say was—my grandfather. Then there was Garland James. He was my uncle. You and your little friend there, Flex . . . I'm sure he's standing somewhere close to you like the lovesick bitch boy that he is. Yeah, homie, I had fun pounding your bitch all these years. Oh, sorry, my dear wife. I know your mouth is wide open right now, because how dare I disrespect you, the queen that you are," he said it mockingly. His speech was slurred, and spit was flying everywhere. He wiped his mouth and started speaking again as tears came down his face.

"I loved you, Elana—or shall I say, Dutchtress? Didn't think I knew that? While you were busy

living this double life and shit, killing people and selling more dope than a muthafuckin' hooker sells her pussy, I was busy setting your ass up. Yeah, yeah, I know all 'bout your secret love affair and your love child who bears my name. Why? Why would you hurt me like that? You lying bitch!" he angrily said as he faced the camera. He slumped in his seat and composed himself a little to deliver me another message "*Look in the left drawer in the desk you're sitting at and pull that black box out. I know you too well—better than you think. I have watched and studied your every move. I'm still watching your ass.*

"*In about fifteen minutes, the police will be all over our lovely home of lies that you built with drug-sniffing dogs and gathering fingerprints to tie you and your lover to a few murders in the city. You thought you wouldn't get caught? Well, the joke's on your ass. That bag you have in your hand . . . Go ahead and look in it.*"

I slowly opened the box. The box was small enough to hold a watch. "What the fuck!" I quickly scooted the chair back from the desk and dropped the box. A severed finger rolled out of the box and on to the floor.

"This stupid-ass nigga! I see he wanna play games," Flex said through clenched teeth.

All the anger I could feel was coursing through me at that point. Every thought in me was about getting my hands on Naheri and cutting his fucking head clean off his shoulders. "This lying snake—" I began to say until something else on the screen grabbed my attention.

I watched Naheri get up from his seat, and when he reappeared, he had Junior cradled in his arms as if he were a newborn. I looked at the bruises on Junior's little face and reached toward the screen as if I could feel him. My heart went out to my son. I missed him so much! He was the only one besides his father who could weaken me. I would kill anyone for them. I could see he was sleeping or semiconscious.

Naheri leaned in closer, and in just above a whisper, he said, "*Listen, I will hold to the promise I made to this little dude right here the day I held him in my arms in the hospital and accepted the role you gave me as his father. I played my part well, wouldn't you say? I got him back a little bruised, but don't worry; Daddy is taking care of him,*" he said with a smug smirk on his face. "*The promise I made to him was to protect him from any hurt, harm, or danger—even if that is you.*" He looked right into the camera again, this time as if he were staring right into my soul. Through gritted teeth, he said, "*With that, say goodbye to my son! I will be sure to tell him you died a champ. Oh, and don't bother destroying this DVD, because I have a little surprise in store for you.*" He started laughing and doing a countdown like a rocket launch. I was confused. It looked like he had lost his mind. I had to find him and get my son away from his crazy ass. But I couldn't figure out what he meant until I heard what sounded like sirens—and then a loud, thunderous boom.

"Dutch, watch out!" Flex said as he dove and threw his body on top of me to cover me from flying debris.

I saw smoke and fire coming from the laptop we had just watched the DVD on. "Flex, Flex!" I screamed his name. I heard sirens as smoke filled the room. Gingerly, I eased from under Flex and was a bit dazed, "Flex! Flex! Get up!" I shook him as his body lay there motionless on the floor. I regained some of my composure and tried tugging and pulling on his arm.

"Come on, Flex. Kajaun, don't you do this to me! Come on! Get up!"

He still didn't move. I slipped on something on the floor as I tried pulling him one more time. Then I heard another loud boom.

"Oh my God, no!"

Chapter 20

All Hail the Queen

I could hear sirens all around me as I desperately tried to move. The smell of smoke was filling my nostrils. My legs felt as if sandbags were tied around them. I struggled to move, and now I felt pain intensified throughout my entire body. I remembered trying to wake; then an explosion rocked my entire house.

"Flex, Flex! Oh my God, Flex, where are you?" I tried screaming, but my mouth didn't feel right. It felt as if my jaw was hanging. I tried opening my lips to call out his name again, but no sound came out. My body wracked with pain as I lay underneath a piece of the desk that had fallen on top of me after the explosion. Suddenly footsteps, followed by unknown voices, filled the room. I wanted to get up.

"Damn, Doug, this looks bad. Looks like we have two bodies over here!" I heard one of the voices yell across the room. I felt whatever was pinning me down being lifted up from on top of me. "We have secured the structure. Send in the medical examiner. Looks like we have one fatality," the man said as he pushed a button down on what sounded like a two-way radio. I knew I had to make a move, a sound, something to get their attention. I felt someone kneeling over me.

"Mmm, mmm," I faintly moaned.

"Did you hear that?"

"Yeah, sounds like it came from one of the victims over there." I could hear footsteps rushing toward me. One of them lifted my wrist.

"Send in the EMT. We have one with a faint pulse," he spoke again.

"Hey, Doug, check that other one over there." I heard footsteps stepping over the debris on the floor. I assumed that was this Doug person. "No, this one is DOA," he loudly said across the room.

My heart felt as if it were snatched from inside of my chest. He had to be talking about Flex. "No! No!" I screamed, but no sound parted my lips. I tried once more to move, but my body wouldn't allow me to. I lay there in pain. My heart and body ached. I couldn't believe the love of my life, my friend, my lover, my son's father . . . Flex was dead. At that moment, I wanted to die, but before I take that final nap, Naheri will pay for this.

Chapter 21

Cold Hard Facts

"Look, I'm going to make the best of this. I don't want to hear any more about it. Just accept the fact we cannot go back there," I said to my mother for the one-hundred-thousandth time. By now, I knew Elana was dead. I had to break the news to Junior when he felt better. I knew my actions would bring about the destruction of my unhappy home. After being played for a fool for years, then to the downright disrespect, I'd had enough. She was the reason my brother was killed, and her lover was the one who delivered that fatal bullet. The first time I laid eyes on her, I wanted to look past her beauty and curves and place a bullet right in her dome, right there on campus, but I didn't. Instead, I made the stupid mistake of falling in love with her. Damn! If only I would have stuck to the plan and finished her off, but her smile and warm eyes captivated me. I got lost in her smile. There was something about her and the way she would look at me as if she were looking right through to my soul. How could I have fallen for the person who was a part of taking my family member's life and our demise? I must somehow get past all of this and make life better for my son, the only good thing from my union with her.

I looked over some pictures and papers I'd stolen from her private desk in her penthouse office. She didn't know I knew almost everything she has done. I am using every piece of this to take back what is rightfully mine, for my son and me. "At the very least, she owes me that much," I said aloud as I looked over the bank statement I found inside of the papers.

Chapter 22

Time to Hit 'Em with the Switch Up

I lay in this bed for what seemed to be an eternity. I heard different voices on a daily basis, but the one voice I long to hear is gone. I can't believe I lost the two people I love the most in this world, my son Naheri Jr. and his biological father, Flex. My husband Naheri took my son and left to punish me. I knew one day my lies would catch up to me. The way I felt about Flex and our lives, I should never have married Naheri. What I wouldn't do or give to have them back. So many things I would do differently. It would have been just Flex and me. We would have Junior right now, and Flex wouldn't be dead. I would have never gotten mixed up with the cartel. Our lives would have been so different.

"Aw, Mrs. Dolvan, how are we feeling today? I see your temperature is up a little," I heard what sounded like my doctor say as she examined me. I wanted to move, say something to let them know I was ready to get out of here. I want to find Naheri and take great pleasure in making him pay for causing me all of this pain. Most importantly, I wanted my son.

"Well, we're going to make sure you get better; you are too beautiful to lie here," she said in a lustful tone. I found that odd that someone who is supposed to be nursing me back to health is lusting over me.

I tried moving my arm. It felt as if a sandbag or heavy object were tied around my wrist. I couldn't move. *Damn! I need to get out of here. Flex, I need you,* I cried on the inside. I knew that would never happen again. I will never forget the last thing I heard before they took me from the shambles and debris that I used to call home. "This one right here is DOA." The words of the EMT have permanently been set on replay when I'm awake. I refuse to believe he is gone. He grabbed me to shield me from the blast. I must admit I have truly underestimated my unseen enemy. As soon as I get my chance, I'm out of here.

"Hello, Dr. McKinley, is it?" I heard an unfamiliar voice.

"Yes, I am. How may I help you?"

"I'm Detective Hudson. Here's my card. I'm here again to question Mrs. Dolvan. Is she awake? We need to hear what happened in her home last month."

"No, she is not. Unfortunately, her injuries were so severe we had to place her in a medically induced coma. As of today, there is no change in her condition," I heard the doctor as she lied.

The fact that I could hear every word from two weeks ago had me even more curious about why this doctor would lie. I lay still as I heard the detective firmly state once again that it's important that he speaks with me when I regain consciousness.

"Never mind him, my sweet Elana. I'm gonna take good care of you. I won't let anyone touch you," I heard the doctor whisper in my ear as she planted a sloppy kiss on my lips. I was so shocked and surprised. I didn't know her from a hole in the wall, and it seemed she was feeling me in ways I have never asked for or even wanted. I wanted to open my eyes as she gave my lips a sloppy and wet assault, but I couldn't. Soon, she will be a major part of me getting out of here and out of the trouble I was in.

“Dr. McKinley, you have a patient in th—” I heard the nurse say as she entered the room.

“Ye-yes, Nurse Cole. I’ll be there shortly,” she responded nervously. “Okay, I’ll let the attendant know that you will be in shortly,” she said with an inquisitive tone in her voice. I heard the nurse’s heavy feet as they hit every tile on the floor until she was out of the room.

“I’ll be back, and when I do, we’ll finish where we left off from,” she softly whispered in my ear.

This doctor has been coming at me for the last week. The first week she seemed so caring in a doctor-type way. Now, every day this week, she’s been getting touchier and touchier. What the fuck is going on here? Where exactly am I? Why can’t I wake up? It was all exhausting to try to remember each moment before the blast.

I knew one thing was for sure and two things that were certain . . . I was going to get my son and place a well-deserved bullet right in between Naheri’s eyes.

Chapter 23

A Deadly Dick

I arrived at the hotel dressed to a tee. I looked like a million bucks. I picked one of the best hotels with the prettiest views. I only carried a small bag because I wasn't staying long. It was just a quick stop before heading into a life of no mess or drama or craziness.

"Hello, may I help you?"

"Yes, you sure can. I would like a room with an ocean view. And send some of your finest . . . As a matter of fact, I would like a bottle of Dom Pérignon. Nothing but the best for my lady," I laughed and placed a Black Card on the counter.

"Ah, Mr. Bastion, is it? How long will you be staying with us?" the hotel clerk asked eagerly as he examined the card. To say that I was living it up was putting it mildly. "For the night. I'm here on business, and I want the best wherever I lay my head," I said in a cocky tone.

When I got to Kingston, I searched through the briefcase I'd taken before I left the house. I was curious to see just how much of Elana's little double life that she was leading had she put away. There was no way if she survived that she would live the lavish lifestyle I helped her lying, conniving, deceitful ass build. I felt she owed me that much. When I searched through the papers in the case, I discovered she had several bank accounts. Each had over $10 million apiece. Some were in the States, and others were overseas in the Cayman Islands. When I tallied up all of them, she had managed to hide close to a hundred million dollars in there. I was in shock, and when I proved she was my wife, the bank was more than willing to allow me access. It had been months now, and I still hadn't received news if she was dead or alive. But what I do know is that I am gonna party and live off of her ill-gotten fortune.

"How ya wan me, daddy? Dem wan face up or down?" I looked over at my lovely choice of the evening. A medium-built, dark-skinned, Jamaican goddess draped across my arm. "Yes, you can have whatever you like," she playfully cooed as I lightly slapped her across her bottom. I was in the mood to have some fun tonight, and she was going to be my freak. Money, I have learned, has a way of making the strongest person weak, and the sexiest, prettiest woman lose herself in every sense of the word.

"I'ma tear that ass up. I want that porn star treatment," I said to her as I slid the key card in the door of this five-star hotel. When I opened the door, she looked around the room. The expression on her face showed she was past impressed with the layout of the room.

I watched her sashay over toward the king-sized bed that was adorned with plush blankets and pillows. She plopped her body on the bed with her hands over her head and ass jiggling as she landed on top of the blanket that was fit for a king.

"Come here, girl, I want to taste you," I said as I kneeled by the bed. I placed my face close to her stomach. The smell of strawberry and cream was a welcoming smell to my nostrils. Her skin was even more perfect as I got to touch it. The smoothness of her skin, the heart-shaped beauty mark reminded me so much of Elana.

I wanted to feel her, taste her. I missed my wife. After all she had done, I still loved her. I thought of the last night we shared. How her body responded to my touch and how she threw it back at me. I knew she had to have loved me. The way her pussy purred when I stroked her . . . I stood up. It was like a mirage; I could have sworn Elana was standing in front of me. Welcoming me to touch her hard nipples and gently stroke her round, tight ass. Was I dreaming?

Elana's voice seemed to be dancing in my thoughts "Naheri, baby, I'm yours. Take me," as if it were her pussy I was munching on. I heard her sweet voice ravage my thoughts.

"Come give daddy his dinner," I said as I parted her neatly trimmed snatch in my face. I licked and slurped all on her sweet pussy. Taking the tip of my tongue, I gently stroked every inch of her clit.

"Hum, um, yes-ya wan me da . . . ddy."

I was so into devouring the sweet pussy in front of me until I heard the Jamaican goddess's voice. I was so wrapped up in my fantasy of Elana. I slightly lifted my face upward to look at her face. That's when I noticed she was, in fact, a look-alike of my dear wife, Elana. I was so into feasting on her as if she were my last meal. I had her body shaking from pure ecstasy. I never stopped. In fact, I continued vigorously. Never taking my eyes from her, the more I watched her head rear back in ecstasy, the more I licked. I startled her when I forcefully grabbed one of her nipples and roughly twirled on them with my fingers.

"Boi, dat lickel hard der. Release mi nipples. Ouch!" she said in pain. I didn't stop. Before I could climax, in one swift motion, I rose and snatched her from the bed. Then roughly, with no remorse, made her kneel in front of me. The look she had was pure ecstasy. But in my mind, all I could see was Elana and how badly I wanted to punish her. I took my ten-inch penis and shoved it into her mouth, almost down her throat.

"Gr . . . gr . . . wha . . . fu . . ." were the muffled gurgling sounds coming from her as I made long thrusts inside and out of her mouth. She tried her best to accommodate this lovely assault, but it became too much. I pumped and pounded on her mouth as if I was fucking her pussy. "Yes . . . Take this dick, bitch. Ooh yes . . . Elana!" I yelled out as I held a firm grip on her head. The more I pumped, the tighter I held on.

"Aaah . . . sliii . . . mmm . . . aaah . . . yes . . ." I moaned in pleasure as I released a load of semen in her mouth. When I looked down, I noticed there was a mix of vomit and blood running down her lips. As soon as I released her head, she slumped to the floor, motionless.

Reality set in. I was so rough that I choked her to death with my dick.

"Shit! Sweetheart, wake up," I nervously said as I tried to shift her body in a more comfortable position. Her eyes were open in shock. I kneeled and closed her eyes shut as I shook my head in disbelief. I was so out of the moment I didn't feel her pushing and clawing at my thighs the whole time.

"Sorry, my Jamaican princess," I said as I picked her up from the floor and gently laid her on the bed. Her naked body was drenched in sweat. After I placed her on the bed, I walked into the adjacent bathroom and got a warm washcloth to wipe her face. "I'm so sorry. None of this is your fault," I remorsefully spoke to her as I wiped her face clean of the vomit and semen. I took the towel and placed it on the nightstand and cleaned her body up. Then I slowly dressed her back in the clothing she was wearing and placed the covers on top of her. I made it seem as if she had fallen asleep. I checked the room over as I got dressed, making sure I didn't leave anything with my real name or any of my prints.

What the hell has become of me? I've done the unthinkable. I wiped the bottle of Dom Pérignon clean. When I was sure everything was in place, I discreetly slipped out of the door down the back stairs.

I briskly walked to my Bugatti Veyron. *Chirp, chirp*. I hit the alarm to unlock the doors. Then I discreetly looked around and got in. On my way leaving the garage I spotted a man whose features looked vaguely familiar, but I kept on driving right out of there. I didn't want to be anywhere around when the body was discovered. I turned on my CD player and pressed the button on the remote to number seven. The sounds of John Legend's "Who Do You Think We Are" played at the highest level I could put it. The last part of the lyrics hit me right in my heart, as it had been for the past year. The life I had grown to live with Elana was all a lie. I often went back to the day I found out about her and Flex's affair. After all that went down with her, she turned me into a killer. The well-respected doctor I once was is now a thing of the past.

A phone call brought me back to reality. "Hello." I pressed the Bluetooth button on my console.

"What time you think you'll be home? Junior has been asking for you, and this little one is kicking me like crazy. I think he misses his dad."

"Hey, honey, I'll be there in about thirty minutes. I had a patient at the last minute. Do you need me to stop and pick anything up?" I said to my wife, Netta.

"No, honey, just come home. Junior has been a little uneasy, and your mother . . . Well, your mom is your mother," she said with disappointment in her tone.

"Baby, it'll only be a little while longer; then you, our kids, and I will be in our own little world. I plan on moving her and my father in a home of their own soon. If I haven't said it to you lately, thank you for coming into my son's and my life when you did. I feel like the luckiest man alive," I said as I tossed the Jamaican princess's necklace out of my window as I steered down the highway on my way home to my family.

The lie rolled so easily from my lips. It could have been unnerving, but I was used to it now. This is just another piece of me Elana had taken to the grave with her.

"I'll be there shortly, and please let Junior know that I'll have his favorite."

"Okay. I love you, honey, and be safe," she said warmly.

"Back at you." I took a deep sigh and hung up.

My thoughts went to Junior and his condition. He was still recovering. The injuries he sustained at the hands of Rasta proved to be more serious than I first thought. When we made it over to the island, he was put into a coma for over a month. He was beaten and kicked in his head and ribs multiple times. One of those kicks to his young ribs almost severed his spinal cord. This left him partially paralyzed. He just recently regained some mobility in his legs. It has been a hard, long road, and some days, I wished he had his mother here with us, but she was the reason he was like this. I'm glad I sent her ass straight to hell where she belonged.

I sometimes have dreams of me choking the life right out of her. I would watch as her eyes rolled to the back of her head while I would say, "Die, bitch, die." And she would be no more. But then, of course, I woke up, and it was all a dream.

Before I got closer to my house, I pulled over to check with my team. Since my grandfather's and my uncle's death, my brother took over. He was a major supplier on the island. I wasn't gonna be in that. But one thing my brother always valued and protected was family. I had to make sure that the situation at the hotel wouldn't come back to bite me in the ass.

"*Who do we think we are? Who do we think we are, baby? We've got a lot of nerve, girl; we walk around here like we own this place.*" I continued to listen to the lyrics. Each word had me. I loved my wife, but Elana owned my heart.

"Hey, Spunky, do me a favor. Handle a situation for me. I left a small tight package at the hotel by the shoreline. Can you get at it for me?" I said to my brother when he picked up the phone.

"Ha-ha, what have you gotten your lame ass into this time? I swear, yo' ass need to come on the team and help me run this shit. This better not be like that last one," he said with a light chuckle.

I took a deep breath and didn't respond. My silence told the answer.

"Damn! What the fuck you thinking, man? You can't be doin' this shit and think shit sweet. I got you this rip, but one more time, lose my number," he said and hung up.

I know he was mad and always says he won't help me, but that was five bodies ago. He always said the same thing. I smirked confidently, knowing he'll take care of my situation. I turned the radio up again and continued to get lost in the song as I reminisced about the life I used to have with Elana.

I had two brothers and two sisters. We all went to school in the States, and they came back to Jamaica. While I was with Elana, she didn't care to ask about my family too much. Due to my mother's dislike of her, I thought it was best to elope. My parents kept their distance while we were married. When Elana was pregnant, I could count on one hand the number of times Mother came to the house. It didn't matter, though, because I loved Elana. I had forgiven her for the devastation my family went through. I moved on from it and forbade my parents to ever talk about it. Then when Junior was born, it was the happiest moment in my life. I thought we could live the life we built together. But Elana got sloppy. I had my suspicions, and that led me to unearth those horrible feelings and wishes I once had when I set out to get her ass.

Now my life is no different than the one she lied to me about. I met my new wife while she was on vacation here. I was drawn to her. Her likeness to Elana was uncanny, and I felt like it was Elana and me again in the good days of our marriage. It was a whirlwind affair. Quick, fast, and in a hurry. After we had our fun while she was here on vacation, she left for California. We talked, texted, and Skyped every day for a month straight. Then when she told me that she was prego, I went into overdrive. I immediately asked her to marry me and come to live in Jamaica. She wanted nothing more than to spend the rest of her life with me. I was overjoyed, and now life is different, at least on the surface.

Elana was gone now. I was sure of it. My sources haven't reached out to me after they confirmed that the house did in fact explode and bodies were being carried out.

Chapter 24

Mother Is Getting under My Skin

I drove off the highway and followed a narrow road which led to my estate. I owned ten acres of land. It was a huge area where your neighbor was at least two to three miles away. I had the main house smack-dab in the middle that took up about two acres and was gated. My family occupied the rest of the land. A house per acre. Of course, I had the big grand house. Most of the older people in my family were centered around the estate. My brothers and sisters chose to build their mansions far from this one. I never understood why, but I didn't question it because I just left when my maternal grandfather and uncle died and instead of killing one of the person's involved, I married her.

I reached the entrance to my estate. "Wha ah gwan?" I said to the guard as I pulled up in front of my heavily guarded home. The gates were tall and surrounded the entire estate. The crest of my family sat proudly on the front gate. Two bald eagles sat with a watchful eye over the land. My grandfather always said, "Never sleep always. I mean, always keep your eye on the prize." He taught me at an early age that an eagle has a very keen vision and rarely missed its mark. I couldn't get caught slipping. Even from the grave, Dutchtress had a watchful eye. I needed to stay on my toes.

The guard opened the gate after he saw my car slowly pull forward to wait for the gates to open. I gave him a slight nod as I proceeded to drive up the long driveway. I took the sights in around me, all of the stone statues of angels and red cobblestones that aligned the driveway.

This estate was well cared for and had been in my family for centuries. My grandfather said his grandfather passed it down to the family. Each male was heir to the so-called man-made throne. "Family first" is the phrase my grandfather pounded in our heads ever since we were small children.

"Hello, honey, how was your day?" my lovely new wife said to me as I walked through the foyer of our home. Netta waddled her way over to me. She was about seven months along in her pregnancy. She was cute to me; her features were so innocent. She painfully reminded me of Elana when we first met. Before all the evil and destruction. I knew about Elana's life, but I didn't know it was that deep, and she was the queen on the throne.

"My day was fine. I had a few patients today. It wasn't anything worth getting excited about. Ah, how's Junior?" I asked as I placed a small kiss on her lips.

"He's fine. He started saying a new word today. I couldn't quite make out what he was saying, but it sounded like d-d-dma. Something like that. I was happy that he was saying anything." She rubbed on her protruding belly.

"How's daddy's princess today? Have you been feeding her? I want her to grow up nice and strong."

"Yes, she has been doing nothing but making me eat. I swear I have gained about twenty pounds carrying your princess," she smiled.

"Netta, baby, it's almost time. She'll be here soon enough; then we can hold her and introduce her to her big brother. I bet he'll be so happy. That will help him get better. I feel it considering how his mother left him the way she did." I rubbed her stomach as I beamed with pride. Finally, my life seemed somewhat normal again since I have a wife, and I have my son. Soon, my family will be complete when my little princess arrives. Yes, life, my life, was looking good. And I hope that witch is turning over in her grave. I hope she is rotting in hell.

I kissed my wife and walked out of the foyer. I went into the kitchen where my mother was sitting with Junior. I watched for a second as she fed him. She spooned his food into his mouth, reminding me of when she used to do the same for me when I was younger. Although he was getting better, my heart ached for the turnaround he had to endure because of his low-down dirty bitch of a mother. If it weren't for her and her web of lies, he wouldn't have had to start life all over again. His mind and actions were that of a 3-year-old now.

I took in a deep sigh, fixed my face, and walked into the kitchen. "Ah, hello, Mother. Here's Daddy's little man. How have you been today?" I said as I reached down and picked him up from the table. I tickled his sides and watched him laugh. He giggled and laughed like he did when we were all a family.

"Naheri, did you hear me? I said, have you made plans for us to go back to Chicago yet?" my mother said as she nervously shook her leg up and down. There was fear in her eyes.

"We've discussed this already, Mother. I told you soon. I have to put some stuff in order here; then we'll go back. What's wrong with you? Why are you acting nervous?" I looked her in the face as I put Junior back in the chair.

"Pst, how do you plan on handling your little wife, or shall I say the Elana look-alike? I swear, if you men would think with your head up top and not the one down below the world would be a better place. And don't think I don't know what you have been up to, Naheri. I know you like the back of my hand. How long do you think you're gonna get awa—?"

"Shut the hell up, Mother, before she hears you. I mean, come on, why don't you announce it to the world? And how do you know anything about what I have been up to? All you need to be worried about is taking care of my son," I said to her in a low, callous whisper.

"Boy, look here, your brother can't keep nothing from me. I'm Momma. You been selling that girl a dream from day one. Do you think I'm blind? She has a strong resemblance to Elana." My mother had a way of getting under my skin, but she has sacrificed her life for me. All I want is for all of us to get what we want. If I told her that I love my wife and that I planned on leaving her and my father here while I take my family and skip off into the sunset, she might do something to my wife and my unborn child.

My mother played a major role in some of the moves my brothers made. If she felt my wife was going to be an issue, she would not hesitate to remove her and my unborn child out of the picture. I looked her in the eyes, wanting nothing more than to tell her where she can go and to leave me and mine alone. But the only thing I could muster was, "Yes, you're right, Mother. I got this under control. I'll stick to our plan." After confessing this huge lie to her, I walked out of the kitchen. I needed to get out of her sight and out of this house and fast. Soon I would.

Chapter 25

The New Me

I sat in the bed with thoughts of Flex consuming my mind. I knew the other half of me was gone. With the police no closer to finding Naheri or my son, my days and eventually my nights had become full of sorrow. I had become so vulnerable that all of my hard work—everything I spent my life building—was diminishing and fast. I lay in that hospital bed for the latter part of almost a year. This Dr. McKinley kept the police from me. She would always come up with some lie or excuse for them to stay away for long periods of time. She told the detective I was in a coma and never regained consciousness. He bought that for a while until he tried going to court seeking a court order to have my physician switched. He almost got his wish, that was until there was an injunction filed by someone not to have that done. I often wondered who that could have been. My mother is dead, and I have no living relative besides my son. I know Naheri didn't do it. He wanted nothing more than to see me dead and rotting in a grave. My heart aches for my son and Flex, his birth father, the love of my life.

I finally was able to escape from the hospital with the help of Dr. McKinley. She got a cadaver body, close in appearance to mine, and declared me deceased. After all the paperwork was filed and everything was confirmed, she snuck me out of the hospital into one of my hideaway homes, not in my name. Thank goodness I had enough sense not to put it in my real name. It was a quiet little house not too extravagant on a quiet block. No stragglers walking about. No hustlers on the corner, and most of all . . . no Naheri. It had a garage which was great. It was easy to sneak me in here without anyone knowing because I didn't know if Naheri was still watching me. Shit, close to a year has gone by, and there was no attempt on my life at the hospital, so he must think I'm dead.

For some odd reason, this doctor had an obsession with me that was seriously unhealthy as hell. But I decided to use it to my advantage.

"Thank you, Mita. I sure appreciate you. All the lengths you have gone to keep me safe, I appreciate them." She looked over at me with a smirk on her face; then she slowly walked over and gave me two small pills.

"Here take these. They will help you relax." She smiled and watched me swallow both pills. I didn't question her. She was the reason I was sitting in this house. If it weren't for her, I would have been locked up for life. Soon, I started feeling woozy, almost as if I wanted to go to sleep. I tried sitting up, but my legs felt like concrete was wrapped around them, and neither they nor my arms would move. I could still see and hear everything. Mita walked over and stood in front of me and began to undress. She kneeled down and started to caress my hair and kissed my lips. I made a motion to move back from her unwanted touches. When she kissed my lips roughly, I tried lunging at her but to no avail. I was stuck.

She smirked. "You like that? Do you feel good yet? Let me make you feel even better . . ." she seductively said.

"What was that? Mita, what the fuck are you doing? I don't—" I tried to move my lips, but

I couldn't even feel them. The more I tried to speak, the more my words sounded garbled. She took off all my clothes and continued her little trick on me. Unable to move, I watched as she knelt down and spread my legs wide. She placed her tongue on the inner part of my thighs.

"Just lie back and relax," she said as she smirked and began feasting on my pussy. I wanted to cut her head clean off her shoulders, but I was immobile. I was forced to let her have her way with me.

I watched her head twirl around and round in a circular motion as she licked and slurped on my clit as if she were devouring her favorite meal. I tried one last effort to shove her, but everything went hazy and blurry. Then it went dark.

Dazed and confused, I struggled to get my bearings. When I finally came to, I moved my hands up and down my body and felt that I was semi-dressed. I eased up a little and saw some sex toys sprawled throughout the room. When I turned my head to the left, I saw a huge, long black dildo and some anal gel along with a few more sex toys. I was on the bed. The last thing I remembered was that I was sitting on the sofa in the living room. I looked on the other side of me and saw Mita sleeping with a huge smile plastered on her face. I slowly got up from the bed trying not to disturb her and keep my balance at the same time. I moved at a snail's pace trying my hardest not to fall. I saw a shirt on the edge of the bed and grabbed it as I slowly exited the bedroom. In shock and feeling my kitty pounding like I had a long night of hard-core sex, I saw her briefcase she left on the table. I went over to it and noticed there was a lock on it. I looked at the numbers on it and saw that some of them were not aligned. Once I nudged the numbers into their place, I tried to open it. The buckles at the top popped open. It made a sound, so I stayed still listening for Mita. Then I heard her snoring.

I opened the briefcase. I wanted to see if Mita had any drugs in there that would knock her ass out for good because after this little episode, I was done. Now that I thought about it, no wonder she didn't object when I told her I wanted to leave the hospital. She couldn't wait to do these sick things to me without a chance of getting caught.

The only things I saw were some papers and file folders. I grabbed one of the folders and examined it closer. There were pictures of me, Naheri, Flex, and my son. The ones of Flex and

I were older photos, but Naheri's and Junior's looked more recent. I searched some more. The next folder I picked up had Flex's name on it. There were photos of a charred body and an x-ray of what looked like a chest. I could make out the rest, but it was gruesome. My heart sank once again when a picture of my love Flex was on the next page. His eyes were bright and that smile . . . the same smile I lost myself in a long time ago. Thoughts of him consumed me. The last moment of his life was spent trying to save me. I wanted to be with him. I felt like I couldn't breathe without him. As a tear started to form in my eyes, I laid the folder down and picked up another one. I took a deep breath when the next picture was one of my son. His eyes seemed low and hazy as if he was semiconscious. But underneath that, I noticed a slight grin on his face. It was a faint one, but it was so close to that same smile his father possessed. My hurt feelings came and swept all over me. I totally forgot about what Mita had done to me. Then at that very moment, I saw a folder with Naheri's name on it. Inside were a few pics of him and a huge check for $1 million made out to "Dr. Mita McKinley."

I was even more confused. I wanted answers, and I wanted them now. I managed to wipe away the tears that decided to cascade down my cheeks. The more I thought of what could be, or what the hell was going on, the more I wanted answers.

I looked through her briefcase some more and came across a few small white oval-shaped pills much like the ones she gave me. I picked the baggie up containing the pills and saw the number "7.5" on the top of the pills. I wondered what they were, so I went over to my laptop. "Zopiclone 7.5" came up when I typed a brief description and the numbers on Google. "A strong sedative, known to help with difficulties sleeping," I read aloud. Every word pissed me off more. According to this site, this pill has been used to render a person helpless if given in higher doses. I wanted to run in there and slit her fucking throat.

I sat stunned for a second or two; then I remembered my trusty, dependable "right arm," the one I can always count on underneath the cabinet. I walked over to the cabinet. It's been a long time, but in all my hideaways, I hid my weapons throughout just in case of an emergency. When I got in front of the cabinet, I looked up in the mirror that hung just above and caught a glimpse of myself.

The sight of my once nicely done-up hair lying flat, matted to my head, threw me off. My eyes were puffy and red from constant crying. My always nicely groomed, expensively manicured nails were a thing of the past. I had let my depression take over my life. Even my money was almost gone. I tried checking my offshore accounts and found out they had been wiped out. I knew Naheri was behind it. From what Mita told me, she had me declared dead and signed my death certificate.

To the world, Elana Dolvan was no more. She made it look as if I'd succumbed to my injuries from the fire.

She had me in a position where I would be left vulnerable, depending on her. Even my so-called trusted soldiers left me standing alone. I stood in the mirror for what seemed like an eternity, contemplating every thought, every moment, and all of the people who have crossed me. I was so consumed with anger the more I thought about it. I reached down under the cabinet and grabbed my machete. No matter how hurt or depressed I was, I never leave my most trusted weapon.

"Mmm, time will take its toll. The deceit, the backstabbing . . . and heads will roll. Dem wan test me? They will see there will never be another, not one, no bitch like me," I said as I looked at my reflection in the mirror. I smiled knowing the destruction I was ready to put on those who had crossed me. I thought of ways I was going to find my nothing-ass husband and save my son. I want to make sure Naheri pays with his life for taking the love of my life, Flex, away from me. I continued my slight rhyme aloud just above a whisper as I turned the shower on.

Chapter 26

Flex Is Back

A smack hit my cheek. Hard and fast. Then another to the other side. I couldn't move. I was tied tightly to a chair. The room was dark but had enough light for me to see that I was right where I needed to be. The last thing I remembered was trying to climb a fence on the grounds, and when my feet hit the ground, I was met with a hard hit sending me to la-la land. This was not how I planned it.

"Yeah, ya wan fuck wit' my shit! Ya tink ya gwan come in mi spot and take what's mine!" I was strapped down to a chair as this big, black, and real ugly Jamaican sumo wrestler-looking dude pounded away on my ribs. I didn't know how much more of this my body could take.

"This . . . all . . . your bitch ass . . . got? It's gonna take a lot more of that . . . bitch muthafucka, to kill me," I said panting and out of breath. The pain was horrible, but I had to do what I needed just a little bit longer before shit got real.

"Ah, ah . . . fat muthafucka," I said as I laughed and spat blood on the floor. There was no way I was dying like a punk, not like this. The look the big dude had on his face was pure anger. I continued to taunt him some more. With each punch he delivered, I envisioned my son's and Elana's face. I knew they needed me.

This muthafucka was sicker and stronger than I thought. I heard a cracking sound when he hit my rib one more time. The powerful force behind his punch nearly knocked the wind out of me. He drew his fist back one more time to deliver a punch dead center in my jaw—but that's when the door came crashing down halting him in midswing.

I thanked the heavens that the cavalry had finally arrived.

"Yeah, nigga, let's make this shit fair, shall we?" my boy said as he rushed over and knocked the big dude out with the one hitta quitter. He hit that fool so hard he went crashing to the floor. The other dude tried to flee the scene, but he was met with a bullet to his knee, toppling him over in agony.

Peanut, Knight, and Vell rushed in behind him with guns drawn.

"Damn, niggas, what took y'all so long? Shit, he almost killed me."

"My bad, homie; you know we not from 'round here. These muthafuckas don't speak no English, and it smells like shit. Damn! Let's hurry up. Get yo' shorty and be out," Vell yelled out as he untied my hands from the chair.

"Shit, man, this shit is fucked up, a'ight. I got word my son is on the top level of this muthafuckin' mansion."

"Man, how the hell they knew you was here? We kept this shit on the low once we got confirmation he was here."

"Man, this shit was mapped out like a top secret mission," Knight and Peanut said as we all stood over the guard that got his knee blown out.

I looked at each of them wondering the same thing. "Pick that bitch up. I'ma show his ass what it really is." Knight stood at about six foot five and was 240 pounds of pure muscle. He worked out. He had no problem lifting him up and putting him in the same chair I had been tied in. He made it seem like that man was a little rag doll when he tossed his ass on the chair, then quickly tied his hands to it.

"So, I'ma ask you this one time, and one time only. How did you know I was in town?"

"I—"

"Make sure you answer wisely, homie, 'cause your life depends on it."

He looked me up and down and started laughing. Both sides of his lips were curled upward as if he smelled something foul. He sat up straight in the chair. "Ya tink mi scared of you?" He hawked up a nasty glop of spit and aimed it in my direction. It narrowly missed my shoe.

I stepped back a little and looked at him smirking and said, "That was some nasty shit. Ya muda teach ya that?" I said, mocking his voice. "How did you know I was here or alive?"

I gave him one punch to the gut and another to the eye. Then I drew back one more time and delivered a blow to his lip. Blood started spurting everywhere.

He flinched his body down in pain; then he slowly raised it back up and started laughing. "This nutin'; ya hit like a bitch." He spit more blood on the floor. Peanut rushed over and kicked him in the back of the head like he was a karate ninja or something. We all looked at Peanut and laughed.

"Damn, fool, don't kill his ass. I need to find my shorty. You been watching too many of them damn flicks, Joe. Nigga, we use hands or guns, not yo' fuckin' feet," I said as we all burst into laughter.

I was getting tired of the games by now. I leaned down and forcefully grabbed the dude by the back of the neck. "Where's my son?" I said with spit flying all over his face. At this point, I was angrier than before, and time was running out. He wasn't giving answers fast enough.

Images of my son being hurt or Elana in so much pain invaded my thoughts. The more I envisioned them, the more tears I saw on their faces. I looked him right in the eye. "I see you a loyal muthafucka, huh? You tryin'a be a rider at the end of the day, huh? Okay, have it your way." I raised my Glock 9 mm up and placed the tip right on the temple of his head. I put my finger right on the trigger and slowly began to pull. Sweat beads started dripping from his matted hair. For the first time, I could now see fear start to form in his eyes. I felt nothing, and he looked like he bit off more than he could chew. He was about to lose his life over something or someone who didn't give two shits about him.

I got one more inch closer to pulling the trigger. "Wait, wait! What ya wan know?" he said trembling.

"Dis not mi fight. Mi not gwan meet the Grim Reaper for a few coins. Dem holy one knows all.

'Im see ya every move, boi. He eyes everyw'ere. Da boy safe. He roots of the holy one. No one touchin' 'im. Da holy one wan ya dead. Ya can't come back from dead no more. He 'ave the witch, Dutchtress. He cursed to make ya and her pay for da lies and the murda ya put on 'im family," he nervously said as he shifted in the chair.

I wondered who was back in the States after Dutch. There was no way I was gonna let that happen. But I have a huge problem. Naheri knew I was alive and knew enough to send someone to kill me.

I turned my back toward them trying to put some answers to my questions. The who and the where came to a halt when I heard three loud pops. I quickly turned back around to see the big guy's head seeping blood and a gaping hole in the side of his temple. Peanut stood with a smoking gun in his hand. "Nigga, why the fuck you do that? I needed to get some more info from him! P, man, what the fuck is up with that?" I yelled.

"Man, Flex, that nigga flinched, and I thought he was about to up itchy on us so, I swept him first," he said shrugging his shoulders looking like he didn't care that he'd just murdered my only chance to find my son in this big-ass maze.

Something wasn't sitting right with me about that. It was too quick and messy. Besides, his excuse about why he shot him was lame as hell. The one thing I have learned the hard way is, money and power are an evil that can turn family against family, son against father. Hell, a mother would even sell her child to get a touch of the almighty dollar. I felt like I had someone paying me back for my good deed with no strings attached. It was my duty to come to Jamaica and find my son.

"Fuck! Damn, man, how we gon' get to ya shorty? Peanut, man, that shit was some foul shit, nigga. You always on some Rambo-type shit," Vell said as he took a look outside the door.

"Man, let's roll before somebody comes down here. I know they heard that shit. That was some sloppy work, Peanut," Knight said as he nonchalantly walked toward the door. We all hurried to the door which led up to the main floors of the house.

By the time we made it to the top, we could hear some Jamaican goons heading out the door. We all were in stealth mode maneuvering through the house. I peeked into the first room we came to, and no one was in there. We moved slowly across a long hallway to another room.

I looked into that room, and there sitting in a chair holding her stomach and singing was a beautiful female. She was an eye-catcher, and she resembled Dutch. I watched her hum and sing light lullabies as she looked out of the window.

"*La, la, and the cradle will fall.*" Her mellow, soft, and soothing voice almost had me lost in thought for a moment. I started to reflect on the rare moments when I was able to see Elana and Junior as mother and son. Elana would try to use her soft voice when she sang to him. She couldn't hold a tune in a bucket, but she tried, nonetheless, especially when it came to Junior. When he was fussy, her singing always made him cry more. It was still a sight to see. One of the most cutthroat bosses in the Chicagoland area was reduced to a pile of girl when it came down to showing love to her son, our son. What I wouldn't give to see her in moments like this again.

"Hey, man, what you gon' do? Just stand here staring at the bitch or make a move?" Vell said in a whisper, tapping me on the shoulder. I stared at the lady a little more because her features looked familiar, I was trying to place if I'd seen her from somewhere before. Her resemblance to Elana was enough to stop me from moving in quickly and blowing her brains out.

"Yo, Joe, he right. Did you forget there is about a hundred mad Jamaican muthafuckas that's gonna get hip to the mess downstairs soon enough and come hunting for our asses?" Knight sternly said as he kept watch in the opposite direction.

I was about to make a move toward the beauty, "Ah, ah . . . Help, hel—" she screamed. I rushed over to silence her by grabbing a glass vase that was on a table nearby. I hit her with enough force to knock her out. I didn't know who she was and what part she would play in this deadly game Naheri set up, but one thing was for sure . . . She was coming with me. I had a feeling she was going to be my ace of spades.

I threw her over my shoulder, and we all made our exit without alerting anyone. Due to the huge plot of land, we were able to scope out a weak spot in Naheri's security and took advantage. Money talks and Naheri wasn't treating his men right. I found out that some of his security men were planning on robbing his ass anyway, so I just gave them an incentive to help me out to make their story believable. It was simple. We take the girl, and they come in take what they want; then they leave, never returning. It was easy to get into their simple-minded heads. Now my next move in this chess game has to lead me to victory.

Although I was disappointed that we were not able to thoroughly search the house for my son, I know by taking his pregnant woman, it would bring him to his knees. After all, Junior ain't his blood.

Chapter 27

Death Is a Good Look on You

I drove down the narrow road heading to my house. I looked toward the mango trees when I saw headlights coming, but I thought nothing of it. I continued to my house. I pulled up at the gate, but the usual guard wasn't there to let me in. That was odd. I shrugged it off and thought maybe he went to take a dump or something. I punched in my code, and the gate opened. I drove up to the house, and again, I didn't see anyone patrolling the front of the house. Now my mind was uneasy. I parked the car quickly and ran into the house.

"Baby? Where are you?" I didn't hear any footsteps.

I immediately ran up the stairs dashing into the nursery. A vase lay on the floor broken. I quickly ran through all the bedrooms searching for someone. "Net, Netta, baby, where are you?"

I yelled as I rushed from room to room searching for her. I halted in my tracks when I spotted a long line of blood trickles on the floor, leading toward the back stairs. I feared the worst. I quickly ran down the stairs with my heart pumping fast. Horrible thoughts invaded my mind. Is my wife dead? Has my son had been taken again? From the moment I saw the bodies of my henchmen laid out on the floor of the basement I knew then that my plan was unraveling at the seams. The one moment I feared most was now here.

"Net, Netta, baby, where are you?" I yelled louder as I rushed from room to room searching for her. Frantic, I continued to run throughout the huge house in search of them.

I had built a panic room in the house. My mother sat there with Junior in her arms as she watched me on the monitor losing my mind.

When my mother heard the commotion downstairs, she grabbed Junior and rushed into the panic room and quickly locked the door. Then she called her eldest son who instructed her to keep the door locked and stay there until he came. She was able to see everything from the high-tech monitors that had been installed. She didn't bother to get her husband so that he could be out of harm's way. She looked on as she shielded Junior's eyes from the sight unfolding on the monitor. She watched as her husband's head exploded like a melon dropped on a concrete floor. Blood and brains painted the wall of the study. She closed her eyes in hurt for the love of her life being murdered, and there was nothing she could do about it.

"I knew this was going to happen, that damn Dutchtress," Mother spoke out loud in anger.

Junior looked up at her. "Mamma, I want Mommy," he said with his innocent and sad eyes. It had been over a year since he had seen his mother. He'd just started sleeping through the night without calling out for her. It was almost as if he knew she was still alive.

"No, Mommy is in heaven, Junior. Didn't Mamma tell you that? No Mommy, but you have me." Mother bowed her head. A silent prayer escaped her heart for her husband. She waited and waited until she heard a loud bang at the door.

"Mother, it's me. Open up!"

Hearing the sound of her older son Kainmen's voice and seeing him on the monitor, she knew it was safe to open the door.

"They killed him; just shot him in cold blood," she hysterically said as she fell to my knees crying.

Kainmen's heart hurt over the loss of his father, but now wasn't the time to show sadness. They had to get out of there and fast. "Come on, Mamma," he said sternly. His jaws were clenched tightly together. His anger was boiling at this point. Not only did Flex and his boys break through the fortress of this large home, but they killed his father. All because of this little boy Naheri is claiming to be his own. Kainmen was so angry he lifted his Glock and aimed it right at Junior's head. Junior sat in the panic room with his head turned, playing with his favorite toy, so he didn't see what was happening.

Just as he was about to pull the trigger, my voice roared.

"What the fuck you doin'? That's my son—your damn nephew. What the fuck!" I screamed as I ran up and knocked the gun from my brother's hand.

We scuffled for the gun as my mother screamed in terror at both of us. There was no way she was about to let us kill each other or Junior. This was her family, and Dutchtress was behind all of their pain.

"Stop! Stop! Now! You're scaring Junior," she yelled as we threw punches in each other's direction. My desperation and anger gave me strength that my brother had never seen before.

I showed what my brother was trying to bring out of me the whole time we were growing up. It was meant for me to take over the empire our grandfather built.

I finally released the hold I had on my brother's throat and quickly picked up Junior and rushed out of the room. Kainmen looked at his two guards who stood by the door unsure if they should kill me or just let us fight it out. He gave them a head nod, and they lowered their weapons.

"Why the hell did you do that, Kainmen? You . . . You . . ." I said with my eyes full of tears and my voice weak. The pain I was feeling at this moment couldn't even begin to match the anger I felt for Dutchtress and Flex.

"Ma, if it weren't for that little boy and Naheri's fuckin' obsession with that heartless bitch Dutchtress, Daddy would be alive right now. And you wouldn't be in so much pain."

"I know, Kainmen, but Junior is family. Blood or not, he is my grandson, your nephew. There will be no more fighting between you and your brother. The only person we need to be finding and killing is Flex. I thought for sure he was dead."

Kainmen straightened his suit and brushed off his shoulders. Mother saw the look in his eyes and like she knew all her children, his thoughts were not ones of relief. He had the same look in his eyes she used to see in her father's eyes when a bloodbath was about to happen.

Chapter 28

Mita's Confession

After looking through the briefcase and finding all those folders, I decided to get some answers. I went to the kitchen and filled a glass with water from the faucet. I drank the water like I haven't had any in days. I filled it again and downed the water. My balance was back, and my dizziness was gone.

"You awake?" I asked upon entering the bedroom where Mita lay resting peacefully, unaware of what was in store for her.

"Mm, yeah, I'm awake," she said with a smile on her face right before she remembered where she was and what she had done. Mita quickly sat up in the bed. "E . . . lana . . ." she said stammering over her words.

I just gazed at her as I held up one of the sex toys in her view. Her eyes widened. Her expression was like a deer caught in headlights. She was caught.

I walked over to the bed with slow, calculated steps. Mita reached for the sheet to cover her body. "Oh no, don't be shy now. Let's look at all of that." I snatched the covers from her naked body. The look I had in my eyes made her cower toward the headboard.

"Look, I'm sorry. I thought you were into me. I mean, you did kiss me back. So I thought it was time to take us to the next level." Mita began inching toward the nightstand.

I watched her and allowed her to move closer. Close enough to open the drawer. Then I watched the shock and horror displayed on her face and started laughing.

"Is *this* what you were reaching for?" I held up a small caliber .22 Smith & Wesson handgun.

Mita lowered her shoulders down in defeat. "So what are you gonna do to me? I-I know you are mad, but please, please, spare me. When Nah—"

I heard her getting ready to say the name of the person I wanted more than life itself to take his last breath. "No, continue, please. This should be interesting. So you were saying that Naheri did what?"

Mita inched her body toward the edge of the bed in hopes that I would show her some forgiveness and mercy.

"Last year, before your accident, Naheri's brother Kainmen approached me about handling you. He asked me to give you enough drugs to kill you at Naheri's party. I told him there was no way I was going to jeopardize my career for him and his desire to kill you. He laughed at me and threated to kill my family. I agreed to do it, but when I saw you, there was no way I could kill you. You were, I mean, are the total package. Beauty, brains, and power. I could not believe the information he gave me on you. After I changed my mind, I went to Naheri thinking I could get him to help me out. I asked him to get my family to a safe place away from his brother."

I walked over to the chair on the side of the bed. All of my attention was on Mita. I picked up one of the dildos that she had left on the floor. My thoughts went back to the night of the party. "That's why when I first saw you in the hospital you looked real familiar to me. You were one of the guests at the office party. I thought you were one of Naheri's colleagues. But that still doesn't answer how, or why, you would take over my life the way you have. I mean, when they wheeled me in that hospital, I was all but dead, and you, you nursed me back to health. Then . . ." My anger was building up again. All the unanswered questions I had were making me more and more ready to slash her throat. Mita, full of fear to make a sudden movement, slowly rose to her feet and stepped in front of the window. I noticed her make a hand motion in front of the window.

"Oh, no one will be driving by. This is a very quiet block; mostly elderly people live around here. So guess what? It's just you and me. Isn't that what you wanted?" I walked over and placed my hand on Mita's shoulder, gently rubbing it, giving her a sense of comfort. "Don't be scared. I just want answers. So tell me how my husband Naheri played a part in this." I gave Mita a slight smirk when I noticed her look down toward the evidence from the night before sprawled across the floor. I gave her a warm smile. "No, don't worry about any of that; it's okay. If I wasn't so drugged up, I might have enjoyed it." Mita sighed, relieved. "Okay," I said, "back to how Naheri played a part in all of this, how you took care of me."

Mita took a deep breath. "I want to say I'm sorry. I only wanted to keep you safe. When Naheri got my family to safety, he told me that everything was okay. And that he and your son would be leaving for Jamaica. When I asked him about you joining him, he got a crazy, mean scowl on his face. I didn't pursue it further. He just told me that you and he were getting a divorce. I found that odd, since the last time I saw you both, and you looked happy. When he and I were in medical school, you were all he would talk about. The opportunity never came for us to meet when we were at college because I stayed in the books, and eventually, my hard work paid off. I was given a scholarship to Princeton in the middle of our school year, so I transferred. But you were all he would talk about when you guys first met. He would tell me about you and the long dates and even longer conversations. I was happy for him. After I left, we stayed in touch as often as we could. Then life happened, and we lost contact."

Mita's demeanor turned from calm to shaky. She looked at me with pleading eyes. "Do you mind if I get a cigarette? I said I was gonna quit this nasty habit, but . . ." she nervously chuckled. She walked toward the nightstand and got a cigarette out of the box. I could see her hands shaking as she lit it.

I watched her as she took a deep pull from the cigarette. Smoke filled the air. She took one more long pull. As she began to speak, smoke from the cigarette escaped her lips.

"When Naheri and I connected back up, the first time was that night at the party. He kept a watchful eye on you. Every move you made that night with that Flex guy he knew about. He was a little tipsy . . . No, he was a lot tipsy, and he was about to make a scene, so I took him to an empty room, and that's where he told me the whole story. Every move you made. From your affair to the murders he planned on pinning on you. He even told me his real name. I was shocked at first, thinking it was the alcohol talking, but seeing my friend, a man I considered a brother, in so much pain, I had to do something. When he drunkenly asked me to help, I said anything I could to keep him from making a scene and destroying everything he worked hard to build.

"Again, I thought it was the liquor talking, so I didn't put much into it, that was . . . until he showed me a file with pictures and other incriminating evidence. I briefly looked at the file and put it back in the drawer. I thought he was crazy; I found out just how crazy when he came to my house and demanded I help. I had to help him, or he would have killed my entire family. I'm so sorry." Mita started crying, holding her hands over her face. She cried and cried. "I looked at him as he pleaded with me to help. I still didn't think he was going to do anything. That wasn't the Naheri I knew. Months later when he showed up at my house and asked me if I was ready to help, I told him no, but he used the fact that he helped hide my family from his brother, and that I owed him. When he showed me a picture of my mom and sister bound and gagged, I agreed to help. I didn't know what he had planned but when I saw you in the hospital scared and bruised . . ."

"So what you're telling me is that he had this planned all of those months? When you saw me in the hospital, what? What was your part then?" I asked seething with anger.

I wanted to slam her head down on the nightstand. Not only did she take advantage of me, but she raped me. All while my manipulating husband took my son, killed the only man I truly loved, and to top it all off, he stole my fucking money. In my mind, all of that was about to be rectified. Starting first with Mita. I held Mita's hand and looked deeply into her eyes. "Look, Mita, this is no one's fault but your friend's, my husband, Naheri's. You did keep me alive, and I'm grateful for that." I held Mita in an embrace that seemed to calm her. "Mita, when was the last time you spoke to him?"

Mita looked into my eyes. "He called me last year to make sure you were dead. He told me that my family was safe, and I no longer owed him. He also told me they were staying at his childhood home in Kingston, the home of his grandfather. The very home he and his brothers grew up in."

I knew the home she spoke of. In fact, it was the home my henchmen invaded several years ago. The very home I slit the throats of Naheri's grandfather and uncle. I found this to be the perfect time to kill two birds with one stone.

I led Mita back over to the bed. All of the toys and evidence from the night before still laid in the open. I tried to imagine what had happened. All I could remember was passing out, and Mita hovering over me. I gently laid Mita on the pillow. I seductively rubbed her shoulders. When she saw that this was about to go into round two, thoughts of her ravaging me the night before probably entered her mind. She smiled and began to coo. Then Mita felt something stiff and long entering her wet box. She looked up at me with a loving smile on her face. I smiled and gave her the impression that I was into it. She threw her head back in passion as she felt the long stiffness move in and out of her cave. When she heard a click, she looked back up into my eyes, which now were cold and empty.

"So this the shit you like, huh? I don't do bitches."

"Pew, pew" rang out in the air. Her stomach exploded. The bloodcurdling yelp she released as two shots from my .38 snubnose entered her body through her wet box. Mita's eyes stayed open in shock as she took her last breath.

I got up from the bed, walked into the bathroom, and turned on the shower. When I looked over at the wall, I saw the small radio. I turned it on and found the station I loved so much. As the classical music interrupted the silence in the house, I made motions as if I were conducting an orchestra. I looked back at the bloody mess on the bed where Mita's lifeless body lay. I smiled, excited about the face-to-face I was going to have with my son and my soon-to-be-dead husband. Then I stepped into the shower and allowed the warm water to cascade over my head. "Soon, you will see what it is," I spoke out loud as the music from Johann Sebastian Bach played through the small radio.

Chapter 29

Naheri, All Lies Tell Truths

"Look, I don't care what it takes, find that muthafucka!" Kainmen's voice boomed from the other side of the room.

I just sat there in shock and agony. Not only did Flex kill my father, but my wife, my sweet wife was missing. They took her too. I looked back on the surveillance tape, and to my shock and pure dismay, I watched as Flex and his crew tore through my secure and gated home and took things that I held near and dear to me. My wife was unconscious as they tore through the house looking for what looked like a way out. When they came upon my father lying asleep on the couch, I watched in pain as Flex made sure he put a bullet through his head. I could hear my father now, "*You should have left this alone when you had the chance, son.*" I had to sit back and wonder if Elana was alive too. I picked up my phone to call the only person who would know the truth about that. She promised me. I'll kill her and her whole family if she double-crossed me.

The phone rang for a moment; then the voicemail picked up. I hung up and called right back. This time, on the third ring, someone picked up. "Mita, Mita," I called out to her in desperation. Still no answer. I could hear breathing on the other end. "Mita, this is Naheri. I need to speak to you about my wife. Did you kill that bitch as we discussed? If you di—" I heard laughter erupt from the other end, and then the call was terminated. I called right back, only to be met with the voicemail again. I wasn't sure if that was Mita. All I knew was whoever it was found something I'd said real funny. A sick and eerie feeling crept over my body. I will never forget her laugh. It was the devil herself. I looked over at Kainmen and swallowed a huge lump that seemed to have formed in my throat.

"I need to go back to the States. Junior and I are leaving tonight."

Kainmen looked over in my direction with a menacing stare. His eyes seemed cold and empty. If looks could kill, my son and I would be dead right where we sat. Kainmen nodded to his guard that stood at the door. Then in a loud booming voice, he said, "Leave? Leave now? Are you fucking serious? This shit is all because of you and your weak-ass moves. When I sent Rasta to kill that bitch, all you had to do was . . ." He stopped talking. By this time, I sat Junior down in a chair. I looked in the face of my son. His resemblance to his mother was enough to shake my cold heart. The feelings I had for her were not all the way gone. In fact, she haunted my every thought, even at a time like this. The long scar that adorned the side of Junior's face brought back the reality that they almost killed him. No matter blood or not, he is my son, and I am his father in every way that counts.

I stared at Kainmen. "*You* are the one who unleashed that fool on my family and me. Because of you, an innocent young woman lost her life. And my son, my son is starting all over because of that savage beast who damn near beat him to death. You did this to your nephew and for what—to get back at my wife? You—"

"See, that right there is what I'm talking about. You still, after all of this, you consider that dead bitch your wife. And because of this little retarded muthafucka who ain't even yours, our father is dead. The bitch killed our grandfather and uncle; then you sitting here raising her damn son like he's yours." He lunged toward

Junior. I drew my hand back and punched him in the mouth right before he could make contact with Junior. The commotion caused the guards to rush into the room and break us up. Once again, our mother rushed in. Her face was stained from the tears she shed.

"Go and kill each other; go ahead and hurt me some more. My husband is dead, and that's my grandson. Yes, my grandson," she said with a mean scowl on her face as she stared directly at Kainmen. "The more you two fight, the more she wins. I mean the devil wins," she chanted as she turned and walked out of the office in Kainmen's house.

I stood there panting and breathing hard, trying to catch my breath and protect Junior at all costs. I was confused about why Mother would say she wins. Hell, Dutch was dead, and I have her son. The only part I underestimated was that damn Flex. But soon, I'll correct that.

I picked Junior up and stormed out of the room and out of the house. I wanted to be as far away from my family as I could get. I strapped Junior in his custom-made car seat. I was going to a hotel for the night. I needed to get some rest and clear my head. I was going crazy. I missed my pregnant wife and needed to see Flex take his last breath. I caught a glimpse of Junior in the rearview mirror as I got in the driver's seat and strapped my seat belt across me. "It's okay, li'l man. We'll find Netta, and we'll all be a family again. She's your new mother."

"Mommy," he said making a well-formed, understandable word.

My heart pained me each time I watched him struggle for a sentence. This was so unfair. For the life of me, I couldn't understand why this was happening. Just a year ago, our lives were so different and happy . . . or so I thought. But, of course, like anything good, nothing lasts forever. My main concern at this point is making sure that bitch Elana was six feet deep. I picked the phone up one more time in hopes of reaching Mita, but no answer this time. In fact, the call went straight to voicemail. I had a feeling once again that my world was about to be uprooted and shaken to the core.

My phone rang. "Hello," I said as I answered it. Kainmen screamed into the phone something about me and leaving the family and our mother when she needed us the most. I listened for a short moment, then hung up on his ass. I didn't want to hear shit from him after finding out he was the one who sent the very man who put my son in the state he was in. After driving a little more, I finally came to a stop at the nearest

Knutsford Court Hotel Inn and booked a room for Junior and me. I was going to be up early in the morning to get out of this country, back to Chicago to find Flex.

"He'll be worm food by sunup." There's one thing I know for sure with a dude like Flex. He only knows one way to survive, and that is in the streets, and, of course, he will not do it in unfamiliar territory. "So Chicago it is." I spoke aloud as I sang along to Bob Marley and the Wailers' "I Shot the Sheriff." "*It was I who shot the sheriff, but I did not shoot no deputy.*" I sang the lyrics as if I held the smoking gun in my hand right then and there. In my mind, Flex was the sheriff, and I shot his ass dead.

I pulled up in front of the hotel. When I got out of the car, I looked around to make sure I didn't see anyone who would be following me. At this point, my brother and I were not on good terms. In fact, in my mind, if I saw him at this moment, I would put a bullet clean in his head.

I noticed a tall redhead standing across the street. She was tall and thick. Her skin was a caramel brown. She seemed to be in a heated argument with some man. I noticed another big, burly looking dude come over and lift the man from his feet and toss him to the curb. He jumped up with fear in his eyes and took off running in the other direction. Then the redhead looked around and sashayed back into a building. I read the sign above the entrance, "Club Ready Red." I got Naheri Jr. out of the backseat, making a mental note to myself that while he was asleep, I would check this club out before we headed out the next morning.

I got us a room and made sure I had Junior down for the night. It wasn't hard to do with all the commotion he experienced earlier. He was fast asleep once he hit the bed. I sat for a second flipping through the TV channels. There was nothing on to bore me to sleep. Television over here was not like the States. I turned to a station that was playing videos. "*Just gimmie the light and pass the dro . . . some of them move like a Spiderman.*" Sean Paul's hit *Gimmie da Light* was on. I watched the woman in the video move her hips with sexy dance moves. That put me more in a party mode. I wanted a stiff drink and some hot pussy. My mind flashed back to Ms. Red I'd seen earlier. My brief glance at her body was enough for me to get a stiff one in my jeans. I turned the volume down, made sure Junior was out cold, and slowly crept out the door on my way headed to my next level of passion with Miss Red.

Chapter 30

Mona Red

"Hey, put that box over there. And make sure all of the condoms are in stock. I don't want that shit from last time to happen again," I said as I directed one of my assistant managers.

"Yes, sure thing, Miss Mona. Did you order the new kneepads? Some of the ladies were complaining about the old ones. They said when they are giving head they can't stay on them a long time," I laughed.

Slynn was my partner in crime. We came from the States a few years back and found a gold mine selling pussy over here. Adult Yankee pussy was the hottest thing around. When I got over here in 2010, I started off small, but today, I own and operate one of the most popular brothels Jamaica has ever seen. Politicians, hood ballers, everyday workmen from all walks of life who may be different on the outside had one thing in common: the love of pussy, and they didn't mind paying for it.

I made sure everything was well stocked before we opened up for the night. Earlier, I had a problem with one of the regulars not wanting to pay, so my bouncer had to rough him up a bit. Then I noticed a face I hadn't seen in years. I could have sworn—no—as a matter of fact, I *know* that it was Naheri. Before I moved over here, my girl Elana introduced us. Back then, I had black hair and was a few pounds heavier. When I got here, I started working out and toning up and dying my hair its signature color, red. I remembered when I didn't have a dime to my name; then Elana hooked me up with the bread I needed to get started over here. I will forever be grateful to her and my cousin Flex. I hadn't heard from either of them in a while. I decided to call the one number back home who could give me the 411 on them. When I learned that Elana was dead and Flex was too, one of our real close associates put me up on what was really going on and gave me a number where I could reach Elana. When I called her, she confirmed everything and let me know she was looking for Naheri, and he'd taken her son. When I saw him earlier, I knew he wouldn't be able to resist all of *this*. When I noticed him watching me from my peripheral view, I made sure my tight, round ass was in plain view. The gap I have between my legs made it better. That gap speaks volumes about a woman's sex. In most cases, it means you have some good pussy. That couldn't be any truer in my case. When I told Elana they were here, she asked me to stall him for a few days. She was on her way.

He wasn't bad on the eyes, so this would be a pleasure for me, and my girls would make him never want to leave. I grabbed a glass and some ice and poured some of the top-of-the-line Jamaican rum in it. Then as the sound of the ice crackled from the rum, I heard someone ask, "You mind fixing me one?"

I had my head downward as I poured. When I heard that question, I slowly lifted my head up to give whoever this was "the business," till I noticed these sexy brown eyes and almost flawless bronze skin adorned with nice long locs. When he smiled, I almost came in my thong. When our eyes met, it was confirmed in the flesh. Naheri was here.

"Sure, baby, no problem," I said as Naheri took a seat at the end of the bar. He was looking good to me. "Where you from?" I asked him with a smirk. He took a nice gulp of the rum and placed the glass down on the bar. "I'm from 'round here.

Surprised you don't know who I am. Well, I'm Naheri, and you are . . .?"

I thought for a second he'd figured out I knew him from Chicago, but when I noticed the lustful look in his eyes, I knew then he was clueless. "My name is Mona, Mona Red. Nice to meet you, Naheri, or should I call you Adonis?"

He laughed. "Now, why would you call me Adonis?"

I bit down on my bottom lip. "'Cause you look like a Greek god to me." I hoped my straightforwardness didn't scare him off.

"Well, thank you, Goddess Red. You lookin' delicious enough to eat to me." He had a look on his face full of lust. If I wasn't on a mission, I could get lost inside of that fineness, but I had to stay the course. I motioned for Slynn to come over. "Hey, escort our new friend over to the VIP. Make sure he stays happy and satisfied."

Slynn seductively sashayed her hips. She made sure her round bottom was at full attention and very noticeable to him. Like a dog in heat, he followed every sway and curve she threw at him.

He managed to snap out of his trance long enough to ask me, "Will you be joining us, I mean me?"

"Sure, give me a few minutes to situate the bar, and I got you. Mi wan give you a new ting," I said to him as sexily as I could in a broken dialect. I watched as he and Slynn entered into the VIP section. His broad shoulders and massive legs had me wanting to hit that in the worst way. I made a mental note to enjoy every inch of him. As soon as I was sure he made it in, I quickly picked up the phone and called the number Elana told me to call whenever I saw him.

"The pigeon is on the wire," I spoke in code to the person that answered the phone. In so many ways, I owed Elana and the help she gave me before and after I left Chicago. I hurried and hung up and made my way inside of the VIP. "Hello, there, handsome. Let's share a toast . . . to new friends and great times."

"Sure thing, my sexy red. So how long have you been here on the island? And is it true what they say about redheads?" He took a sip from his glass.

"Well, I have been here my whole life. And, yes, the saying is true. Redheads put the F in fuckin' and fun." I smiled and took a sip from my glass. He looked at me funny. "What's wrong? Am I too forward for you?"

He chuckled. "Not at all. You are just the way I like it. Straight; no chaser." He inched closer toward me.

The scent of his cologne filled my nostrils. He smelled like a bag of money. The scent he wore I'd smelled it before on some of my wealthiest cliental.

"Um, you smell good enough to lick on," he said to me as he took the tip of his finger and traced along the side of my arm. "Is that the exotic scent of J'Adore for women? There's something about that smell that drives me crazy. You mind if I get a little closer? Girl, you gonna make me eat my snack right here and now."

I was so into his swag and the game he was throwing my way I almost forgot to keep an eye on him. There was something about him that had me wanting to bust it wide open, but I couldn't allow him to go there or take me there.

"Slow down, handsome. I got a surprise for you." As wet as my kitty was for him, I had to play it cool. I gave my bouncer who stood at the door a head nod. This wasn't the regular head nod; he knew exactly what it meant. About two seconds later, two tall, dark-skinned, long-legged goddesses walked through the door. Identical twins; one rocked a short bob, while the other one wore a long, Brazilian weave. Almost identical in size, only one had a huge donkey ass, and the other had huge breasts. They both walked over and sat on either side of Naheri, which was good for me because I didn't know how much longer I could stick to the plan.

"Here you go, baby; enjoy the appetizers before the main course," I said to him with a smile on my face as I stood up and let them have at him. He reared back in the booth as the sexy duo stood and circled their hips and grinded on each other. They gave each other seductive feels and rubs as Naheri sat back and enjoyed the show. I watched him as he got turned on. He licked his lips and rubbed his manhood through his jeans. I poured him a glass of Hennessy. This time, I slipped a molly inside of his glass, a small pill filled with different types of drugs guaranteed to make him horny and who knows what else. Then I sat down next to him as he watched the show. I passed him the glass as soon as the pill dissolved. He hadn't noticed. His eyes were glued to his two personal porn stars in front of him. He gulped the drink, and almost immediately he felt it. He stared at me with hunger in his eyes as he licked his bottom lip and started kissing my arm.

The two ladies were so into doing each other they didn't even pay attention to him as he pulled his massive dick out of his jeans to stroke it. I took my leg and raised it in the air as I moved to the beat of the music. Beenie Man's "King of the Dancehall" was playing loud. The beat of the music was electrifying. He stood up and put his manhood back into his pants, then reached for my hand to join him in a dance. He started slowly grinding, then dropped it low around my waist. He took in a deep breath of my kitty as I worked my hips and kitty in front of his face. He came back upward and stopped just above my ear. "Let me touch that pussy. I wan' take my tongue and tickle that clit some. Sit on my face. Mm, girl, I want you now." He sounded so hungry and horny. I knew the drug had taken effect.

I took him by the hand and led him out of the VIP area. I gave Rachel "the look." No one was to disturb us. She took her client and turned her back toward him as she gave him the backward cowgirl move. She winked to let me know she understood. When we got inside my back office, I completely lost control. I was feeling horny and off my square.

He grabbed me by the breasts and started biting them. I felt pleasure and pain at once. "You like that?" he said lustfully. I threw my head back in pleasure as he ravaged my body. He lowered himself to the floor in front of me and tugged at my thong with his teeth.

"Yes, take all this pussy in your mouth."

He ripped my thong off; his eyes widened with delight. "Damn, baby, even your pussy hairs are red. I like it," he said as he placed his tongue on my clit.

"Mmm, yes, mmm," I moaned with delight. He sucked me until my body shivered. I'd had my experience with head before, but he was a true professional. His tongue technique had me coming in less than five minutes, and that was a first for me. I couldn't let him punk me out like that. I lowered myself panting and breathing to his dick and took that massive pole out of his jeans and placed it inside my mouth. I bobbed my head up and down faster, slower, swirling my tongue on the tip of his manhood. He moved my hair from my face so he could get a better view.

"Ah, shit, sl . . . ah, shit," he said as he rammed his manhood deeper down my throat. I took every inch like a champ. I continued until I felt his legs start to buckle from underneath him. My head was spinning by then. But I couldn't stop. I swallowed every drop. Was he was done releasing his load into my mouth? I did a quick headstand. He placed his long, thick shaft down my wet hole as he stood up straight inside of my legs while I hung upside down. The position we were in was straight from the Kama Sutra. He was thrusting up and down like he was dipping a tea bag. In and out, slow, then fast. He had me going so hard I was coming harder than I'd ever done before.

He grabbed my legs quickly and took a hand full of my hair. "I love the way this red shit looks in my hand. Come here, bitch," he said in an angry, stern tone. He spun me around and started ramming his manhood inside of my anus.

"Ouch, you're hurting me," I said, almost screaming.

"Oh no, Ms. Mona Red, or shall I say Ramona. Didn't think I knew who you were? I remember your flat ass from Chicago," he said as he rammed his dick deeper inside of my anus until come and blood started flowing down my legs. He continued his humiliation and assault. "Didn't think I'd remember your ass, huh? Well, guess what, bitch?" he said as he continued to thrust.

With every word he spoke, he rammed his massive penis inside of me. "Didn't think I'd remember your fuckin' cousin, Flex? That muthafucka ruined my life." He went so deep I thought he was coming out the front. "Yeah, I knew you when I first came in the door. So yeah, take this dick," he said panting. "Yeah, this the dick you want, the dick you need. Oh yeah, this is the dick you will *die* for." I felt a swipe across my neck and blood started pouring from it. I tried holding the wound to stop the bleeding. The more I tried to inch away, the more he continued to ram himself inside me until he came.

Blood rushed out of my neck as if someone turned on a faucet. "Be sure to tell your girl, my bitch of a wife, I said hello." The last thing I heard was an animalistic grunt from him.

Chapter 31

Dutchtress Gonna Give You What You Want

"What the hell you mean? I sent you to do *one* thing, and you fucked that up?" I hung up the phone in his face. I had no time for excuses. I was on the plane jetting to Kingston. Mona called and told me she had Naheri right where I needed him to be. She said she saw my son with him earlier that day. But if I knew anything about my conniving husband, she was not to underestimate him. I'd done that before, and look where I am now—without my son or the love of my life. My heart was heavy once more. The only thing that has kept me going since I killed Mita was the fact that I knew all was not lost. My money was low, but the ones I have helped along the way saw fit to help me. Not only did they help, but also they supplied. Elana was legally dead, but Dutchtress was alive, well, and ready.

I walked over to the bar stocked on the private jet I'd borrowed from one of the Kristen Brothers. They were two of the most ruthless drug lords in Columbia. Cartel ties came in handy. They owed me. When I came aboard some years ago, they had an uncle that was fuckin' up the family money. They couldn't get rid of him; it went against the family code. But neither Flex nor I was a part of the family. In fact, the old bastard tried to step on my toes, and I wasn't having that. When the brothers came to me and gave me a proposition I could not refuse, it was settled. Their uncle, Uncle Karry, had to go.

The night of the murder they made sure their father and mother were gone with them on a cruise for a few days. I set up a deal to cop some product from Karry to send to my people in Hillcrest. When he called me over, he thought he was gonna get his old dick wet. I wasn't the average thug-looking chick, nor did my looks resemble a gorilla, either. In fact, I was what you would call "thicker than a Snicker." My body was my most dangerous surprise. None of the men in the organization took me as the nightmare their mother warned them about, but to their dismay, I was that . . . and much more.

When I met up with Karry that night, it would change my life forever. I sat across the table from him and looked him square in the eyes. When he reached under the table, he came up with a Glock 9. This was the type of firepower I loved. He aimed it right at my head. I smiled. He looked confused. "You're not scared, *puta?* You're about to meet your Maker," he said, laughing with the gun still aimed at my forehead.

"See, the difference between you and me, you fat, sloppy muthafucka, is the fact that I fear no man." I laughed at him, staring right down the barrel of his gun as if he said a joke. Just like the archangel he is to me, Flex came behind him and put one right in the back of his head. I watched his body fall like a ton of bricks on the table. Then I walked over and laid a passionate kiss on Flex's lips.

"Here, baby, I thought you'd need this," he said to me as he lifted my prize possession, my double-bladed machete.

"You know me too well, baby." I walked over and lifted Karry's head up from the table. I took the machete and severed his head from his shoulders. "Give me the duffel bag, bae." He passed me the bag, and I placed the bloody head, along with a few pounds of cocaine, inside of the bag.

A few days later after the brothers got back and word had spread about their beloved uncle, a bounty was placed on the head of the person who did this. Of course, no one ever came forward. After it died down some, the brothers made good on their word. They called me to their yacht on Lake Michigan. I showed them their uncle's head. One of the brothers threw it overboard, and the other gave me my new world. I became one of the most powerful bosses Chicago ever saw. My name rang loud in the street. Dutchtress. But to the world, I was Elana Dolvan.

When I made moves, I took no mercy. I guess that's because of my mother and crackheaded-ass aunt. I owe all that I am and all I have to Flex. He stood there with me, even when I left to pursue a career and education. He found me and never left my side.

"Fasten your seat belt. We are about to enter and land in Kingston, Jamaica," I heard the pilot say over the speakers. I sipped the last of my rum; then I started feeling nervous. A year has passed since I have seen my son. I wondered when I finally lay eyes on him will I be able to look past the fact that he looks so much like Flex? My heart ached for them both. I missed Junior's little smile and bright gray eyes. And the way he tilted his little head slightly when he would try to get his way. Much like Flex, with his steel-gray eyes and his cocky smile. He always had me in full confidence that he had my back.

I felt a tear start to well up in the corner of my eye. "Flex, why did you leave me? You said us against we, death before dishonor. Baby, I miss you. I need you," I spoke aloud as I felt the plane start to descend for our landing. A lone tear cascaded down my cheek.

"We have landed safely, ma'am. Enjoy your stay on the lovely island of Jamaica. Make sure you take in some of the beautiful sights on your visit." The pilot was very polite. He made the flight over very pleasant. Being here for a nice visit was the furthest thing from my mind, however. When I get my son to a safe place out of harm's way, I am going to unleash pure hell on Naheri's entire family.

I kissed a necklace that Flex had given me two years ago that read "*Forever us against we*." "Be with me, baby. Our son needs me. I love you, Flex."

Chapter 32

All of the Queen's Horsemen

"Come on, Flex, man, what we gon' do with her? Her ass heavy as hell, and trying to get a pregnant bitch on the plane is hard as fuck," Vell said as he paced the hotel room floor. Knight didn't say a word. Instead, he focused on Peanut. From the time they were in the basement, he felt something wasn't right with their longtime friend.

"What's wrong, Joe? Why you looking like that?" Peanut asked as he sat on the windowsill.

I was so into Netta, and how much she resembled my beloved Dutch, I hadn't noticed Peanut acting nervously.

In fact, the only one who paid full attention was Knight. "Man, nothing, man. I'm just trying to piece some shit together."

"I feel you, man. We got to be out of here. I'm ready to get back to my fam, my city, the Chi," he said with a little too much eagerness for Knight. Vell stopped pacing the floor long enough to catch the expression that adorned Knight's face. In his mind, something wasn't right with the way Peanut had been acting. If they weren't in a rush to get out of that death trap saving Flex, he would have called Peanut out on it. The one thing Vell hated the most was a disloyal muthafucka.

Vell walked over and stood close to Peanut. He noticed a light blinking from the side of his pocket. Vell looked over at Knight, who then looked over at me. I then took notice of the building tension in the room. Netta lay unconscious on the bed. Her stomach moved up and down as the baby switched its position. I was relieved we hadn't hurt her baby. I nodded toward Knight. "Aye, Joe, let me step on this balcony to get some air and call Polu. Let that nigga know to get shit ready." Knight nodded his head but never took his eye off of Peanut. Vell caught the hint and turned his attention back to the light inside of Peanut's pocket. He wanted to know what that was and where it was coming from because Peanut had his cell phone in his hand already. The light blinked faster and faster.

I stepped onto the balcony and took a deep breath. The fresh air and cool breeze were welcoming to me. I started reminiscing on the times Elana and I came to the island. It was supposed to be business, but before it was all done, we turned it into pleasure. Every time I thought of her, my heart ached. I would touch my chest and remember what those days meant to both of us.

The way I found out about her death was too much for me to take. I vowed then that I would find my son, our son, and make Naheri pay for what he did. He took her from me. He killed her. I couldn't believe she was gone. I thought back to the time when Dutch and I danced on the beach to Sean Paul's "Still in Love" which played softly on my iPod. "*I'm still in love with you, boy . . . oo.*" It felt like she was standing right in front of me as I remembered her singing to me that day. "Damn, I miss you, baby girl. Until we meet again, save me a seat in heaven, or in our case, throw some ribs on the flames for me."

I stood in my thoughts for a little while longer—until a loud crashing noise caught my attention. I turned around to see Knight picking Peanut up by the throat and slamming him on the floor as Vell held Netta down.

"Aye, what the fuck you doin', Knight? What the fuck's goin' on?" I yelled as I ran inside from the balcony. Vell had his hand covering Netta's mouth. "What the fuck! Vell, man, what the hell happened?" I asked again confused and shocked.

"This mutha . . . This nigga is a fuckin' rat, Flex. He set us up," Knight said breathing hard as he tightened his grip on Peanut's throat.

"Ma-an, I-I don't know what you talkin' about. I ain't no rat, nigga. Let me go," Peanut said as he struggled to break from the hold Knight had on him.

"Bitch, if you scream or even say a syllable loud, I'ma snap your fuckin' neck," Vell said as he slowly moved his hand from Netta's mouth.

"Man, this nigga foul, Flex. He has been workin' with that nigga's brother for the longest. That's why when he came to you about the whereabouts of Junior, it was all a setup," Vell said with sadness, then anger in his voice as he looked over at Peanut.

"Flex, it's true, man. Look at what this nigga had on him," Knight said as he passed me a small device.

"Look at it. It's a GPS. This nigga is leading them right to us. I'm guessing we got a few minutes before shit gets real. When ole girl came to, she looked at him and called him Maurice. That's this nigga government." Knight was way past angry. If I wasn't mistaken, I could have sworn I saw a tear fall on his cheek.

"This some fucked-up foul shit, Peanut man. We go back to the cradle. How could you, man? Why?" Vell was so angry he charged toward Peanut as his feet dangled from the floor.

I couldn't believe everything. I took the GPS device and smashed it to the floor and stomped it. Then I walked over to Knight. "Let him go, man. Let him go!" I bellowed. Knight looked at me with a mean scowl on his face. "Bro, I got this. Let him go." He took one more look at Peanut and dropped him. Peanut fell to the floor gasping for air and holding his throat.

"Flex, man, they lyin', I swear. Man, fam, we been down like four flat tires for life. Why would I go against the family, man? Come on," he said as he pleaded his case. Knight rushed over before I could stop him and kicked Peanut right in the face. Trying to pull Knight back was like trying to stop a charging bull.

"Fuck you mean, nigga. Fuck you mean? I *trusted* you; *we* trusted you. You lyin'-ass, bitch-made-ass nigga." Knight tried to get one more good kick in. I pulled him back with so much force he almost flew through the bathroom door.

"Enough! I said I got this." I watched Vell make a motion toward Peanut. "Whoodie, I got this." I calmly walked over to Peanut and helped him up from the floor. Then I looked back at

Netta. The cold stare I gave her let her know that by all means, she and her unborn child will die if she doesn't tell the truth. "Do you know him?" I asked her.

She lowered her head. "Yes," she said in a low tone.

"Speak up, shorty. I wanna make sure I heard you correctly. Do you know this nigga?"

"Yes, I know him."

I chuckled lightly. Inside I was fucked up. Peanut was my li'l nigga from the hood. I practically raised him, fed that li'l nigga, and taught him the business. I didn't give him; he earned. I always go by the code if you give a person food they will eat for that day, but if you teach them to hunt, they will eat for a lifetime. I looked him in the eyes. I wanted him to see the pain *and* pleasure I will soon be having.

"Flex, that bitch lyin', I swea—" I placed my hand over his mouth.

"Go ahead, sweetheart, tell us where you know him from."

She cleared her throat, then looked over at Peanut who had pleading eyes begging silence. She turned toward me. "I know him from my brother-in-law Kainmen. Last year when we all took a trip to Chicago, I was in the car when he and another guy met with Kainmen and my husband, Naheri. I didn't notice him at the time until I heard someone mention the name Dutchtress. That made me take notice because I'd heard my husband mumble this very name in his sleep. When Naheri and I were back at the hotel, he told me everything. Even told me the names of the men they'd met with. I watched him that night put an envelope up in a safe. He told me if anything ever happened to him, give it to the police. He said he didn't trust the guys." She looked over at Peanut who was now sitting in a chair as Vell towered over him.

"Go on, finish," Knight bellowed across the room in a tone that could almost shake glass.

Netta nervously rubbed her hands together and continued to tell us everything.

"The fact that he met with this nigga and sold you out, us out . . . Come on, Flex, let me kill this disloyal-ass nigga right here," Vell said as he pulled his gun from his side.

"Naw, man, not right now. We ain't got that much time if this shit is true. That GPS shit got them muthafuckas on us like white on rice. So we gotta wrap this shit up."

I turned back toward Netta. "Please, sweetheart, continue." I wanted her to trust me, and I wanted to make her feel at ease.

"When Naheri told me that his son's mother died in a fire, he said you were with her, and the one who set it was you. So, he went on a search to find out if you were, in fact, dead. That's when he came across your brother over there. Then Kainmen, Naheri's brother, got involved and found out about you still being alive and . . ."

"And what? Go ahead and finish." As she opened her lips to speak, we heard a loud booming sound down the hall.

Vell rushed to the door and opened it to peek out. He quickly closed it. "Come on, let's get the fuck outta here. The nigga down the hall at the wrong room," Vell said as he rushed over to the balcony. The good thing about the room was we were not too far up so climbing down was not as hard for me, Knight, or Vell. But getting Netta down and Peanut would be the hard part. I wasn't done with Peanut. I wanted to get some more answers from him before I put his ass down for an eternal nap.

"Get up, nigga, let's go." I snatched Peanut up from the chair. Then I rushed Netta over to the balcony. We tied sheets together quickly and used them as a rope. Knight took Netta on his back and climbed down first. Vell was next; then I forced Peanut down before me. By the time we got to the ground, I heard a blast from up in the room. I rushed over to a cab, and we all got in.

"Where the fuck you supposed to pick up your money, you bitch-ass nigga?" I asked Peanut as he sat scared in the middle of Knight and Vell. I sat Netta close to me. Peanut's head hung in shame.

"At the airport," he said in a low voice. "Dude got a private plane waiting for me to get back to the Chi." He lowered his eyes toward the cab floor. I looked at him with nothing but disgust and hate in my heart. The man I thought of as a brother turned out to be a foe. "I should have listened to Dutch when she tried to warn me about you when you were coming up in the ranks. She always told me to keep an eye out on you. 'The worst thing you can do is let a hungry dog know where you keep your food,' she would always say. But I stood up for you. Hell, we all did, and *this* is how you repay us." Knight sat quietly looking out the window. Vell kept a mean scowl on his face as he focused his attention solely on Peanut.

"I wanna know one thing. Who was this other muthafucka who betrayed us?" Knight asked, never taking his attention from the window. The stern tone he used had Peanut scared to speak.

I looked at him. "Yeah, Peanut, who is it? I mean, since the cat's out of the bag and shit, you already know how this shit roll. 'Honor the family, death before dishonor.' Remember? That shit used to mean something to niggas. Now it's all about self. Me against we, that's how muthafuckas like you get down now." I was past mad.

After this last year, almost losing my life and losing the love of my life, and our son, the last piece I have left of her all taken from me, I wanted to reach out and blow this nigga's brains across the backseat of this car.

"Man, what the fuck would y'all have done in my place? Money was low, and the streets was dry. I was barely eatin'. I mean, me, my moms, and my girl with my shorty on the way . . . Damn, Joe, y'all tell me y'all wouldn't have went for the money?" Peanut asked in his defense.

Knight slowly turned his head from the window to face Peanut. "Nigga, you mean to tell me you put *money* over family? For real? Fool, when your ass was breaking and had nothing to call your own, family, *this* family, fed you and yours. When your moms sat out over on Sixty-third and Laflin, and you called me at 1:00 a.m. to help, nigga, I got up out of some good pussy to help. Better yet, when them Mexicans over on Forty-third and Honore offered niggas ten stacks for your head, we went to war for you and dared any nigga to touch a hair on top of your fuckin' head. *I* saved you; *I* made you; *I* gave you—bitch." Knight reared up and beat on his chest with every word. This touched him far worse than it did us. I didn't know about the hit that was on Peanut's head.

"Look, man, the way I see it, y'all, my so-called fam, gon' kill me anyway. So what I did that shit? If that bitch Dutchtress hadn't killed my uncle and started all of this shit, maybe I would have done shit different. I was gonna make sure I stomped on that bitch grave when I got back to the Chi. Oh well, I guess I will have the bitch suck on my balls while we both burning in hell."

I lunged over before anyone could react and started beating him with the butt of my gun. The muthafucka had the nerve to speak of my love like that. The one who made sure his disloyal ass was fed and protected. I beat him until he was unconscious. In my rage, Netta cowered over in the corner. Knight looked on, and Vell grit his teeth.

"Kill that nigga," Vell said aloud. I stopped when the cabdriver shouted from the front of the car.

"Ya no do dis, er, not in mi ride." He started to pull his cab over to the curb. "Get out, and get out of mi ride. Get—"

I placed the gun directly up to his nose. "You really want to do that?"

The cabdriver looked down the barrel in fear. "No . . . No."

"Good. Keep driving." I put the gun back down as Peanut's blood trickled down my hand.

Knight looked at Peanut's unconscious body. "I should have let them niggas smoke his ass."

"It's all good. We got something for this fool," Vell said as he shoved an unconscious Peanut to the floor of the car and put his foot on his back. Netta slowly repositioned herself back in her seat. Fear was etched all over her face.

"Where to now? Until this fool regains consciousness, we don't know which airstrip the plane is at," Knight spoke as he lit up a Black & Mild cigar.

"Hey, yo, driver, what you know about Mona Red?"

He looked through the rearview mirror, and his eyes were full of terror. "She runs the brothel across town."

"Good. Take us there." I sat back in the seat with my eyes trained on the driver and Netta at the same time.

Chapter 33

Long Live the Queen

Dutchtress

I exited the plane with my Versace wide-rimmed shades over my eyes. I felt something in the air. I didn't know if it was because of the fresh island breeze or the bright blue sky. All I knew was it felt different. I had been so down in my spirit for the longest of times, but being this close to my son restored my hope. I envisioned several thousand ways I was gonna kill Naheri the whole trip over.

"Ma'am, can mi take yo' bags?" an attendant asked me as I stepped into the carport area.

"Yes, you may, and can you tell me where I can get some of that good ganja from?" In this part of the island, it was legal to smoke weed. I wanted to get in contact with a good connect. If I knew the trade like I know I do, Naheri's brother would be wrapped up with it as the big man. I waited for my car to pull up. The attendant told me where to get some good stuff and a nice hotel just on the other side of town I could lay my head at in peace. But that was the furthest thing in my mind. Mona already told me the hotel Naheri was staying at with Junior. "Take me to the Knutsford hotel." The driver pulled off.

We pulled up in front of the hotel. I looked around before I got out of the car. I couldn't take a chance on Naheri spotting me. "Take me around the back. I want to enter through the service door." The driver looked confused. When I slipped him a hundred-dollar bill, he shrugged his shoulders and drove around back. I asked him if he knew where Mona Red's spot was, and he informed me that he knew exactly where it was, and he had a good connection in there if I needed a job. I lightly laughed. "No thanks, selling pussy ain't my forte." He shrugged his shoulders again and opened the door for me to the back entrance. I walked around to the front desk through the service doors. As I was approaching the desk to check in, I noticed a little boy sitting on the couch in the lobby by himself. My heart almost leaped from my chest when I noticed his wavy hair and bronze-colored skin. He also had a pair of almond-shaped eyes. I looked closer as I was about to run over to him. When I lowered my shades to get a better look, my heart felt like it had sunk to the bottom of my stomach. It was not my son. I put my shades back on and turned toward the desk to check in. "Room 520," the clerk said with a huge smile on his face. I picked up my oversized bag, and the lobby attendant grabbed the rest.

I walked back over to the elevator and got on looking down at the floor the whole time. I felt like I was so close yet still so far away from my son.

I opened the door to the room. The view was breathtaking. When I turned around to the lobby attendant who'd carried my luggage up, he asked, "Will dat be all ma'am?" His hand was behind his back.

"Yes, thank you. I will need a car later. Can you ask the front desk to have one ready for me in about an hour? Once I settle in, I'm going to hit the town."

He walked out the door after he agreed to let them know about the car service. He was all smiles after the hundred-dollar tip I put in his hand.

I picked up the phone to call Mona to let her know I was here. I hadn't heard from her since yesterday. But she told me she had Naheri on lock and would hold him there with an extended party he looked like he would love until I got to him. The phone rang about four times before her voicemail greeted me. I didn't think too much of it. Maybe she was tied up with a client. I was about to take a walk into the bathroom when there was a light knock at the door. "Who is it?" I tried my best to disguise my voice.

"I'm Sistren Mary, mi waan Priors yah."

I understood her words even with the heavy dialect. I needed every prayer I could use if I was gonna get my son back and have my revenge on Naheri. I slowly approached the door with my trusty friend behind my back. I wanted to make sure this wasn't an ambush. I was most certainly going to be ready. "Pardon us; we want to offer you prayer."

When I opened the door all the way, I laid eyes on two short, dark-skinned women in nun attire. Nothing was odd about them. I remember from my days here, the island parish would send the nuns out to pray with tourists and islanders alike. They say no matter where you are, if you won't come to Jesus, they will bring him to you. I graciously stepped aside and allowed them in to pray for me. I bowed my head to receive the prayer. I hid my machete on the side of me, not wanting to scare them.

After a few moments, "In da name of da Fada, Son, and Holy Spirit. Amen," I heard the lighter skinned nun say. She held my hand and gently rubbed the top of it. She looked me in the eyes deeply as if she were trying to see into my soul. "E, mi waan tell you dis. Nothing is worth losing your soul over. Stop da blood fire. No one will survive, not even ya soul. By morning sun, the love you lost will be found."

I removed my hand from hers as I felt a tingling sensation travel through my body. I couldn't say what it was, but it did shake me some. It was as if she was prophesying. I have lived a cat's life span and know well enough some things can't be explained.

"Tank ya. I be sure to remember dat," I said in my broken dialect.

The nun smiled and stepped closer to me. "Chile, no mind me and all ya waan be lost. I say ya go back to ya home and live. No good gonna come from this. I speak not of mi self, but the Fada dat sent me to ya."

Her eyes threw me off a little bit. They were glossy and colorless, almost the color of two silver dollars. The other nun who had stood quietly as I was prayed for and received my prophecy took the arm of the sister. They both began walking toward the door. "Thank you. What are your names?"

"Sister Mary," the one who was guiding her to the door spoke first.

"I am Sister Mary as well." She stopped with a wide sweet smile across her lips.

"Good Sisters Mary, I want to thank you for the words and prayer," I said with my mind still focused on what she'd said to me. The fact that she knew about my life and the love I lost and will soon gain again was shocking, but I had to realize it came from a higher power.

"Again, thanks."

They continued to walk out the door until the one whose eyes were colorless stopped. "Remember dis day. All who do shall reap wahn ey sow. Choose this day what end ya waan be on when the smoke clears. And the bloods seeps into the ground. No waan cr . . ." She stopped midsentence and rubbed my hand lightly. Her eyes once again had me mesmerized.

They had no pupils as if she was blind, but her words chilled me right down to my bone. She released my hand and walked away. I stood there for a moment. In my heart, I knew her message was saying for me not to kill, just get my son and leave. But there was no way I could do that. If I don't kill Naheri and his brother, there is no way either of them will allow me to live my life peacefully with my son. Besides, Naheri owes me over a year of my life that he stole. He took the two most precious things near and dear to me . . . my son and Flex.

Chapter 34

Kainmen

The Ruling

"Make sure she's gone. With a woman witch like that, you can't make any mistakes with her." I could still hear my grandfather saying this to me some years back. "*But, Gramp, she is no threat. How could a little female ruin anything for us and what you have built?*" I can recall that whole conversation as if it were yesterday. Everything he said to me about that evil bitch was true. After that day, she was behind my uncle and grandfather getting killed. She came like a thief in the night and killed them both. I found my grandfather lying in a pool of his own blood. I remember flipping him over on his back as he gasped for air. The cut on his throat

made it impossible for him to breathe. All I could make out of his words were, "*Ki . . . ll. her. Dutchtress must die.*" These were the last words he muttered to me. I knew then she was the one who caught one of the most notorious drug lords slipping. Every day since then, I have hated her and anything that is her, including my stupid, naïve, fool-in-love-ass brother Naheri.

I sent him to the best school in the country to get his doctrine, and when I found everything I needed to know about Elana, I sent him to the same school to kill her. She was young but vicious and callous. But what does he do? The fool falls for her. He went against everything that's family. My grandfather and uncle died at her hands, and all he could do was think with his dick and not his brains.

The day I heard about him getting married, I told him he was dead to me. But when he later told me about his plan to kill and destroy her, I was all for it. I wanted her and anything that had to do with her . . . dead. That's why I sent our cousin Rasta to her. I knew if Naheri didn't go through with it, he sure would.

I need to drink. I grabbed my nearest pair of black-on-black John Lobb Italian loafers. I also had my white Dolce & Gabbana suit laid across the bed. The one thing my grandfather taught me was never to let the world see you sweat. Always look your best. I walked into the bathroom and started a nice long shower.

My mind was no clearer than before. I wanted to find my coward-ass brother and kill his so-called damn son. "Damn, dumb mutha-fucka," I said as I slammed my fist against the nightstand. Naheri was beginning to be more of a headache. Family or not, I'm going to have to deal with him. "Come in," I yelled.

"I just wanted to see if you need anything before I take off for the night, sir," my personal assistant Gina said as she came to the door. She had one of the most innocent faces I have seen in years. Secretly, if I weren't married to the life, she would be wifey. But I couldn't chance anything getting in the way of me taking this game to the next level.

"No, that's all. Have a good night and be safe."

"Oh, I see you're going out tonight? Where ya goin'? I may wanna go. Might wanna shake some ass." Gina laughed and gave me a "but I'm serious" look. I couldn't take my eyes off of her. Even if I couldn't commit to her, she would always hold a place in my heart.

"No, Gina, you might want to go home. Get some rest before tomorrow. Besides, ain't your rude boi at home?" I said with sarcasm. I wasn't happy about her having a man in her life. But it isn't fair of me to have her put her life on hold for something that may never happen between us.

"Kainmen, why don't you stop with the games? You know just as well as I do that no one else is in my heart but you. But I guess I'm not good enough for you to make it official, just a good fuck." She turned in a huff to walk away.

I gently grabbed her by the arm. "Gina, stop it. You know I can't do that. It's too dangerous. If anyone who wants my head on a stick knew what you meant to me, they wouldn't waste any time getting to me through you. And I-I . . ." I tried hard to bring the words out. They seemed to have gotten stuck in my throat. Her eyes pleaded with me to say what she already knew.

"You what, Kainmen, you what? This is torture. Just say it and put me out of my misery." She grew more frustrated with me.

The outside of me was hard as a brick, on the inside, I was screaming "I love you, Gina, I want you. Have my babies. Let's jump the broom and make a life." Everything in me wanted to say all of this out loud to her, but I couldn't. "Gina, the times we shared were good and fine, but there is no way we can be together. My life is too dangerous. I care for you too much to just let you be hurt because of me." She looked sad and defeated. In one last attempt to get to me, she quickly reached for me, pulled me closer to her, and planted a wet kiss on my lips. I couldn't resist my sexual attraction growing in my boxers for her. I gave in.

We lay there in the aftermath of some mind-blowing lovemaking. I wished I could lay here with her forever. I wrapped my arms tightly around her as I imagined our forever fairy tale. I was caught up in it until I heard her soft voice as she caressed my chest. "Kainmen, I knew I loved you from the first day we met. Your dark chocolate skin tone . . . Even your long thick locs were so attractive to me. The very attribute you had that I found most intriguing was your eyes. They sang a sad song to me. Not weakness but sadness, as if you were missing something . . . or someone. The lighter shade of brown was as dark as coal to me." I felt her hold on to me a little closer.

"Listen, I know you're a man with much power, and you can have as many women as you want, but when we're together, you make me feel like I'm the only woman in the room. You smile even when you don't think I see you. Kainmen, please tell me what makes you so distant. Why can't you love me in the open? The way you make love to me, or the way your head tilts to the left when you are nervous, or the way you look when you talk about Jack and I being in a relationship . . . Kainmen, why are you like this? Can you just give us a try?"

I looked right into her eyes. I could see she meant every word she said. "Look, it's complicated. I'll leave it at that," I said as I moved my body from our embrace to sit at the edge of the bed. I took a deep breath, then looked back over my shoulder to her face. She had a small frown on her face, but love was still in her eyes. She searched my face for answers. "Look, Gina, I have been taught all of my life never trust anyone who is not family. The day my grandfather left this earth was because of a woman, and my brother with his dumb ass married the bitch. So, no, I won't be jumping over the broom or walking down any aisle any time soon. Better yet, this was a mistake. See yourself out." I stood up and walked into the bathroom and slammed the door. It hurt me to talk to her that way. But I couldn't allow her to be my distraction. I turned the shower on once again to get cleaned up. I'm about to hit the club. By the time I stepped out of the shower, Gina was gone.

I love her, and nothing will ever change that, but right now, I can't entertain love. I want to kill this nigga and anyone who is close to him. He doesn't think I know about his cousin Mona Red, but I'ma about to pay that bitch a visit. Maybe get her to suck my dick first before I shoot her in the head.

Chapter 35

Naheri

The Day of the Geechie Is Coming

"Hello, Mr. Dolvan, will you need anything tonight, sir?"

The hotel desk clerk called out to me as I was almost breathless rushing past the front desk. I managed to get out, "No, I'll be okay." I rushed to the elevator. As soon as the door opened, I stepped in and frantically pressed the button labeled six. As I impatiently danced in one spot, it seemed like the elevator was going slower than usual. I counted the numbers on the elevator keypad as each button lit up. When it finally got to the fifth floor, it stopped. I watched as two nuns slowly stepped on. I politely nodded, waiting for the doors to close. One of the nuns pressed the number one button.

"Oh God," I said a little louder than I'd intended to because I knew this old elevator was going to take us down instead of up.

One nun turned toward me. "I'm sorry, son. I meant to allow you to go to your floor first."

The other nun turned to face me. Her eyes were steel gray with no pupil. From my years of practicing medicine, I knew she was blind. I stepped back a little. "No . . . No, it's okay, Sister. I can wait," I said nervously. There was something about the way she looked at me. Not because of her blindness, but it was as if she were looking right in to my soul. She offered an innocent smile, then turned back around to face the elevator doors. As badly as I needed to get up to the room so Junior and I could leave first thing in the morning, I couldn't get the way the nun looked at me out of my mind.

"*Ding*." The sound of the elevator doors opening brought me out of my trance. As the doors opened, one nun began leading the blind one off of the elevator. However, the blind one stopped in the middle of the doors. Never turning toward me, the same one with the steel-gray eyes began to speak. "What you seek is not 'er. You will not find it, because it is seeking you. Every man must face ah music and 'tone for their action. You have to seek da Fada for help. Leave da bloodshed," she said, her voice filled with sadness and despair as they continued into the lobby.

I just stood there in silence and shock. Who was this woman, and where did she come from?

A man entered the elevator drunk and staggering around, barely able to stand. "Nice to see y'all too, Sisters Mary," he yelled out as the doors started to close once again. He struggled to push the button for his floor. Finally, he pressed the button for the seventh floor. I once again looked at the keypad as the numbers lit up. When the doors opened, I rushed off the elevator, almost knocking the drunk man to the floor. "Aay, bumbaclot," he said as the door closed. I was about to push the door to get it to open up again, but decided I would just let it go this time.

When I got to the room, I slowly opened the door and tiptoed inside, making sure I didn't wake Junior. I was grateful he was still asleep.

Quickly, I walked over to the bathroom and closed the door. I turned on the shower. I wanted the water as hot as my skin could stand it; then I undressed. When I got down to my wife beater, it was covered in blood. Mona's blood. I looked under the sink for a plastic bag. I found a small one and put the shirt, along with my socks and anything else I had on inside of the bag and tied it tightly. Once I was fully undressed, I got under the water to wash all the blood away. Thoughts of Elana started ravaging my mind. Her smell, the way her thick hips use to sway. Then I could see the look on her face the last time I saw her.

As the water ran down some more, I envisioned my lovely Netta. I wondered what they were doing to her. I knew the way Flex thought, so I had a strong feeling she was still alive. I have something he wants, and I know he will use her to bargain for it. "I'm so sorry, Netta. I love you," I said just above a whisper as the water cascaded down my face. I wanted what I wanted. Things were out of control; first my wife, and now my father. I wondered when this would be over. The nun's voice also ran through my thoughts.

She told me death was near. "Please, Lord, don't allow Netta to pay for my mistakes. And please forgive me for all of my sins," I said aloud as I turned the water off. "Oh God, please hear my prayer. This is all my fault. I love too hard, too fast. I loved Elana, and she still has my heart. Maybe I should have tried to fix us before I took that drastic measure. I hope she is resting in paradise in your arms, but please, don't let my Netta be my punishment," I spoke to myself as I looked in the mirror. I needed to get some sleep before the morning flight. I have to get Netta back.

Chapter 36

No Boundaries only Blood Bond

"Mona, hey, Mona, you here? It's me, Fle—" I walked through the bar calling out for my cousin. I called and called and got no answer. Knight and Vell held Peanut and Netta by each arm, making sure neither of them got away. Peanut was going to pay dearly for his betrayal, and Netta was going to be just what she is . . . a bargaining tool. When I got closer to Mona's office, I heard faint cries. The door was slightly cracked, so I pushed it opened to see who was crying. I laid eyes on Slynn, Mona's right hand, her sister. She held a bloody body cradled in her arms, rocking back and forth, much like comforting a baby. Slynn looked up at me, her eyes full of tears and pain.

"Who . . . Who is that?" I said, stumbling over my words in fear that what I felt was true. I looked at the body Slynn cradled. The first thing

I noticed was the red hair on whoever it was, and it was female. "Slynn, I said who the fuck is that! This bet' not be my peeps, man," I said in a cold, nervous tone. Judging from the red hair and the body shape, I immediately knew it was my cousin. Slynn just continued to rock her back and forth. When I got closer, my fears were confirmed. My cousin, my beloved cousin, was lying in her best friend's arms, eyes wide open with blood covering her entire neck and clothes.

"Slynn, Slynn, what the fuck! What the fuck happened?" I yelled at the top of my lungs.

By this time, Vell, Knight, Netta, and Peanut were close enough to see Mona's body lying slumped in Slynn's lap. Netta held her hand over her mouth in shock.

"Wha . . . Who is this?" Netta managed to say before she turned and vomited on the floor.

"Vell, take her ass outta here," I said as I stepped in front of Netta to prevent her from seeing Mona's body any further.

"I told her to be careful . . . I told her to be careful," Slynn repeated, still rocking Mona's body.

"How long she been like this, Slynn?" She didn't say a word. She was in a trance from shock, and grief consumed her. "Slynn! Slynn, baby girl, you have to tell me who did this!" I shouted to her as I pulled her up from the floor.

"I told her he was no good. She told me she could handle him. She said he was a lightweight."

Slynn sobbed louder as she placed her head on my chest. She was so messed up in the head she couldn't even form a sentence to tell me anything. Instead, she pointed over to a small monitor that sat on the top of a cabinet on the other side of the room. I looked over in the direction of the monitor and noticed a DVD player underneath it. "Take Netta and that snake out in the lobby. Make sure no one comes in." I looked at Vell and Knight. Before walking over to the monitor, I grabbed a tablecloth off one of the tables and covered my cousin.

Then I walked up to the monitor and noticed it was a base for a surveillance camera. I could see the live feed of me looking at myself on the screen. I looked at the DVD player and pressed play. The images appeared on the screen. The audio was real low, so I pressed the button to turn it up. I heard Mona and a man having sex. I could hear the skin-on-skin action. They were not in the camera's view until Mona was flipped on top of the desk and getting long dick from behind. That's when I saw the face of the man who has caused me so much pain and misery that could last me a lifetime. Naheri was fucking Mona, saying things so disrespectful and cold. Then in one long stroke, he placed his hand around her neck with a small blade in between his fingers and slit her throat. Blood gushed out as if a faucet had been turned on. I watched in anger as Mona took in her last breath. In a fit of rage, I flung the monitor around and broke the DVD player against the wall. "I'ma kill his ass if the last thing I do. I'ma kill him!"

The noise caused Knight to rush back in to the office. Confused, he asked, "Hey, what the fuck happened, man? Who did this?"

I didn't say a word. I just heaved my chest in and out trying to calm myself. "He killed her, man. First, the love of my life, and now, my cousin."

"Who killed your cousin?" Knight asked, ready to shoot the next thing moving. I just stood there clenching my fist tightly with a look of murder on my face. Knight looked over at Slynn. She was crying, staring at Mona's body covered on the floor.

"Why?" Slynn said, holding her hand over heart.

"One of y'all tell me who the fuck is behind this," Knight demanded.

I looked at him with pure fire in my eyes. "That fuckin' Naheri did this. I saw him on the DVD slashing my cousin's throat." I hit my fist against the table. A shot coming from the other room caused us to run out of the office. Peanut lay on the floor holding his right arm as blood gushed from a bullet wound.

Netta screamed, "Stop him! Please, he's gonna kill him. I'll tell y'all everything," she yelled.

"The muthafucka was trying to run. He a fuckin' snake, I don't care how you put it. He double-crossed us—his so-called family, his bros . . . *us*. I see no need to keep him alive," Vell said as he held the smoking gun to Peanut's head. "Why, man, why? We been more than family, nigga. How could you turn like this? Why? For the almighty dollar?" Vell was within inches of pulling the trigger. Slynn fell back down to the floor, still upset about her dear friend.

Suddenly, they heard the wind chimes on the front door make a noise, and a female voice yelled out, "Hey, is anybody here? Mona, Slynn? Where y'all at?"

"We're back here, Brandi," Slynn called out to her. When she made it over toward Slynn, she looked at her then back toward me; then her attention diverted over toward Peanut who was lying on the floor whining in pain.

"What's going on h—" Her words suddenly stopped as she gazed down at what looked like a body lying on the floor, then looked back up at Slynn. Judging by the way Slynn was so upset, it had to be someone close to her. "Come on, y'all, put the guns down. Slynn, who is this, and what happened?" Brandi walked over and put her hand on Slynn's shoulder.

Slynn began to tell Brandi the body on the floor was that of their beloved friend and sister Mona. Hearing that, Brandi hugged Slynn so tightly. Tears fell from their faces like rainwater.

"Pick that nigga up and put his ass in the chair," I said to Knight as he stood over Peanut who was still lying on the floor. "Slynn, did Mona say anything about where this fool was stayin'?" Slynn released Brandi long enough to tell me everything Mona had told her about this dude. She told him everything except why and who she was doing this setup for.

"All I know is she told me she was holding him here for a friend. She never told me the friend's name. Oh my God, how could he just kill her like this? The way she was when I first came in . . . Not even a dog deserved to die like that," Slynn spoke through her salty tears.

"Don't worry, Slynn, this fool is gonna pay. Did she tell you where this dude was stayin'?" Vell asked as he slammed Peanut in the chair.

"Or better yet, do *you* know, seeing as how you keepin' secrets and shit?" Vell stared Peanut right in the eyes.

"Naw, man, I swear, I don't know nothing about this. All I know is I was supposed to get you, Knight, and Flex here; that was it," Peanut said as he lowered his head in shame.

Vell huffed and walked off. Brandi looked at the trio and the pregnant woman who looked terrified. Netta trembled as she watched the veins on the side of Flex's forehead begin to form.

"Wait, wait. Mona called last night and asked me if I wanted to come in and get some of this hot trick she was workin' on. I told her I couldn't because I had a private party of my own. I asked her who the trick was, and she told me some dude from the States, and that he was good looking. She said he stayed over across the street at the big hotel, Hotel Knutsford," Brandi said as she began recalling the conversation in her mind. The Knutsford hotel was one of Kingston's more reputable hotels. Many diplomats and people with money stay there whenever they visit the island.

I looked at Peanut with disgust and hate written on my face. Knight and Vell did the same.

"Come on, help me clean this place and take care of my cousin's body. Slynn, where is Mona's car?" I asked, knowing my cousin had a whip. Slynn walked over and gave me the keys to Mona's Jeep Cherokee with vanity plates that read "Red's Baby." Vell held on to Netta. Peanut didn't put up a fight. He stood as Knight and I carefully picked up Mona's body and placed it in the back of her truck. Slynn and Brandi stayed behind and cleaned up. They would make sure the place was spotless.

They all loaded up in the truck and covered Mona's body. I got in and sat in the driver's seat and took a deep breath. My heart was hurting for my cousin, and her dying this way was no good. I wanted to give her a nice resting place. There was no way I could get her back home, not without the police getting involved. I looked through the rearview mirror into Netta's eyes. "Do you know of a nice, peaceful, secluded section on the island?"

"Yes, over on the north side of the city, close to the ocean. There's very little traffic in the heart of this park, and it has a nice flower garden,"

Netta said as she stared at Flex through the mirror.

Once again, her similarities to Dutch took my attention. I couldn't break my gaze off her. "Flex, man, let's go. We have got to lay Mona to rest; then we go see that fool. Even if it takes all night, his ass will pay," Knight said, bringing me back to my reality.

"A'ight, let's go." I started the engine and pulled off in the direction Netta told me about. Then Naheri was my focus, getting my son back, and making him pay dearly for taking another person out of her life.

Chapter 37

Kainmen's Law

I was so glad when I pulled up at the spot that I didn't get right out. Instead, I stayed in the car and peeped the scene. I parked in front of the hotel across from Mona's brothel. I knew my eyes were playing a cruel game on me because I could have sworn I spotted Flex and Netta, along with Peanut and two other guys I didn't know. I watched as all of them piled up in Mona's truck and loaded up something in the back. They had no idea I was close, close enough to take them all out. I clenched my gun and just when I was ready to jump out and spray all of them, a truck parked directly in front of me, blocking my view. My anger forced me out of my ride. I inched closer behind the truck, quickly ducked down, and crept up from behind the truck ready to empty my clip . . . but they were gone. I was pissed. I looked up and down the road and could see red taillights in the distance. Fuck! I couldn't jump back in my car and try to follow them now because by the time I headed in the direction I saw the red lights, they would have been gone. Besides, there were too many possible turns they could make, and I wanted to see his face when I blasted that ass.

I tucked my gun back into my waist and decided to enter Mona's spot. As soon as I opened up the club door, the strong scent of bleach overwhelmed my nostrils. Two females were cleaning the place. The look on their face showed my presence was a shock. I remembered the taller one from some of my many visits here.

"Ay, baby girl, wha wrong? I don't remember your name offhand, but you seem down. Is there anything I can do to help?" I walked over to her and saw the tears all over her face. That was my confirmation that something bad went down.

"We're closed. Can you come back another day?" the shorter one with the brown complexion said with a slight attitude. I almost reached back and slapped the taste from her mouth. I gave her a stern look to let her know if she said one more word, she would be breathing her last breath.

"Anyway, baby girl, as I was saying, do you need my help with anything?" I said as I walked her toward the back of the club where the smell of bleach was stronger.

She stopped me before I got to the part where the office was located. "My bad, baby girl. You don't want me to go in there. I'm sorry if I'm intruding." My curiosity was getting the better of me. Before I could take another step, her friend raced back there, almost knocking me down to close the door.

She looked at her friend. "Slynn, don't you think you and your guest should go back up front? I don't want anyone coming in. We ain't doing no business tonight. Sir, I'ma have to ask you to leave." Brandi gave Slynn a knowing look.

"Yeah, she's right, but thank you for trying to help me. What's your name? You look real familiar to me," Slynn hesitantly said.

"No need to thank me. It's just when I see a beautiful woman in need, it's in my nature to help. Besides, I heard this was the hottest spot in town. Ya know how to party."

She smiled but held a questioning look on her face.

I had to smooth it over. Her friend looked me up and down as if she was saying, "Fuck you, nigga." I turned to walk toward the front when I heard her friend say to her in a hushed tone, "Girl, we ain't got time for this shit. Like how we gonna survive, and who this fool is who killed Mona?"

"I know, Brandi. He didn't mean any harm. Right now, I need to get this place cleaned up and lie down. My head hurts."

I slowed my stride toward the door and stopped when I heard her say Mona was dead. I know fuck boy Flex ain't kilt her, but who did? This nigga bring nothing but misery and sadness every place he go.

"Ayo, baby girl, you mind if I leave my number with you? Maybe on a better day we can hook up, ya know, spend some time," I said as I called toward the back of the club. I held a small card in my hand. Slynn smiled and reached out to accept the card . . . until her friend slapped it out of my hand.

"I know you. You that muthafucka that got the big-ass house up top. You and your brother . . . Wait ah minute. I know your brother too, that sick fool. He killed my girl last month. Slynn, get the fuck away from him," she said as she stood between us.

Slynn looked at her, then at me. "What are you talking about, Brandi? What brother?"

"Slynn, remember when we had this guy acting up in here last month . . . getting rough with Renee? Well, this is him. I remember that night he went in hard. Almost broke her nose and fought Derose. It took the whole team to put him out."

"Ma'am, I have no idea what you are talkin' about" I lied with a smile. In fact, I remember her too. That night she was the one who called the police on me. I was about to come back and shut this shit down, but Mona brings big money to the island. I refused to fuck up the churches' money, as we say.

"Stop lying, Slynn. Remember when I told you Mona called me last night to join the party? Well, she sent me a photo of the guy. He looked familiar like I knew him. The fact he was sexy didn't hurt, either, so I looked him up on Google. There was a picture of him and this guy right here standing in front of a mansion. They were featured in the Social section about some of the wealthiest families around. I remember the dude's picture because my girl has been missing for a while, and his brother was the last one with her. How I know that? She was staying at my house, and she had the guy's picture in some of her things. That's when it hit me, who the guy was, and where I remembered him from. I couldn't make it to the club. I tried calling Mona, and when she didn't answer, that's when

I decided to show up early today and see how her li'l date went and warn her about the guy."

I just listened to her go and on. Then I drew my hand back and slapped the spit out of her mouth. I had enough. There was one thing I will not stand, and that is a female thinking she can talk flip to me, then live or be able to talk about it.

"What the fuck!" Brandi said as she lunged at me. She was wildly swinging blows and connecting some of them to my face.

I caught her by the hand and slung her so hard, she landed against the bar knocking over every bottle and glass. She lay there unconscious as Slynn screamed at the top of her lungs. I didn't want to do it, but I had to. I drew back once more and punched her right in the face. What the fuck has Naheri's stupid ass done now? I didn't have time to worry about that. I reached out swiftly and grabbed Slynn by the neck. I was choking her almost unconscious. I couldn't take a chance of her tipping the police off or her letting Flex know.

I watched as her eyes began to roll in the back of her head until I heard . . . "Muthafucka!" I turned toward the sound, and the side of my face encountered the side of a glass bottle. I released Slynn and held my head. Dazed a little but angrier than anything, I lunged at Brandi and wrapped my hand around her neck, shaking her like a rag doll. I felt the life leave her.

"You stupid bitch," I said as the blood ran down my face. I wanted her to die. Suddenly, *"Click"* is all I heard. I released Brandi, and her lifeless body hit the floor. I turned around to stare . . . right down the barrel of a Glock 9 mm . . . and a very healthy-looking Dutchtress holding the other end.

She smirked. "I see some shit never changes. Nice to see you, Kainmen."

I held my hands up in submission. I knew if I made a move, Dutchtress would blow my head clean off my shoulders. "I see death looks good on you, aye," I said smiling. There was no way I was gonna die kissing her ass. I could see the hate in her eyes. At any moment, she could pull the trigger.

"Not as good as it will look on you. So tell me, where is your sorry-ass brother? Better yet, where is my son?" she said through clenched teeth while she held the gun in my face.

I knew my options were few and far between. I had one chance to grab my Glock from behind me. "Look here, I'll bargain with you. My brother's stupid ass already is dead to me, so how about we work together and kill his ass? So what you think about that?" I said trying to sound as convincing as I could because the first chance I get, I'm blowing her fuckin' head off. I hate her just as much as she hates me. There will not be a second try. She will be dying this day.

"You sound . . . stupid . . . as . . . hell," she said laughing as if she heard a joke. "I don't believe that, Kainmen. Who in the fuck do you think you're talking to? Better yet, fuck your information. I'll find him myself. You two dummies never learn, do you?" She began circling me with the gun. I felt a sharp tug at the back of my shirt. She found my gun.

"Shit," I said just above a whisper.

"See, Kainmen, you should know me better than that. After killing your grandfather, I was trained by the best. I'm not one of these dummies you run into, the ones who fear you. Muthafucka, I know how you work, and what drives you. And that would be me. You lived your whole life eating, sleeping, and breathing me. I'm in your soul." She continued circling me slowly and cautiously. "See, unlike you, I never send a soldier to do a general's job. Your grandfather underestimated me, as did you, I see. Naheri was, well, I thought he was a good dude, ya know, husband material and a good father. Had I known he carried your sorry-ass blood, I would have long ago slit his fuckin' throat in his sleep."

She stood right in front of me with my body towering over her, and she pointed the gun right at my Adam's apple in my throat. It was close enough to when I swallowed my saliva, I could feel the tip of the gun. I knew then my life would be over. The look in her eyes was as cold as ice as if she had long ago lost contact with her emotions.

"Come on, sister-in-law, we can fix this. I swear I do—"

"Shut the fuck up! I wanna know one thing and trust me, I *will* know if you're lying. See, dealing with your snake-ass brother all these years has changed me. I trust no nigga! I can see shit for real now. Did you send Rasta to my son?" She waited for my response; then she stepped up closer as my heart pounded hard against my chest.

At any moment, I would be breathing my last breath. Everything was like it was going in slow motion. I discreetly raised my hands. In a split second, I dove on the floor. I heard the gunshots ring out as I felt a sharp pain in my shoulder. Dutchtress opened fire as I dove behind a table, then a booth. I didn't have my gun. I had one chance to get to the door. I lifted my head up slightly and watched as she held a gun in each hand, firing away. She hit any and everything. I noticed Slynn in the corner balled up in a fetal position. I crawled over toward her and snatched her up. Using her as a human shield, I ran toward the back door. Every bullet landed in Slynn's body. All I heard as each bullet ripped through her flesh was her bloodcurdling screams. Dutchtress never let up. She continued firing away.

Chapter 38

Us against We, Death before Dishonor

"Man, I need to go back right quick. I lost my chain. It's back on Mona's desk. I must have lost it when I saw that video and started throwing shit around."

"Dude, fuck that chain. Buy you another o—" Vell said as Knight cut him off with a look that would scare the hardest man.

"He need to go back, so let 'em," Knight sternly said as he shifted his body to face the road.

Knight could see that chain meant a lot to me. It was the last thing Dutch gave to me before our world became so full of hell. It was the only thing I clung to besides our son. I had nothing left of her. I couldn't even say goodbye to her. No service—nothing. That chain was my lifeline to her. I wasn't going to leave the last thing I had of her. I got to an open field and made a U-turn to go back to the club. We weren't too far from the club, so we arrived back there within fifteen minutes.

"Y'all wait right here. This should only take a minute. I'll be right back."

When I jumped out of the truck in the front of the club, all I could hear was gunshots. I quickly grabbed my snubnose .38 I kept on me at all times. The only way I could get it here was to fly a private plane over to the island because of the tip Peanut gave me . . . only to find out it was a setup. I rushed inside, hoping that Naheri hadn't come back to kill Slynn. Knight was right behind me. I could see that Vell had Peanut and Netta out of the truck and walking toward the hotel across from the club. All I could think of was Slynn. She was the last one connected to me besides Mona. I rushed in gun drawn and spotted Brandi dead on the floor. Then I heard another gunshot. When I got closer, my eyes laid on a female holding two guns sending bullets anywhere they could land. She pulled the trigger of one of the guns, and it was empty. The glass behind the bar was exploding all over the place as she freely released her bullets. I snuck up behind her ready to splatter her brains all over the wall until I saw a guy with long dreads ducking and dodging out of the back of the club. She took a step to chase him, and I grabbed her. She tried to shoot over her shoulder, but her gun was empty now.

She kicked and screamed, "Let me go, let me the fuck go now! As soon as I get loose, I'ma kill you, whoever you are!" I held her tighter, and her voice sounded just like my love. But I knew it couldn't be her.

"Stop moving; calm the fuck down," I said as I held her tighter. All of a sudden, she stopped. She just stopped kicking and moving and dropped her arms in defeat. I released my hold on her. She stood there with her back turned toward me. I lowered my gun but kept it by my side in case she got it twisted.

"Flex?" she said in a low, meek tone.

Her voice sent chills down my body. There was no way this was her—my love, my life, not the one who I would have died before I dishonored her.

"How do you know my name? What kind of sick joke Naheri got you playing? I swear to God, I will—" My words were caught in the air.

I laid eyes on her. To say I was in disbelief would be an understatement.

"Kajaun, babe, is that you? They told m—I heard them pronounce you . . ." She couldn't complete a full sentence. Her tears started streaming down her face. I had no words myself. I stepped closer to examine her face, hair, and those eyes. Everything screamed Elana. But they told me she died.

"Elana, they said you were gone, babe . . . . That you?" At this time, my tears were welling up in my eyes. I didn't wait for an answer. I picked her up in my arms and kissed her so deeply, my tongue almost touched her tonsils. If this was a dream, I didn't want to be woken up. If this was a cruel joke by Naheri, I didn't want to end this moment, this second, with her.

She pulled back with tears flowing down her face more than before. "Babe, it is you. I heard them pronounce you dead. I felt as if I couldn't breathe without you. Kajaun, babe, I missed you." She planted soft kisses all over my face. I was so lost for words, all I could do was kiss her again, and again, and again.

"Babe, I have missed you. When I tried to find you, they said you were dead. After the explosion, as I lay on the floor semiconscious, I heard them say you were DOA. I went so deep in depression, I didn't even see the setup they had for me. Naheri paid one of his doctor friends to kill me. But instead of murdering me, she nursed me back to health. She thought she and I would be a couple. Babe, I was so messed up without . . ." She kissed me again and touched my face, chest, and head . . . anywhere on my body to make sure I was real.

"Dutch, it's me. If this a dream, don't wake me. Babe, I've been searching for over a year for our son. That's what led me here." I paused for a second to look her in the eyes one more time. I was in such shock I forgot about Knight and the rest of them. "Dutch, they said you died, and you'd been cremated. My whole world has been nothing. Every day, all I could do was think of you. I even have the chain we bought each other. That's what made me come back to get it. That muthafucka killed Mona. Man, he killed my cousin like she was nothin'." My eyes fell to the floor.

"Who killed her, Flex?"

"Naheri. He did this, and he still has Junior. I went to his estate, and it was a setup. Our own did it. You remember that li'l nigga Peanut?" I asked. I could see her mind working.

"Flex, look, I'm so happy to have you in my arms right now. I've missed you so much. Every day was like living in hell. When I first got—" Her emotions started to get the better of her. "When I found out that you were gone, it hurt to breathe." She stared into my eyes once more and touched my arms. Then she rubbed my face again.

"I can't believe this. It's really you. Standing right in front of me! Many times during my recovery I thought you were standing there, but you weren't. I would open my eyes, only to find out you were gone, and the hurt was far worse than any pain I have ever felt in my life. The only hurt that could equal up to that was the day my son was stolen from me.

"Flex, baby, I need to make sure you're real. I feel you and hear you, but do you know how long I have dreamed of this day? I longed for this day like I need air in my lungs." The smell of his favorite cologne was a welcomed invasion in her nostrils.

"Yes, Dutch, I do know what it feels like. Babe, living without you was torture. I missed that smile, your laugh, and the way your round hips would jiggle like Jell-O whenever you're in a hurry. Or the way your nose would crinkle when you would get pissed off. I even missed your singing. I had days when I would have given anything just to hear you hit a note like you do. So, yes, I do know what it felt like. Losing you was as if I lost my sight and I lived in darkness. I love you," I said as I pulled her closer until there was no room in between us. Not even the air in the room could seep in the embrace we held. If I could have wrapped my body inside of her at that moment, I would have.

Time and space knew no boundaries . . . that was, until "Ayo, Flex, let's be out. What you doing up in here? The people have been tryin' to—" A now bigger and much-taller Knight came through the door. His eyes widened in shock as he laid eyes on Dutch. "Dutchtress, is that you?" he said stammering through his words. He cautiously walked over toward us and stared at her from head to toe as Flex held her in his arms. "Bu . . . But my people, our people, said you were dead. I mean, the whole city was on lock trying to find out where they had taken you, or shall I say, your body. I mean . . . How? When?" He touched her arm to see if she was there in the flesh. He looked at Flex, then back at her.

"Damn, nigga, what's wrong? Cat got your tongue?" I said with a slight chuckle. She still held on to me tightly. "Okay, babe, you can let go now. I won't move." I started laughing.

Knight was right. We couldn't stay here. It was getting late, and we had to find that bastard before he left the island.

"Where are you staying?" I asked, anticipating the answer. I didn't want to leave her side. I wanted to stand there forever and a day, but with Kainmen and Naheri on the loose, there was no telling when they would strike, so we had to stay a step ahead of them. "Naheri's brother knows we're alive, so I know he's forming some retaliation right now. We have to find out where Naheri and Kainmen are."

"Dutchtress, where have you been?" Knight said, still in shock.

"If there is one thing I taught you when you were coming up in your ranks, that is you never underestimate me and how far my reach extends. Not to be counted out, but be unexpected." She gave Knight a wicked smile.

"Flex, baby, we have to leave this place, but this is where I am. I'll be at the hotel across the way called the Knutsford. Room 520. Meet me there in an hour," I said as my anger began to resurface. I thought about the hell I went through this past year and the hurt I suffered at the hands of those fucking brothers.

"Wait, Dutch, I can't let you out of my sight. Please come with us, babe, please. I have to take Mona's body and lay her to rest. And we still have this matter with Peanut to deal with. As a matter of fact, Knight, can you drive the truck and . . ." I wasn't about to let her out of my sight. "I know you like the back of my hand, and I know you got a whip outside, so let's do this tonight. Knight can drive Mona's truck, and we trail him. I'm not letting you go, not now, not ever again." A serious expression was on my face. I wasn't going to take no for an answer. I could see her looking around the bar and felt her pain when she looked toward the back office. "It's not your fault."

All of the glass and blood, Slynn and Brandi's bodies lying on the floor underneath all of the debris was more motivation to do whatever was needed to get our son back and kill those two bastards and all members of their family. It was time to wipe their bloodline from the face of this earth.

Knight, who was now focused, said, "I can drive. Are we ready?"

"No, I don't have a ri—" Dutchtress began to say until I picked up some keys off the floor.

I noticed a huge crest emblem on the key chain.

"Oh, I do now. Meet us outside in front. Knight, be careful, brutha. That means that fool is lurking about." Knight nodded his head in agreement and rushed out the door.

Our eyes met once again, and we both smirked, almost as if we had the same thought. When love is as deep as ours, no matter how much time passes, we will forever know each other's thoughts, moves, almost the pattern of the way each other breathes. Without spoken words, we both grabbed the unbroken liquor and started throwing the bottles everywhere. After the last drop was drenched on every piece of furniture, we walked to the front door. I turned and took one last look at Slynn and Brandi's bodies on the floor and said a silent prayer for Mona. Without so much as a flinch, I struck my lighter, showing nothing but a high flame. Just when I was about to toss it in the room, I remembered something.

"Wait, wait a second. I forgot something," I said and took off toward the back to Mona's office. In a split second, I was back holding the chain in my hand. "Okay, we can bounce now." I kissed her lips. "I couldn't lose this—or you—again." I struck the lighter once more and tossed it in the room. The fire started quickly, and within seconds, the room was engulfed in flames.

When we got outside, I spotted Kainmen's 2012 Land Rover parked across the street. We jumped in and got directly in front of Mona's truck so they could follow us. I told her the destination. I remembered it from my many visits, and I agreed it would be a perfect low-key resting place for Mona.

After an hour of driving, we arrived at Mona's final resting spot. Vell and Knight, and even Peanut, helped get her body out of the back of the truck, and we all carried her closer to the sound of the rushing water. It was dark, so the only light shining was the full moon and the headlights of our rides.

"Sorry, my friend. Rest in heaven, Mona. Ms. Ruby, take care of her for me," Dutch said aloud as we let her body go in the secluded part of the island.

I prayed that no matter what I have done in this life that my prayer be heard. Dutch caressed my hands as we walked back toward our rides. I lifted her hand up to my lips and kissed every finger on it. "I'm never letting you out of my sight, ever again. Once we get our son back, we will be that family," I said kissing her hand.

"I wouldn't have it any other way."

We got into the trucks and drove out of the area. I was happier than I had been in a long time. I wished this feeling could last forever, but I had to be realistic. Shit was about to get real. On the outside, I smiled, but inside, I was preparing for a battle that could end with both of us dead for real this time.

Out here, my ties were limited. When I faked my death, it was easier. After the explosion at the house, I was fucked up for real. My body was bruised internally and out. I remembered when the EMTs came into the office moving debris around me. I thought the fight was over, and I would never be able to be the father I knew Junior needed. As they moved the debris from me, someone felt for my pulse. The voice wasn't familiar at first, but then he spoke again. I was fighting hard to move. To make them aware that I was alive and needed medical attention. Without seeing or hearing Elana, I felt that maybe death was best for me if I couldn't help her.

Suddenly I felt hot air by my ear. "Flex, don't worry, I got you." Then I heard the same person say something about a DOA. I tried to move but couldn't. I must have passed out due to my injuries 'cause it all went black.

When I finally did wake up, all I saw was darkness and smelled the odor of plastic. Then I felt the heat of light over me. I could barely open my eyes. I thought I was dead. I could feel someone touching my body, and I tried to make a loud sound, but only a soft moan escaped.

The light was causing my eyes to hurt, and I could no longer hold them slightly opened.

Although there was some ringing in my ears, I heard that voice again.

"Yo, get him right. He in bad shape. I pulled him out of that explosion you been hearing about."

"You know this dude?"

"Yeah, he helped me when I was down, and now I can pay him back. The life I used to live was never a nice one, and when I didn't want to do bad anymore, he allowed me to leave without consequences. Just get him right."

"Who is he?"

"It doesn't matter who he is. Just get him right."

I remembered that conversation like yesterday. Come to find out, it was my right-hand man back in my early days. We broke bread, robbed, killed, and hustled years before Dutch and I linked back up again. When he lost his newborn baby and girl to some shit we did, he vowed never again to pick up a gun or weapon in his life. He came to me like a man, and I respected him for that. My crew didn't like it and thought he would turn snitch on all that we did. I wouldn't let that go down, so I sent him to school and made sure he kept his promise by never coming around him again.

I realized that he was the EMT on the scene, and he was the one who got me out of there, knowing the life I lived. When I could sit up and talk, he told me he was forever indebted to me, and he had fixed it so whoever was trying to kill me would think they had been successful. I was grateful. I knew that not everybody was cut out for the life I lived.

Chapter 39

Naheri

The vibrating cell phone on the nightstand kept going off, back-to-back, for over an hour. I picked it up. Each time the name Kainmen was displayed on the screen, I slid my finger across it to ignore the call. "Ugh," I said as I placed the pillow over my head to block the sunlight.

I hadn't gotten much sleep. Junior tossed and turned all night. After I murdered Mona and got into bed to get a little sleep before we left in the morning, I finally got Junior settled; then my cell kept going off. I put it on vibrate after the fifth call. There was no way I was letting the sound wake Junior up.

"Damn, what the fuck does he want?" I was way past pissed at my brother. I was out of here; I needed to find Netta. She didn't deserve any of this. I almost threw my phone into the wall because I heard it vibrate once more. This time, I picked it up and turned it off. Then I cut it back on again because I didn't know if Netta was trying to call me. I was in no mood to hear Kainmen's threats or the speech on how Junior's not my son, and he's the reason our father was dead, blah blah blah. I didn't have the energy to deal with him, not right now. I finally eased myself from under the cover to sit on the side of the bed. I gained my composure enough to get up and open the curtains. The sun hit my eyes immediately. I looked at the view of the ocean in amazement and peace. Then I slid the window open a little to smell and hear the ocean breeze. I took in a deep breath, just appreciating the moment.

Soon, I looked over my shoulder at Junior. I turned back to take one final look out of the window when I felt my morning wood rise. I walked over to the bathroom and began to relieve my bladder.

"Ah." I released what seemed like the longest piss ever. The vibrating of my cell phone once again began to frustrate me. What part of him didn't get that I wasn't feeling his rants? He wanted to kill my son. There was no way I was staying around his ass, brother or not. My main focus was on us getting back to Chicago and getting my Netta back.

The vibrating stopped—only to start right back again. Irritated by the constant vibrating, I finished draining my lizard to answer it. I picked up the phone, ready to unleash pure hell on the person on the other end . . . that was until I saw Mita's face appear on the screen. "Where the hell have you been? I need your he—" I said as I answered the phone, then stopped midsentence when the nervous voice of my wife, Netta, spoke.

The voice was one that I wanted to shake the life out of him with my bare hands. Flex sounded so cocky and nonchalant. "Well, well, if it ain't Mr. Man. How's it going, bitch-made-ass nigga? Kill any more women lately? Better yet, where's my son?" he said with a sinister chuckle in his voice.

"If you hurt her, I swear to God, I will make sure yo' ass is dead for real this time. What have you done to Mita? I swear, Flex, you're a dead man," I yelled into the phone.

"Is that so? Seems to me your wife is a dead bitch if I don't get what's mine . . . my son. So what do you say, fair exchange?"

"Fool, have you lost your damn mind? He's *my* son, *not* yours. I'm the only father he will ever know. I tell you what, return my wife unharmed and I will allow you to live. You are, how they say, 'foolin yourself.' First, you thought you could just take my wife; now, you think shit is sweet. You got until 5:00 p.m. to bring my wife to the airport. If you don't, I will have you and your boys floating in the ocean by sundown. Oh yeah, tell Peanut I say good job," I said sternly. I could tell I hit a nerve. He was quiet. Then I heard him release a frustrated breath.

"See, I was gonna do this nice, but I see a bitch-ass nigga like yourself just won't have it. Okay, here it is. My son, yeah, *my* son, *my* blood, *my* seed better be at the groove on the north side of the island by 4:00 p.m., or your wife and unborn child—oh, she told me it's a girl. Congrats. But she won't live to take a breath outside her mother's womb if I don't get my son. Also, your precious Mita . . . Let's just say she is resting peacefully after a hard day's work."

I heard some slapping sound and my wife's scream that will forever be etched in my mind. Then the phone went dead. I tried dialing the number, only to be met with a voicemail greeting. I walked back into the bathroom and caught a glimpse of my reflection in the mirror. The call had me in deep thought. On the one hand, I could save my wife, but I would have to give up my son. I'm the only father he has ever known. How could I give him up? Especially to the very one who destroyed my happy home, causing me to kill my wife and flee the only home my son has ever known. I couldn't think straight. Did she really mean that much to me, or was it the seed she was carrying my main concern?

My anger regarding Flex clouded everything. I could have the child of my blood and a woman who did care for me truly and undeniably. I could give the boy back. Netta and I with our new baby will live a happily ever after. But if I know Flex like I think I do, it won't be that easy. I took the one love he has ever known from him. Now, the only thing I could do was to locate him and kill him. My cell phone vibrated again. It was my mother's picture who was on the screen this time.

I didn't want to answer it. To hear the sadness in her voice was too much for me to deal with right now. The fact that my wife, from the grave, is the reason my father was killed and has broken my mother's spirit . . . Even when my parents didn't see eye-to-eye, they still had a bond so strong, nothing and no one could come between that. When I noticed Junior moving in the bed, then calling out for me, I slid my finger across the screen to ignore the call. There was no way I could deal with this. Between her, my brother, and them having Netta, I felt like I was losing my mind.

"Come on, Junior, let Daddy dress you so we can get some food before we get on this long flight."

"Yes, Dada."

His speech was improving, and I was grateful for that, but we still have a long road ahead of us. For his speech and motor skills to get back to where they were before the brutal beating he got at the hands of Rasta, I didn't know how long it would take. There is no way I am going to just hand him over to that Flex. He wouldn't even know how to care for him.

The more I thought about it, the more I made my decision. There was no way I was letting my son go, and I will get my wife back. I didn't give a fuck. Come hell or high water, Flex is a dead man. I turned my cell phone off. There won't be any time to fight and argue with anyone. My main focus is killing Flex and saving Netta.

Chapter 40

Reunited and It Feels Damn Good

We drove down the highway in front of Knight and the rest of them on our way to lay Mona to rest. I could see in the rearview mirror the faces of everyone. They wondered who I was and why and where this second car came from. All of that will be answered in just a moment, but for now, the breeze from the ocean helped calm me. It was the smell of saltwater and sand that took me back in time for a moment. I reminisced on the moment Flex and I came down here. That was the first time we'd really seen just how much of an important part we were to each other. I remembered those broad shoulders and the tats against his brown, with a hint of dark chocolate, skin. Each tat told a story. The one I will always remember the most is the "None before We, Death before Dishonor." As we drove down the highway, I glanced over to his chest. He wore a black wife beater. I could see the tattoo slightly from the side. "You okay, baby?" he asked as grabbed ahold of my hand. Never taking his eyes off the road, he held my hand on his lap.

"I'm okay. This is a bittersweet moment for me. I hate that Mona got caught up in this mess with Naheri. I underestimated him. Did she know you were alive?"

"Naw, I haven't talked to Mona in years. After she moved here, we lost touch, but I needed to get away from that fool for a second, and her place was the only place I could think of." He lowered his head for a second but remained focused on the road as well. He was good for that, but I could see something else was on his mind. I gently rubbed his hand for comfort.

"I have something to tell you, Dutch. You not gonna like it." My heart damn near fell to the floor in anticipation of what he was about to say.

"You know me, Flex, what is it?"

"Dutch, in that truck behind us," he stopped and took a deep breath.

"Go ahead, spit it out."

"In the truck behind us with Knight, not only is Peanut's disloyal ass in there but Vell and . . . and . . ." He was silent for a second. "I kidnapped Naheri's pregnant wife. Her name is Netta."

The air in the car seemed almost to evaporate. I knew that bastard would go on, but to get away with what he thinks of as killing me and stealing my son—oh no, he was *not* getting away with that. I rubbed Flex's hand once more before turning to look out the window. I was way past pissed, but I didn't want anything to stop my reunion with the love of my life and my son.

"Flex, it's okay. Just know one thing for sure. He *will* pay for all of this. A whole year I was alive but not living. I was lost, and a part of me wished I had died in that explosion. The nights were long, and my days were cold. Now that I have you back, I will never let you go. As for his wife, I can't say what I will do to her. He needs to feel the pain he put me through. He took everything, Flex. *Everything* from me. Yes, I kept secrets, but he had his own." In the middle of my rant I hadn't noticed we came to a stop. When I looked around I could see a shallow pathway that led deeper into a wooded area. We were at the spot where Mona would have her resting place.

Flex put the truck in park and turned the engine off. He took a deep breath. "You ready, babe?" he said as he held my hand tightly.

"No, babe, let me sit here for a second. Before I let Vell and . . . You know what? As a matter of fact, leave Peanut in the truck." A sinister smile crept across my face. I couldn't get to Naheri just yet, but Peanut will just have to do.

Flex placed a soft kiss on my forehead, then stopped the truck. "I'll make this as fast as I can. Have fun, my love."

He closed the door and walked back to the truck behind us. I watched him say something to Knight while Vell opened the trunk. Knight walked to the back of the truck to help Vell. Flex grabbed the arm of a pregnant female and walked her down the pathway. I could see worry all over her face. Murder was on the menu, but not for her . . . not right at this moment. I could see Knight and Vell as they carefully took Mona's body out of the truck, each of them holding her as they walked in the direction of the shallow pathway. I lowered my head so that I could not be seen, not yet. I had some retribution to give. I heard Vell ask Knight, "Who is that man in the truck up there, and why we leaving that mutha-fucka by his self?"

He waited for Knight to respond. Instead, he nodded his head for him to move farther down the pathway. "If you move a muscle while we are down there, I will kill yo' ass with no hesitation, Peanut. Man, I don't see why we have to leave his ass here. He just gonna try to make a run for it," Vell said until were they were out of my sight.

I pulled the visor down and waited. Just like I thought, I watched Peanut open the door and try to make a run for it. Before he could pass by the passenger door, I opened it, causing him to run right into the door. He fell to the ground. I slowly put one foot down on the ground as I reached under the seat. I remembered the first rule of the street: never leave your strap at home and always keep a spare. And just as I suspected, Kainmen had another .38 snubnose underneath his seat.

I got the gun and cocked it as I stood directly over Peanut. He shook his head dazed and confused.

"Oh, I see you think this is a game," I said through clenched teeth as I tightened my jaws. I bit down so hard I started tasting blood. The thought of disloyalty was something I could not stand.

I glared down at him; his eyes widened in shock. "I . . . I . . . They said you were dead."

"Yeah, death does look great on me, don't it? I see you have been a very naughty boy. I mean, what was the first rule I taught you when you came on the team?"

He lowered his head toward his chest. "Always look out for family; none before we, death before dishonor."

"I didn't hear that last part. Speak up," I angrily said as he began to repeat the last part loud enough for me to hear. This time, he held his head higher toward me. I stretched my hand out to help him up from the ground. "Ya know what? I know you are young, and loyalty really don't mean that much to you. It's all about the almighty dollar, right?" His eyes screamed remorse, but his actions told me he would do it all over again if he got the chance. "You know . . . I remember when you were just a teenager trying to make a name for yourself, remember that?" I tried sounding as empathic as I could. "That day when I caught you trying to stick up one of Fernando's boys because he was on the block, you remember that? Where was that? Oh yeah, over on Sixty-ninth and Peoria. Yeah, yeah, that's it." I cracked a slight smile as I reminisced on happier times when I took this little, dirty, determined, go-getter under my wing and gave him food and a place to lay his and his family's head. Now, all I could see was the handiwork of Naheri and his family yet again.

"When Fernando was about to give you that dirt nap, Flex and I pleaded your case, remember that?" He lowered his head once again without uttering a word.

Something was sticking out of his pocket, a small piece of paper. I took it from his pocket and began to unfold it. A small picture fell out of it. It was a picture of a small baby girl with bright eyes and two ponytails.

"She yours?"

He looked hesitant to answer me. Finally, he nodded his head yes. I smirked, thinking about the driving force behind his backstabbing. I could see she had his eyes and mouth. If I were the judge and jury in a paternity case for her, the results would clearly be "You are the father!"

"How old is she?"

"Four months," he answered with his face adorned with sadness.

The mother in me wanted to let him walk away, but the betrayal was too much. If I allowed him to walk away just like I did with Rasta, I would be right back here. I placed one hand on his shoulder to gently rub him, to reassure him that he could be comfortable with me. I looked him deeply in his eyes. Holding a long stare, I wanted to make sure we didn't break eye contact.

"*Psh, psh.*" The swishing sound of the snub-nose equipped with a silencer whistled in the air. His body fell to the ground as blood gushed from his midsection. His eyes still widened in shock as they were fixed toward the sun.

"Peanut, I will be sure to kiss that li'l girl of yours." When I looked up, Flex, Knight, Vell, and

Naheri's wife were coming from the pathway. Vell slowly walked up toward me with his mouth gaped open and eyes to match. "Du-Dutch, is that you? I thought you were—"

"Dead," I said interrupting him with a slight smile on my face. "No, you all should know me by now. Not even death can hold me. How ya been?" I opened my arms to hug him. He reluctantly hugged me back; the shock was still on his face.

Flex walked over and stood next to me with a wide smile. "Looks good, don't she?" he said as he patted Vell's arm.

"But when, where, and how? Come on; they said you died. We even held a vigil for you on the East Side after we got the news. Shit, I even named my new shorty after you, that's how much love I had-I mean got for you. Wow, this is unbelievable." He hugged me a little tighter. I was happy to see some of the family remained just like that and loyal.

"Hey, let's continue this somewhere else. What we gonna do about this fool?" Knight said standing over Peanut's lifeless body. We all stood over him looking down in disgust.

Naheri's wife started to cry loud sobs. For the first time, I was looking face-to-face with the woman who has been taking care of my son. The woman whom my husband had his seed with, but the features on her that got to me the most were the fact her eyes and hair resembled someone I knew too well. I walked over to her with my hand extended.

"Hello. Don't worry; this will all be over soon enough. Just stay in your lane, and you won't end up like this worthless sack of shit on the ground right here."

Knight grabbed a hold of her shoulders and escorted her back to the truck. I watched as her body trembled and shook a little. I could tell she was afraid.

"Hey, I have a room in the hotel near Mona's place. When Mona and I spoke, she told me Naheri and Junior were there, so I booked a room. We can all go back there and wait it out. I have something that I know will get Naheri's attention besides his precious wife." I knew the level of fear she must have felt, knowing how this all was going to end. But her face looked so familiar to me. I can't place it, but I have seen her before.

Chapter 41

Netta's Song

I wondered if she remembered me. I knew she felt something by the way she stared at me as we made our way to the hotel. I wanted to scream out so badly to her just who I was. But I have heard all about her and the ice that runs through her veins. I remembered her just like it was yesterday.

She walked right out of the house like she was a bag of money. I have followed her career for years, from her graduating and being one of Chicago's very own to make it out of the hood. I mean, I thought she was going to end up like our mother . . . the neighborhood crack ho. But she proved me and everyone else wrong. However, I knew deep inside of her was the heart of a killer. I remember the day I discovered she was the one and only Dutchtress of Chi-town.

Back in 2001, while I was in school at Chicago State over on Ninety-fifth Street, I started dating this block boy, Yalow. Yalow was one of those guys who did anything he needed to be on top. He started making moves and getting money, and fast. I never questioned it. I just thought it was part of the trade, you know, street hustler. Then one day, he came to my apartment close to the campus all sweaty and rambling on. "I fucked up. Damn, how could I have been so stupid!" He looked scared shitless. I asked him what was wrong, and he informed me that he took some money from some queenpin named Dutchtress. I could see the fear in his eyes. His phone was vibrating so much he threw it on the bed.

"Shit, baby, I'ma have to leave the city for a while."

I was confused. "What do you mean, babe? Why can't your boys get at her and take her out? You got that pull, use it." He looked at me like I'd just lost my mind. I had grown accustomed to getting spoiled by the lavish gifts he gave me. Coming from a mother like mine I wasn't about to let some bitch fuck that up. I grew up on the streets. My first response was to fuck this bitch up one-on-one.

"Fuck that. Let me at her. Shit, me and my girls will let her know what it is. Besides, you the man on this side of town. I know not one bitch gonna touch you or me."

He chuckled a little and smiled. "Babe, it ain't that easy. This is a fight we would surely lose. As soon as I get settled, I'll send for you if you'll come."

"But, babe, I thought—"

"Babe," he said, cutting me off, "look, I know you my Bonnie, my ride or die, but this is too deep for you. Let me go in here and wash my face so I can get my mind right. I got to get on the first thing smoking outta here." He kissed my forehead and walked in the bathroom. His phone vibrated some more. I walked over and picked it up from the bed, and there was a message from a Peanut.

Hey, Joe, you fucked up to the max! Since you my dude, I'm giving you a heads-up. There's a bounty on your head. What the fuck was you thinking, anyway? Look, get at my people in Arkansas and lie low.

Here is ole girl picture. I could lose my life for this, but you my family, and I can't let you get killed. Joe, leave town tonight!

When her picture came on the screen, I almost passed out. Here I was looking at my own family—my sister Elana. I remembered when I was younger, our mother had a few pictures around the house of this girl I didn't know. When I asked her one day in her state of euphoria from her drugs, she broke down and told me and JJ the whole story. How we have an older sister named Elana. She said she gave her to our aunt because she couldn't raise her. When I went to look for her after our mother was murdered, I couldn't find her. But years later, while JJ and I were being raised in foster homes, I saw an article in the *Chicago Sun-Times* about a bright young woman out of the hood who's making a name for herself. She looked just like our mother; even her smile was identical. I knew it was her, so I cut out the picture of her and kept it even as JJ and I were removed from our mother's house and placed in the system. It was one of the few things I held on to. When I compared her to the picture in the article, I knew it was her.

When Yalow came out of the bathroom, I gave him his phone. He looked at the message, then fear drenched his entire face. He gave me a long goodbye kiss and rushed out. I never heard from him again. Fearing the worst, I did what I had to, to get out of that godforsaken city. Years later, the streets started talking. Word was circulating that the one who was responsible for the murders of my mother and aunt was none other than my sister Elana—Dutchtress. Of course, no one could prove it, but the street had better intel than the police. I have hated her ever since. I spent the latter part of my life wanting her to pay for the misery JJ and I were put in. We were moved from home to home, often abused, and were separated . . . only to later reunite at JJ's grave site. I hated her and blamed her for everything. When I discovered who Peanut was, I put a plan in motion to put him on Kainmen's radar, and it worked. I knew it would draw Flex out, and I already had plans for her son. Naheri was an added bonus.

Normally, Kool-Aid don't pump through my veins, but seeing her in action, I can see the ice and ruthlessness flowing through her. I pray that my little one and I make it out of this alive. I doubt that, however, when she discovers me and what I have done.

Chapter 42

Kainmen's Cost to Be a Boss

I have tried calling this sorry-ass muthafucka all day. "Shit!" I said as his voicemail picked up. I looked over at our mother who sat across the table with what looked like a million and one thoughts going through her mind. I studied her. Her usually stern, calm, and all-together features seemed to become unraveled. "I told you, Kainmen, he's not capable of resisting her."

"Momma, I know, but I sent Rasta to make sure she was dead as a doornail. When I looked her eye-to-eye, all I could see was venom flowing from her eyes. She hates us. I mean *hates* us and anything and everything about us. Momma, be careful. She wants us all dead. I couldn't stand to lose you too."

My mother threw her hand up at me to dismiss the warning. Then she got up and walked out of the room. Adorned on her face was the look of "I wish she would try." Dutchtress or no Dutchtress, my mother was old-school gangsta.

When she closed the door, I heard the locks clink together, indicating the door was locked. I tried calling my stupid brother one more time. Still no answer. He was way past pissing me off. He better hope I remembered he was still my little brother because right now, I wanted to put a bullet in his head. Right between his fuckin' eyes. I still tried wrapping my head around the fact that all of his mistakes were the cause of everything wrong. He had no clue who he was messing with when he married that fuckin' lunatic.

I walked over to my minibar and fixed me a much-needed drink to calm my nerves. Images of the previous hours still consumed my thoughts. One thing is certain: Dutchtress has to die. As each ice cube made a clinking noise as it hit the bottom of the glass, I reminisced on the day Dutchtress killed my grandfather and uncle. Her heartless ass just took them out like it was nothing. I knew I should have killed her son and that bastard side lover of hers.

I sat back down seething with anger. All of my thoughts and everything in me wanted her dead. I started biting down on my bottom lip with so much force I tasted blood inside of my mouth.

Suddenly, someone knocked on the door. "One second," I yelled out to whoever was on the other side of the door. I got up and unlocked it. Gina stepped in, looking just as beautiful as she did the other day, but her eyes were filled with sadness. This had become our normal greeting. So much regret and hopelessness from a love that could never be, because I remained true to my business and family.

"Kainmen, I just came to tell you what your mother said. She told me to tell you that your father's body will be placed in the family crypt. She didn't want to have a service; she didn't tell me why, but she said you would know. Are you OK? I know this is hard, and I'm sorry for your loss."

Her words pierced my heart like a dagger. My father was dead, my mother was broken, my brother has lost his mind, and on top of all of that, the bitch who was supposed to be dead is back with a vengeance. I had to get her—and fast. I looked over at Gina. Her eyes were filled with confusion and sadness once again. I didn't have any clear answers for her. She wanted more than I was able to give.

"Thank you for bringing me the word from my mom. If there's nothing else, you can leave," I stated coldly to her. She squinted her eyes at me with a look of challenge all over her face.

"I know you're grieving right now, but that doesn't give you the right to be so cold toward me. I'll let this one go, but if you ever talk to me like I'm one of your—"

"My what? What? Just another female, bitch, or whatever the saying is these days? I don't owe you or anyone else shit. You can leave and get the fuck out of my face, Gina." It broke me to pieces to speak to her like that, but she had to understand that I needed her away from me. Fast. There was no way I'll let Dutchtress kill her just because of me.

Tears rolled down her face. Her lips trembled with every word as she replied, "So, that's all I am to you . . . another bitch? No love, nothing? How dare you! Who do you think you are? I *will* leave. As a matter of fact, I quit, you heartless bastard!"

I just lowered my head. My silent frustration won this battle. "I'd rather have you safe and alive. If Dutchtress finds out just how much you mean to me, you would be dead." I took a big gulp, finishing off my drink, then slammed the glass down and stormed out the door. I had to get on with my mission.

"You dying today, Dutchtress."

Chapter 43

None before We

The ride back to the hotel was silent. An eerie feeling of guilt and confusion lingered in the air. No one wanted to speak about the situation; no one knew where to start. Two people Flex trusted with his life ended up turning on him, Knight, and Vell.

None of them looked at one another, I guess in fear the other one would question his loyalty, but nonetheless, I wanted to leave nothing to chance. When we made it back to the hotel, I had them enter in the back way while I walked past the front desk. I exchanged pleasantries, not wanting to draw any attention to myself or the new guests entering through the back. I gave Flex the room number in the truck and told him which section of the hotel the room was located. By the time I reached up there, all of them were in the room.

Flex stood over by the window, and Knight and Vell were across the room by the balcony. I watched these three strong men who would put a bullet in someone's head if they crossed their leg the wrong way looking as lost as a baby lamb going to the slaughter.

Naheri's wife, Netta, sat in a chair at the desk in the far end of the room. She looked fragile and worn. I walked over to her and placed my hand on her shoulder. "Look, there's another room right there through that door. Why don't you lie down? We have a lot to talk about later."

She slowly stood up and nodded her head in agreement. She reached out for the doorknob, and I said, "Oh, please don't think you can get out through that room. There is no door in there, and the windows are presently sealed shut. There is central air-conditioning, so you'll be cool. But if you get any bright ideas about leaving . . . Let's just say what happened at the cove will be child's play. Ya got me?" I reminded her with a smile on my face. No more games would be played. It is all or nothing now, and I plan on having it all.

Knight and Vell walked over to help her through with the door. "After she's in there settled, come out later so I can talk to you guys and Flex, but Flex and I will be awhile first," I said as they walked Netta to the other room.

Flex walked over to me and hugged me once more. The lost look that adorned his face had my heart in a million pieces, but I did what had to be done because of our loose ends which got us here in the first place. I held him tightly. The pleasant smell of his cologne filled my nostrils. I missed the smell of Sean John for men. The cologne and his body chemistry mixed just right. It was not overbearing or weak but just right. I rubbed my hands down the sides of his arms making sure I touched each crease of his well-defined muscular arms. I loved him and missed him as if I missed the air I breathed. The feel of his shoulders had me ready. But I needed for him to understand me. The old Elana was gone, stolen from this earth too soon, but my love for him remained. I looked him deeply in his eyes. I needed to search his eyes. They have always been the window to his soul for me. All I could see was a hint of confusion and some pain. But the joy in them was there. It was evident when I saw the slight gleam in those gray eyes.

I grabbed his hand and led him into the bathroom. Then I turned on the shower. We undressed each other and stepped under the warm water. We washed each other as if we were trying to wash away the last year of our lives. I felt all of his pain and his love with each stroke.

"Baby, I love you," I said as I lathered his back with soap. He stepped closer under the water.

"I love you so much, Dutch, I—"

"Shh, shh, let's just have this moment." We finished washing each other in the shower for a moment. The silence in the room was understood. We stood face-to-face.

I rubbed his arm to sooth him as he searched my facial expression for answers. "Let's not talk, please. I just want to make love to you. After that, then all of the questions we have can be answered."

"Okay, baby, I have missed you like nobody's business," he said with his hard dick trying to bust from the opening in the towel.

His arms wrapped me up so fast I could hardly catch my breath or balance myself as we made the short stroll that seemed like it was forever over to the bed. He sat me down gently. He held me so tenderly, gently placing kisses on my lips.

"I want this moment to last forever, Dutch. I love you and missed the hell out of you."

I stared intensely into his eyes. I wanted him to know what this moment meant to me. I gently stroked the side of his face. "You don't know how I dreamed of this day, this moment. Kajaun, you are my everything. The nights I woke up in a cold sweat calling your name . . . Every time I would hear a song that we listened to, I thought of you, and my heart broke over and over and ov—" The tears streaming down my face interrupted my words.

"I got you. I'm here now," he said as he kissed my lips.

I gave him every inch of me. Anything I felt that would hold me back from making love to my rib, I pushed it to the back of my mind and released it. He stood up and reached out for me to join him. We stood face to almost face. He kissed my lips once more, then watched lustfully as my towel hit the floor. "Damn, you still sexy as fuck, shorty." He took my hand and spun me around like a ballerina. He made sure every inch of me was in full view.

Then he planted small kisses on my stomach, a peck here and a peck there. He used his tongue to make a trail down to my navel. Then to my pelvic region. Right above my kitty. He was teasing me. The softness of his lips on my skin caused the flow of wetness to drench my panties. I had to restrain myself from shoving his face right into my pussy. Instead, I thrust my pelvic closer to his face. He continued his kisses around every area *but* the spot. "Be patient, baby. I want to savor you, every inch of you."

He laid me back on the bed, then stood over me, watching and licking his lips. Then he lowered himself, and with one swift motion, no more teasing, no inhaling, he just plunged his face right in between my thighs. He sounded like a hungry animal devouring his prey as he slurped and sucked on my clit.

"Oh my God, Flex . . ." I could hardly catch my breath. He played with my clit with the tip of his tongue, first at a fast pace, then slower. It felt like he was writing each letter of the alphabet on my clit with his tongue. The euphoric feeling was better than I remembered it. I grabbed a firm hold of my breasts and squeezed them together, licking them as he pleasured me into a mind-blowing nut. "Oh. Oh . . . yes . . . baby . . . Lick your pussy. All of this is yours," I panted seductively into the air.

I placed my hands around his head to get some relief, but he grabbed them and held them down at my side, locked in place. I tried squirming and moving my hips to get some relief from his tongue assault. But it was to no avail. He just sucked and licked longer and deeper. All the last year with his frustration and pain, missing me, I felt it in his love torture at this moment. "Flex, ba . . . baby . . . Please, no more. I c-a-n't take it. Oh . . ." I moaned as he worked me into another long and strong orgasm.

He finally released me and kissed my trembling body. His face was soaked with all of my sweet nectar. He leaned up to kiss me. I loved the taste of my own juices as our tongues danced inside of each other's mouths. I kissed him on the neck making passion marks as I trailed farther down his neck. I nibbled on his ear, savoring every inch of him as we passionately kissed until I ended up on top of him. I straddled him. I gave him a wicked smirk, ready to have his toes curling and body stiff from pleasure.

"Damn, Dutch, I want this. Fuck that; I want that pussy." He glared at me intensely as I worked my body downward toward his stomach. I placed the tip of my tongue on top of his mushroom-shaped head. I teased and tickled the tip with my tongue. His massive, hard dick throbbed, and my pussy was ready to jump on top of him and work him like a light switch, but I maintained my pace. I circled the long main vein with my tongue, licking it as if it were a melting ice-cream cone. My saliva and his precome filled my mouth. He thrust deeper as I fought against the gag reflex. I relaxed my jaw muscles and increased the suction around the middle of his dick, working it up and down, side to side. I worked my head like a jackhammer up and down on his rock-hard love pole; then I slowed my pace enough to hear him moan with pleasure.

I sucked harder and bobbed my head a little deeper down on his dick until it was touching my tonsils. I felt his hands grab the sides of my head firmly as his body began to shake and his hips swirled and twisted. "Mmm . . . mmm . . . aw . . . yeah . . . sl . . . sll . . . That's it right there." His passionate moans echoed through the room. I gave him the best head ever. I missed him. I wanted him so deep inside of me that he could use my throat to get there; that's how much I loved him.

"Ah, yes, ba . . . baby, take this dick." His voice gave me a burst of energy. I worked his shaft steady and long until I felt his body begin to shake. "Ah . . . Ah . . . Yes! Yes!" his loud, passionate release rang out throughout the room. His warm, creamy nectar sprayed the back of my throat. I didn't ease up the pace, though. Instead, I worked him like a hungry lioness devouring her prey. I didn't stop until I swallowed every drop he had to offer and sucked him dry.

"Damn, baby, you really missed me, didn't you?" he said out of breath, panting hard. I lay next to him. Finally, I felt like my other half was found, and now, I could get back to who I am and what made me.

"Baby, all I know is this is real, and I wish we could lie here in each other's arms forever, but our son needs us." I peacefully lay in his arms drifting to our forever love. I relaxed a little more and began to run my hands up and down his limp anaconda. Once I hit the right spot, he was ready once more. We started hungrily invading each other's mouths once more. I wanted him inside of me. The feel of his body pressed against mine had me so wet. He held me so close to him as he positioned himself on top of me. He spread my legs as he kissed my neck slowly. Biting and gently sucking my neck, the feel of his warm breath on me caused a lone tear to slide down my cheek. He pulled back just a little.

"You okay? Am I hurting you, love?"

"Baby, I'm fine. I'm just happy I have you back. I never thought this day would come."

"Believe that, baby, and trust me, I'm never leaving you, us, again," he said as he grinded his hips and his anaconda found a warm, wet, nesting spot. Once he felt my juices seep down, he thrust a little more until I felt him touching my G-spot.

"Aaah . . . yes . . . ba . . . ba . . . by, take all this pussy; please take me. I love you, Flex. I fuckin' love you."

He filled up every part of me. The more he moved his hips, the deeper he touched the bottom of my love hole. I didn't want him to stop, but the passion in me screamed to meet him with each thrust, moan, and then he released. I scratched his back as I winced from the pain and pleasure of every inch he rammed inside of me. I released loud, passionate screams in the air. I didn't care who heard me. I arched my back. "Aaah . . . Aaah . . . yes . . . umm . . . yes." I wrapped my legs around him. The headboard was moving and banging ferociously against the wall. A year's worth of pinned up frustration and want came rushing out as we released. In unison, we mixed our sweet love juices. He came inside of me, and I poured my love onto his anaconda. I didn't know what was next. I knew I didn't want this moment to end, though. We lay spent, holding each other as we drifted off in a euphoric bliss.

Chapter 44

A Knight's Move

"Yo, let me get that remote," I said to Naheri's wife, Netta, as I grabbed a pillow from the plush and roomy bed. Judging by the expensive things in there, Dutchtress spared no expense with this entire suite. From the rich bedding down to the furniture with gold trim that aligned the walls . . . The windows sealed tight, and the central air was brisk and calming. I smelled some sweet fragrance coming from the unit on the wall. I looked over to Netta as she nervously bit her nails. She walked over to the opposite side of the room to check the door. It opened for her, but only a wall was there. The door gave the illusion it was an exit.

"Look, shorty, why don't you go and take a nice bath and calm yourself. From the sound of things that's going on the other side of that door, this gonna be a long night."

She slowly walked back over to the bed and plopped down. “How could you two be a part of this? You seem like nice men. I really know that Peanut was a good dude. Yes, he did turn on you, but he had his reasons.” She lowered her head toward her chest, then made a sudden jump. “Oh . . . Oh.” I rushed over as she held her stomach.

“Ay, you okay?”

“Yes, I’m okay. The baby just moved, that’s all. It kind of hurts.” She doubled over in pain.

I stood for a second and watched to see if she was lying. I noticed her stomach shift, then settle. The baby had made a huge move. “Li’l momma, why don’t you go in there and take a warm shower? You need to keep calm. You gonna hurt your shorty.” She gave me a weak smile, then rose up to go in the bathroom.

I am a killer by night and would normally choke a female out if it was called for, but this time, something about her softened me. I heard the shower running, then the sweet smell of jasmine and honey filled my nostrils as I stood on the other side of the room. Then I heard a real loud grunt, followed by a crashing sound that caused me to rush to the bathroom.

“Are you o—?” Netta’s naked body spread over the tub caused me to halt.

Her face was etched with pain and fear. I noticed the water still running, and the candles she'd lit were on the floor. I quickly stomped them out before a fire could start. I scooped her body up into my arms. She hugged me around my neck as she screamed and panted. "I think I'm in labor. Please get me to the hospital," she pleaded.

I was a little confused on what to do next. Hell, I take people out of the world, not birth them in. "I ain't no doctor," I spoke as I placed her on the bed and quickly wrapped her up in a towel until I figured out what to do. She squirmed and twisted around, yelling in pain. Vell just stood there.

I went over to the door where Flex and Dutchtress were enjoying their reunion. I was sorry, but that shit was about to be cut short.

Chapter 45

A Family Reunion

"Yo, Flex, Dutchtress, get up! Ole girl in there in pain and shit. She says she thinks she in la—"

When Knight came through the door, Flex and I both were on lock-and-ready mode. Before he could complete his sentence, we both reached under the pillows and got our guns. I held my snubnose .38, and Flex held his .357, both aimed in the direction of the disturbance. When we realized it was Knight holding his hands up in submission and sweat poured from his face, we lowered our guns. My breasts were exposed. Flex stood up and motioned for me to wrap the sheet around myself. Knight slightly turned in the other direction as Flex and I covered our nakedness.

"Man, what the fuck is wrong?" Flex said as he closed his robe.

"Man, ole girl over there . . . I just found her in the bathroom crying and screaming. She said she thinks she's in labor."

I grabbed my robe nonchalantly as I placed my gun back on the bed. I heard bloodcurdling screams coming out of Knight and Netta's room. I have been through too much, seen even more in this lifetime to know when bullshit is in the air. While Flex scrambled to put some boxers on, and Knight's big strong ass looked worried, I shook my head at these two. "Men can be so stupid sometimes," I whispered.

Once my robe was tied, I said, "You two wait right here. Let me go make sure the baby is fine," I said as I walked toward the door into the next room. Flex and Knight both stood there looking unsure of what to do next. They looked like they wanted to keep me from going in there. They had reason to be worried because if I found out the bitch was faking, it would make the decision to put a bullet in her head that much easier.

"But, Dutch, I wi—"

"I got this; sit tight. If she needs to go to the hospital, I'll let you know. I promise I won't kill her or her baby—yet."

I walked into the room. Netta lay on the bed in a fetal position with tears coming down her face. I took a second to assess the moment.

She looked in pain, and her screams were a nice added touch. But one thing was off. As she screamed and semipanted, I noticed her so-called labor pains were not constant, nor did she have any fluids oozing down her legs. As I walked a little closer, I saw when she noticed it was me coming to her aid, she squinted one eye and slightly opened the other one, then quickly closed it.

"So, how you feeling, Netta? Let me time your contractions." I sat in a chair with the clock from the nightstand in my hand. I waited for another so-called labor pain to strike. About ten minutes had gone by, but all she did was whimper and moan. There was no big show of labor.

"Yo . . . ou gonna take me . . . ee . . . to the hospital?" she said with staggered breathing as she looked up at my face while her crocodile tears flowed. I smiled inside at her desperate attempt to be released, but today, she was about to find out firsthand once again just who the hell I am.

"Hold on. I'm trying to see if you gonna need to go to the hospital. I'm timing all of your contractions. This sure will fuck up my plans, but a life is at risk here," I said with a hint of sarcasm.

"Oh yes, please . . . It hurts so bad . . . ouch, ouch."

I jumped up and ran over to the door as if I was in a frantic state and slammed it closed. Then I turned back to face her. I started clapping as if I were at a Broadway play.

She looked confused. “Why are you clapping? Can’t you see I need a doctor? Please, take me to the hospital. Please, I don’t want my baby to die.”

I continued to clap my hands at her stellar performance. She stood up so fast that she forgot that she’d just screamed she was in labor and couldn’t move.

“Help! Help! Can’t you see I need help? You can’t be this cruel,” she yelled at the top of her lungs.

“Yes, I see you do need some help, but it won’t be from a doctor. In fact, the back of my hand will be good enough. Now, sit yo’ four-dollar ass down before I make change.” Her show had really pissed me off; then to say her baby was in danger made me feel some type of way.

“Tell me why I shouldn’t just end your ass right now? Now, tell me, where’s our lousy husband, or shall I say yours, seeing as how I’m legally dead?” The thought of this woman who was clearly a liar and who had been raising my son pissed me off even more.

While she looked like she was struggling with what she should do next, her facial features still struck me as being familiar. I was thrown when I noticed a heart-shaped birth mark on the left side of her cheek, one that was similar to mine and my mother's.

"Okay, so now that your little show is over, sit yo' ass down! What the hell do you take me for? I have had labor pains before, and you sure as hell not in labor. Now, miss, or shall I say, Netta, where's my son?"

She slowly sat down on the seat next to the table. I could tell she was scared but didn't want to show it.

"Look, Elana, I have no idea why you all have taken me. I've been nothing but good to your son. As for Naheri, I didn't have anything to do with him then, I swear."

"Look here; I don't give two fucks about Naheri and all of his low-down dirty antics. All I want is my son and to see Naheri's ass six feet under. As for you and y'all little bundle of joy, well, I'll play that one by ear." I stepped closer to her and leaned down, close to her face. "You have no idea the hell I will unleash on you if you don't tell me where my son is."

Netta began to cry and shake harder than before. The fear in her eyes let me know she would move to the tune I played for her survival.

"Okay, okay. He rented a house on the outskirts of Kingston awhile ago. Not even his brother knows about this one. The only reason I know is becau—"

I firmly gripped her by the neck. "Spit it out. You know this because of *what?*"

"I know this because I followed him one night. At first, I thought it was a house call for one of his patients, but when I realized he let himself inside with a key, I knew something or someone was there that he was hiding. The moment I saw a room with nothing but pictures of you all over the place, I realized his grieving was much more serious than I thought. When he sat down in a huge chair holding what looked to be a nightgown, I'm assuming it was yours, he masturbated. I was sick watching what he'd done. There was a young lady there who resembled you. It looked as if she was about to give him some head. I was about to charge in . . . until he grabbed her by the hair and sliced her throat from ear-to-ear. I knew then I had to do something."

I was confused. She said she had to do something. Tears came down her face, and then she made a facial expression that took me back to a time in my life I wanted to forget and never speak of. Her lips curled on the left slightly, and her right eye twitched. There was only one person other than me who does this, and that was my mother.

"Where are you from?" I asked, no longer able to ignore the resemblance.

When she said the South Side of Chicago, I was thrown way off. Then when she said her old address—the same address where my mother once lived—it hit me.

"How many sisters and brothers do you have?" I asked her.

She started smiling hard and laughed. I thought she was losing her mind.

"Okay, enough of these games, Elana. Your ass far from dumb and nowhere near stupid. You know who I am already, sister dear."

I took a small step backward to focus. "What do you mean 'sister'? My mother had no more kids, and I damn sure don't have any siblings."

I wanted to see how far she was going to go with her speech. Then I remembered the twins Ms. Ruby told me my mother gave birth to.

In a swift move, I rushed to grab a fistful of her hair.

"I will show you better than I can tell you. The fact that you really want to spare your life and this might be true, I will give you the benefit of the doubt. Knight, come here," I yelled out to the next room.

Within seconds, both Knight and Flex rushed into the room. I walked over to the bar and grabbed one of the bags that were in the bottom of the ice bucket and placed the hair in. Then I took another bag and placed some of mine inside. "Here, tell Manju I need this back ASAP. There is no way I'ma take just her word."

Flex stood at the window with a concerned expression as Knight left with both bags. I had no time to play with Netta or Naheri. I wanted my son back and Naheri's head on a platter.

Chapter 46

Kainmen's Revenge

Standing over my father's dead body, I began to think back on the moment I had Dutchtress in my sights and could have taken her life right then.

"Damn! Damn! Find them, fuck boi. I swear to the heavens he will pay dearly for this." I paced back and forth slamming my fist into the nearest wall. The time I have spent searching for Flex and my stupid brother was starting to take a toll on me.

"Look, Kainmen, there's nothing we can do at this point but put your father away in the family's mausoleum with your grandfather and the rest of the family. Don't you think this is hurting me too? My husband and possibly my son have been taken from us. No, there is no way this can just die down. Your brother has made his choice, so now it's war. . . ." My mother's voice trailed off as she sat in the chair holding a Glock 9 mm in her hand. She swished the brown liquor around the ice in her glass. Looking as if she was thinking of her next move, she placed a firm grip on the handle. "First, my son, then my husband. No, no. This bitch has to die." She took a big gulp of her liquor finishing it off.

"Ma! Damn, I know this already. Why don't you go and let me get Pop's body out of here? There is no way he would want you falling apart like this. Meko and Charm, make this happen. Clean this up and let me get my mother out of here. When y'all done, meet me at the spot. Tonight, we finish this."

I lifted my drunken mother from the floor where she lay beside my father's corpse. "Why, why? They didn't have to do him like this." Her voice echoed throughout the room.

"Ma, Momma, let go of him so they can clean this up. Trust me, she gonna pay for this, now move! Please." My anger was getting the better of me. I have lost too much dealing with Dutchress, and I wasn't about to go through anymore. I got my mother out of there and jumped in my car.

I headed toward Mona's club in town. Maybe I could get something to lead me in the right direction. When I got there, it looked like World War Six had happened. The place was burnt to the ground. I walked around there, kicking up ashes from the floor. I was mad at myself. I had him. I was so fucking close.

As I was kicking up the ash and dirt from the floor, I spotted something familiar. I knelt to get a closer look. I removed the black ash and even rubbed it on my shirt to clean it off. It was a chain with a pendant that only my family wore. When I saw the falcon's head on the front and flipped it to the back, I knew I was right.

"What the hell have you done, Naheri?" I was furious at my brother who seems to be leaving lose ends and bodies all over Kingston. If my grandfather were alive, he would lay him down like a rabid dog. Now, it's left up to me.

I stood for another brief second before walking off. "Drive!" I shouted to Manzo as he pressed the gas pedal out of there.

Thoughts of my brother danced in my head. Then I started to think about my dad and how those fuck boys killed him. Like an animal, I started growling and rocking back forth in anger in my seat. "This stupid muthafucka! I swear once I kill Flex, I'ma kill Naheri's ass."

"Calm down, Boss. The first rule you always taught us is to think with your head and not your emotions. First things first. We need to find them rude boys that took out your father; then we handle yo' brother. Now, if you were on some get-out-of-sight-type shit, where would you go? Boss, think wisely because you give the answer, and I know it's right in front of you."

Manzo spoke with truth. I slowed my breathing to calm down; then I started to think. The first question I asked myself was if I were on some kill-and-get-out shit, how would I, the boss, a born killer, get out? I had to admit Flex and Dutchtress's kill game was on point and one to be reckoned with.

I pulled up in front of the run-down hotel on the south end of the island. I couldn't take it any longer. I needed to find my brother and this bitch he has married and unleashed on us. For years, I had wanted her dead, especially when she pawned another man's bastard off on him. He sat there all in love and shit, making no moves or following the plan we had in play.

Getting out of the car, I watched a young female with large breasts approach me as I exited the truck. She looked as if she was once a beautiful woman but drugs had taken her over. "Ya babe wan a date dem der boi?"

"Get the hell away from him. Do you know who dat is? You want live? You gwan, move!" An older female rushed over and grabbed the young woman away. They both began rushing in the opposite direction.

As I approached the front door of the hotel, the heavy scent of crack and propane overpowered my nostrils. Off to the side were some smokers huddled around a lit garbage can.

“Where Minister?” I asked the huge guard that stood at the door. Minister was the man in these parts, and if anyone knew of where everyone could be, he was the one to see. I knew he would know where to find Naheri and Dutchtress.

“Yes, Mr. Kainmen, he’s in his den.”

I opened the door. “Blood crying inna fi yuh heart, eel fi mi wrath know de hurt a suffering yuh will.” He repeated this over and over while holding a crying, naked female by the throat. Her bruised and battered face was covered with hair and blood.

“Please, please, forgimmi,” she cried. He smiled a wicked grin, then sliced her throat from ear to ear. As soon as her body hit the floor like a sack of potatoes, he stepped over her and greeted me with an outstretched hand to shake.

“Ah fi mi broda welcum, ave ah seat.” I sat down in the chair next to the table. He joined me and sat down. Then he reared back in his chair as he lit a long cigar filled with the finest purple weed the island had to offer. He took a long pull, then offered some to me. I refused because I needed my head on right to find my worthless brother and them fools that killed my pops.

"OK, sut yourself. Mi know wah mek yuh deh ya."

"Oh, so you know that I want—no—I *need* to get my hands on my brother and his wife, Dutchtress. She will pay for all of this and more. My silly-ass brother has lost his mind."

"Ah, here," he said as he passed me a piece of paper. I picked it up and read it. There were some directions to an address I knew nothing about. The paper had some blood on it.

"Sorry 'bout dem blood. I had to handle that deceitful bitch. None before we and loyalty is everything to me. I already tracked your brother down. Now, I will tell you, this Dutchtress has been good to me and my people as have you. To find her and Flex I need money." He smiled as he took another pull from the blunt. His eyes began to roll in the back of his head as if he was starting to feel the euphoric sensation from the weed. He slightly swayed from side to side. "Sorry, broda, dis ah som gud dodo. Yuh sure yuh don't want ah lick?"

"No, I'm good. Now, what's this about some money and loyalty shit! This bitch killed my pops and went after my mom. You owe me, Minister. You owe me your life, remember?"

He shrugged his shoulders and continued to hit the cigar as if he didn't have a care in the world. I felt as if he was mocking me.

"No, no, mi don't mean any disrespect, but I am a man with needs and wants. Do you see this mansion?" He pointed around the room. "It cost lots of money to keep this going. Like this dead bitch right here. She stole from me, us, the family, so she paid for it. As a matter of fact, Lucay, put this dead bitch in the garbage where she belongs." Another guard walked over and swooped the dead hooker's body into his arm as if she were just a piece of paper.

Minister continued to smoke and choke as if it was nothing. I was used to killing and smoking and sometimes even having sex in the same room where a body lay. But this time, I felt as if he was testing my gangster. I jumped up and placed a 9 mm Glock under his chin. "You think this shit a game, moda fucka? Shi killed everting mi luv. You gonna tell me where she is, or you won't see the next sun rising." Through gritted teeth, I spoke to him in our native tongue.

His expression didn't change. He seemed unbothered at the fact I held a gun on him. He began to chuckle.

"So you think this is a game? We will s—"

"No, no, brudah. You seem to forget where you are. Now, I will give you dree seconds, and I will forget about this, and you will pay me my money and no harm. But if dree seconds pass, then we handle this like real gangsta, as the Americans say."

I heard guns being cocked, filling the room. I glanced to my left, then my right. About ten men stood with their guns trained on me. The irony of this is, I was the one who trained Minister and gave him his first taste of power when he wasn't shit but a bottom-feeding toad.

"You sure this is how you want it? All you have to do is tell me where to find this bitch, and we'll be good."

He laughed. "Am I sure, am I sure? Seems like I'm the one holding all the c—"

He stopped as soon as he spotted several females dressed in rags and some wore next to nothing to blend in the surroundings, standing directly behind each man he had in the room. Each of them held a Desert Eagle in her hands.

Standing up cocky, I gave him a knowing look. "See, I told you we can play nice, nigga. *I'm* the one who taught you. Now, where is she?"

His expression changed as he realized he was outnumbered. He opened the robe he wore to expose his chest. "You gonna have to kill me because I ain't no rat unlike your desperate-ass ni—" He began gurgling on his own blood. One of my little working assassins crept behind him and slit his throat with a machete.

He began twitching in the chair. I ordered his men to tear the den apart to find anything he may have had indicating where Dutchtress could be. Lucay went right over to his safe and gave me some papers. I thumbed through them and spotted a photo along with an address to find Dutchtress.

Chapter 47

All or Nothing

After getting the DNA results back, it turned out that Netta was indeed my sister. I didn't have time to get to know her that well because I needed to get to Naheri before he does some crazy shit. It had been long overdue. It was time my dear husband and I met face-to-face. With any luck, he'll be sucking the barrel of my .38-snubnose. There was no way all of this would happen, and I didn't get my revenge. I knew Karma was a bad bitch, and she had my name on her list, but before she has her way with me, I was prepared to give my own dose of Karma to some deserving people, starting with Naheri.

"Get me there fast. All of this voodoo and shit, I have got to get to our son." My heart raced in anticipation. After Netta told me where she thought Naheri could be, we all hurried. Knight and Vell trailed us in a car with Netta. I had planned to leave with my son and my one true love. If I remember Kainmen, he was not going to allow his father's death go without war. My only chance was to kill Naheri and take my son back to Chicago. Kainmen knew he had no wind when it came to me and my city.

We drove past this house that was tucked away on a dirt road. It was just like she described it. I almost got out of the moving car, so eager was I to see my son. Before I could, however, Flex grabbed my wrist.

We pulled to the side of the road to get some more info from Netta.

"Look, is this the house or what?" I asked as I got out of the car walking toward Knight.

Netta sat in the front seat of the car with her arms folded. "Look, I said it was, didn't I? You got what you wanted; now, let me go, dear sister."

"Bitch, is you serious? Sister or not, you know where my son is, and all these lies and games you've played for years. I know you mad because of what the past is. By the way, it had nothing to do with me. You should be thankful I don't cut your ass wide open. You helped that muthafucka try to kill me. So, you might want to shut the fuck up," I said, seething with anger.

The way she thought I was just going to allow her to keep me from finding my son . . . No one will ever come between us. I will go to the ends of the earth for mine. Hell, I have looked the devil himself in the face for my son. And now that I have Flex back, we will be a real family. I was so mad, I snatched the car door opened and grabbed a handful of her hair and yanked her from the seat.

"Elana, E—I'm your sister. Come on. It's the house; it is the house. I swear that's where he's at!"

Holding my gun up to her temple, I said, "Bitch, if you playing games, I swear I will murder you right here and now."

"Come on, Dutch, she good, she good." Knight held my wrist before I pulled the trigger.

I slowly looked over my shoulder at his hand, then back up toward his face and down at his hand one more time. "I suggest, if you want to live, you let my arm go. Okay, okay, so you have grown to like this little bitch, I see. But don't forget the hand that feeds you."

Knight slowly moved his hand and stepped back, shaking his head. He glared over at Flex as if he was pleading for me to spare Netta's life, but Flex never took his eyes off me. We were in sync to the core. If I had blown her head wide open, he would have released a few more into her just to make sure she was dead. That's the kind of bond we shared.

When Netta began to shake in fear, I looked down at her very pregnant stomach and had a small piece of remorse, because I'm a mother, and I know what lengths I would go to protect my son, and the hell and hurt I have felt for this past year was nothing I would wish on my worst enemy. I decided to lower the gun and snatched her up from the ground. "Let's go, let's fuck'n go. You gonna knock right at the front door."

I could hear Knight taking a deep breath of relief as I firmly guided her down a small pathway that led up to the house. I was cautious.

"Shh, shh, you hear that?" I said as I heard a child laughing. Netta looked confused,

"I-I don't hear n—"

Just as she about to say she hadn't heard it, the sound of laughter got louder, and it was like music to my ears. I knew it was my baby boy. For a year, I dreamed of his laughter many nights and would wake up in a cold sweat.

"I got it, Daddy!" The child ran to get the ball he was playing with. When he ran up, he met me eye to eye.

"Ma-Mommy! Mommy Netta!" His speech was a little choppy, but I understood what he was saying. I want to hug him so tightly and never let him go.

"Shh, shh, shh-hh, baby." I placed my finger over my mouth. "Yes, it's Mommy, but you have to be quiet. I want to surprise Daddy." I hugged him, and as soon as I let go, Flex picked him up.

"Junior! Junior, where are you? We have to leave. Nana is ready."

Hearing Naheri's voice made my skin crawl. I wanted to walk up to him and put one in his head. I needed to kill him and Kainmen. That will be the only way I can live in peace.

"Son, don't worry. We'll see you soon. Go back to your father," Flex said with a mean scowl. I could tell he was upset. For years, he'd watched as Naheri raised his son and called him daddy, but Flex realized the life he led was no place for a child.

He placed Junior back down to the ground. I turned to Flex, Knight, and Vell. "Take them back to the car for me. I'm going to finish this once and for all."

Flex stood in my face. "Look, bae, I know you are one to handle yourself, and that's all good, but the fact that I'm here, and we are a team, we have to do this together. There is no way I'm letting you do this one alone. None before we, remember? That's how it is and will always be."

"I know, Flex. Out of anyone on this earth, I could always count on you. The year I lost or thought I lost you, not a day went by that I didn't think of you and cried for you. If something happens to me, I want our son to be taken care of. He's a piece of us that I will forever love and cherish. Not even death can separate that. But this one I need to do on my own. Please, you know me better than anyone. Yes, none before we, and I am doing this one for us."

Flex lowered his lips to mine and gently kissed my lips. He caressed the sides of my cheeks, knowing there was no way or time to argue with me. We heard Naheri call out to Junior one more time. As soon as I got word that Minister and his crew knew about Flex and me being in town, I made sure I touched down with him. He assured me on the strength of his two daughters' lives that he wouldn't tell anyone where we were. So, that allowed me to get some of the things I needed to kill Naheri and Kainmen, and even their mother.

"I love you, and if I'm not back in twenty minutes, leave without me. I have something set up for us in Chicago. When you and Junior touch down, go to 11324 South State. They will know what to do." I held back some tears because I knew this was going to be a fight, and my getting out would be difficult.

He held my arms. "Look, Dutch, you are real through and through, so I know you gonna make it back to me and our son. Now, I'm going to go to this car and wait for you. Shit, you won't even need twenty minutes to get the job done."

He walked back toward Knight and Vell. Netta stood looking confused and a little shaken.

"Junior! Junior, let's go. We got to get out of here," he frantically yelled out.

Knight, Vell, Netta, Flex, and Junior all nestled down in the bushes as Naheri's voice seemed as if it was getting closer. Flex had to place his hand over Junior's mouth before he answered. I peeped from the side of the hedge I was hiding behind to see him as he began walking to the other side of the yard.

I watched until I saw him go back inside of the house. Then I slowly crept up to the front door and tried the knob. It opened just as I hoped. When I got inside of the foyer I heard Naheri's mother, "We have got to go. I know Kainmen knows where you are by now, and right now, he's not thinking clearly. To him, you are the enemy and need to be dealt with. I'll be damned if I allow my one son to kill my other son. I love y'all both, and the choices y'all have made cost us plenty." I could tell she was upset as she threw some clothes inside of a bag.

"Go get that boy! I don't want anybody showing up before we can get out of here. He's even talking about killing Junior because of the bitch he calls Mommy. I swear to God, if that bitch were here now, I would kill her with my bare hands." Hearing her speak of me the way she did, I trained my gun directly at her head, then squeezed the trigger.

Before her body could hit the floor, I pounced on Naheri like a beast. I swung at him wildly in the air. "You bitch-made-ass nigga! How could you? You gon' die!" I screamed. He tried holding my arm while I held the gun in the other one.

"Elana, stop! Stop! You need to die, bitch!" He tried to restrain me. I managed to knee him in the balls. Releasing me, he tensed his body tensed in pain. I hurried to cock the gun. "Mommy! Mommy!" Suddenly, I heard Junior call out to me. When I turned in his direction, Kainmen was standing with Junior in front of him, holding a gun to his head.

"Hello, Elana. I see death looks good on you. Aww, don't panic. Me and my nephew were just bonding some, ya know, as family should." His voice dripped with venom. "See, brother, dear, I told you your ass was a sucka. Why ain't this bitch dead already? And you let her kill Mommy? I told you, I told you." He looked over at their mother's lifeless body lying in a pool of her own blood. He gripped Junior by the nape of his neck so hard.

"Ouch, ouch, you're hurting me, Uncle K. Ouch. Daddy, Uncle K is hurting me."

I reached out to grab my son.

"Uh-uh, now, that wouldn't play out well for you. You ruthless bitch. You and yours killed both of my parents. I told my weak-ass brother to get rid of your ass years ago." He scowled at Naheri in disgust.

"If you don't fuckin' let my baby go, I'ma kill your last piece of family you got left." I pointed the gun at Naheri.

"Really, bitch?" Kainmen laughed. "You think I gives two shits about this whack-ass mon? He's fuckin' dead to me." He turned and fired two into Naheri's chest. "Shit, you would have been doing me a favor. But why not do it myself? Just like Cain and Abel, I'm my brother's keeper."

Junior began to scream.

"Shut the fuck up, you little retarded-ass bastard!" Kainmen picked Junior up by the neck. I couldn't hold it any longer. I lunged at him. He pushed me to the floor and shot Junior in the stomach. I was horrified.

"You bitch! No-oo, you punk bitch!" I yelled.

I squeezed my trigger putting one in his leg before he ducked for cover. He put his brother's body in front of him to shield from the bullets flying in his direction. Each bullet tore through his skin. Blood was everywhere, but I wasn't about to give up.

"Look! You might as well come out, you miserable bitch. I'ma make sure you never breathe another ounce of air. Oh, yo' boy Flex dead thanks to my dear sister-in-law slash your sister. That bitch would sell her soul with her conning ass to save her own life. When she seen me coming up on the car, she never said a word to warn them that shit was funny." He laughed aloud. "They didn't even see me creeping up and dropping they ass like a bad habit. She let me grab shorty and ran her ass off in the other direction. Damn, family ain't shit." He laughed harder.

"Yeah, you right. Family ain't shit, just ask your dead-ass mother right here. But the thing is, I got her ass just like I'ma get you."

My heart was all over the place. Flex was dead. Junior was shot, possibly clinging to life, and Knight and Vell, may they rest in peace, were soldiers to the end. I pulled my trigger, but nothing but a clicking noise echoed throughout the room. Out of bullets, I searched around the room trying to find something to defend myself with. There was nothing. I had to get to my son and get him out of there.

Wickedly laughing, Kainmen hobbled over toward me with his gun pointed. I frantically searched around me to see if I could find anything as a weapon, but there was nothing. There was absolutely nothing. If I was going to die, I was going to go out proud and strong like the queen I am.

Standing up to face him, I said, "Take your best shot. I promise you, it better be your best, because if I make it out of here, your ass will not make through another day. I guarantee that." I spread my arms wide, then glanced over to my son where his little body lay on the floor. I wished I could have made it over to him but knew there was no way. Maybe if Kainmen thought he was dead, he wouldn't shoot him again. I couldn't take a chance that a bullet he had for me would hit him again. I inwardly said a prayer and whispered I loved him before closing my eyes.

Next, I heard two gunshots. I felt my chest . . . then and all around my body to see if I was hit. Then I slowly opened one eye to see Kainmen on the floor. Smoke was still coming from the barrel, and Minister was holding a big towel around his neck.

"Fuckin' idiot. Yuh crossed de wrang one. See yuh inna hell, bumaclot."

I rushed over and picked up Junior and rushed out the door. The closer I got to the cars where we were parked, my heart dropped from the sight of blood splatter on the window. Then over on the passenger side, I could see Flex's body slumped over. Across from that car was another one with what looked like Kainmen's boys dead, all laid out in front and on the side of the car.

I'm guessing Minister and his people snuck up and laid them all down. Junior wasn't moving, and although my heart ached, I wished Flex was still alive, but I had to save our son.

I rushed over and put Junior in the backseat of the car Flex and Knight were in. Then I began to pull Knight's body and Vell's out of the front seat to the ground. I didn't want to do them like that, but I had no time to give them a proper goodbye. Then I rushed over to remove Flex. As soon as the door opened, my tears began to fall. I was going to have to leave him. I wished like hell after everything we had been through we could have had our happily ever after.

I reached for his arm to pull him out; then I heard a faint moan coming from him. "Flex! Flex, baby! Flex!" I cried out as his arm moved, and he spoke. Blood was on the side of his ear where the bullet grazed him. I kissed his face and head. "Oh, baby, you're alive. Thank you, God," I yelled out in excitement.

Groggily, he spoke, "Wha-what happened?"

"I'll explain on the way to the hospital. We have got to get Junior there."

I pushed him back in the car and quickly hopped in the driver's seat and sped off.

Making it to the Bellevue Hospital's emergency room, doctors and nurses quickly grabbed Flex and Junior and rushed them in different directions. I waited impatiently to hear a word about both of them. Flex wasn't shot in the head. The bullet just grazed his head, but not deep enough to kill him. At that moment, I thanked Kainmen for being such a lousy shot.

My mind was overloaded, so I decided to take a walk in the building. I walked to the nurses' station where they both were, asking for a good word, but no luck. There wasn't any word yet. The doctors were still working on Junior and Flex, and both were in surgery.

Next, I walked into the labor and delivery part of the hospital. When I was recovering back in Chicago, I would always make my way down to the labor and delivery part. That where I always seemed to have gotten peace. And I was hoping to find it there today.

I watched the newborn babies through the glass. My heart ached for them because they knew nothing about how cruel this world could be. Looking at all the little babies made me smile.

I ogled over them a little while longer . . . until I heard a familiar voice singing to one of the babies.

It was Netta. She was so into the baby she hadn't spotted me watching her. I hid behind a large beam in the middle of the lobby until she finished her visit. "Don't worry, little munchkin. Mommy will be back to feed you," I heard her say as she left the nursery to go back to her room. I waited until she was out of sight before I stepped back to the glass to make sure which baby was hers. I wanted her to feel the hurt I felt. I was going to take her precious gift away but thought no, I had something better planned for her.

I blew my little niece a kiss and walked in the hallway toward the direction I saw Netta going. When I got to the second entrance, I heard one nurse asking another nurse to bring medication in room 74, along with Netta's first name.

I spotted a vase filled with flowers and a few instruments that the medical staff carelessly left out. I was grateful they had been so careless. I picked up the vase full of flowers and a sharp scalpel, and when the nurse left her room, I walked in, holding the vase in front of my face. When I lowered it, by the look on Netta's face, she could have shit herself.

Smiling, I walked toward her and placed the flowers down on the stand. "Wow, welcome to motherhood, sister, dear," I sarcastically said.

"E-e-Elana, how did yo—"

"How did I what? Live? Make it out of the hell you and Naheri dealt me?"

"No-no. How did you find me?" she stuttered.

"Oh, don't worry yourself with that, dear sister. You just gave birth to a beautiful, healthy baby, and she is beautiful. Kind of looks like Momma when she was in her glory days."

She leaned over to push the call button on the side of her bed rail, but I grabbed her by the hand. "Uh-uh. We don't need anyone to interrupt our little family reunion. Oh, how we have so much to catch up on seeing as how we both are mothers now."

"Please, don't hurt my baby. I'll do anything, please." Her face was flushed and filled with terror.

I peeped toward the door to make sure no one was coming. "See, sis, I wouldn't dare touch your baby. After all, I am her aunt. But you, on the other hand, I could care less about."

Taking the instrument, I sliced her across the wrist. She tried to scream, but I held my hand over her mouth. The blood spewed out of her wrist like rushing water. I held her down until she stopped moving. I made sure she was dead by punching a hole in her neck. Her room was a bloody mess. Before I snuck out of the room,

I washed my hands and covered my bloody clothes with a hospital gown that was in her room.

Then I walked back over to the side of the hospital where Junior and Flex were and sat in the waiting room as if nothing happened.

"Code Blue! All medical staff report to room 74. Code Blue!" I heard someone announcing over the PA system. I knew they discovered Netta's body. At the same moment, one of the nurses that I'd asked to keep me informed about Flex and Junior came and gave me some good news. They both were in recovery and will be okay.

Weeks later, they were released, and I couldn't be happier. After Netta was found dead, I waited for a while; then I paid a nurse to give me her daughter, and we all flew back on a private plane to Chicago that Minister provided. I named her daughter after the one female I trusted and admired for strength . . . Elana. She will be all of that . . . and more.